translated from the Portuguese

by **CLOTILDE WILSON**

Noonday Press New York

PHILOSOPHER OR DOG?

(QUINCAS BORBA)

Machado de Assis

O.K.

c. 1

d6-18-54
HR

TRANSLATOR'S PREFACE

Epitaph of a Small Winner and its sequel *Philosopher or Dog?* well illustrate their author's preoccupation with insanity, particularly in the form of megalomania. In an article entitled *Machado de Assis, Encomiast of Lunacy*,[1] several passages of which I shall reproduce here, I have pointed out that in these two novels the nineteenth century Brazilian writer manifests his kinship with the sixteenth century scholar, Erasmus, and the modern psychologist.

In his *Moriae encomium* (*In Praise of Folly*) Erasmus emphasizes the contentment that may be induced by megalomania. "If anyone born a beggar should fancy himself a great prince or the like," he says, "his sort of madness, if (as it is most usual) it be accompanied with pleasure, brings a great satisfaction . . ."

[1] *Hispania*, May, 1949.

He cites the instance of a certain Greek who had suffered a pleasurable aberration, and who, when his wits were restored, "looked upon his cure as so far from a kindness that he thus reasons the case with his friends:

> This remedy, my friends, is worse i' th' main
> Than the disease, the cure augments the pain;
> My only hope is a relapse again."

What is this phenomenon that Erasmus treats humorously in his *In Praise of Folly* but the so-called "pleasure principle" of psychology? To understand insanity we must realize that all men are seekers and all have but one goal in sight—happiness. We call it the "pleasure principle" in psychology. Strange as it may seem, the insane of all people, are sane, if we would judge simply by the success of this great quest— As a group they (the insane) are supremely happy.[2]

In the unforgettable passage of the *Epitaph of a Small Winner* in which Machado de Assis describes the delirium of Braz Cubas, a turbulent vision in which the past ages file before the sick man's fevered eyes, wretched mankind, forsaken by an indifferent universe, appears in eternal pursuit of that nebulous, elusive thing called happiness. Thus does the novelist portray the "pleasure principle" of the modern psychologist. Perhaps no other passage more clearly reflects the author's deeply pessimistic philosophy, for here we see humanity struggling in vain against a relentless fate and seeking with frantic eagerness a chimerical happiness that may fall within his grasp for one brief moment only to vanish the next with mocking laughter.

Machado's characters take refuge from the unfulfillment of their desires and the drabness and insignificance of their lives in the madman's realm of fantasy. Indeed, it is in this implication that only through madness may one attain the illusion of happiness that the author's pessimism reaches its ultimate expression.

Quincas Borba achieves contentment at last through iden-

[2] The Sanity of Insanity, George Estabrooks; *The Scientific American*, April, 1935.

tification with Saint Augustine, with whom he had always felt a close affinity, and his disciple Rubião, though his wealth has been dissipated and though the woman whom he loves receives his attentions with indifference, triumphs over the frustration of reality by donning the crown of Louis Napoleon. Forgotten is all the sad failure of a futile little life in that supreme gesture of picking up nothing and placing it on his head with the exultant cry, "To the victor—" "Consider the typical Napoleon of your local insane hospital. He *is* Napoleon in his own mind. He will write a check for a million dollars or give you a duchy in France for the asking. To be sure the National Bank or the French government might not treat him very seriously, but in his own mind he is very wealthy and very powerful." [3]

Philosopher or Dog? might be considered an elaboration in prose of Machado's famous poem *A Mosca Azul (The Blue Fly)*, in which the glittering blue fly that one summer night flew up from the heart of a rose and buzzed and darted about the head of a poor pariah, symbolizes the delusions of grandeur through which the outcast finds escape from the colorless realities of a humble existence. In the insect's iridescent wings the pariah sees the reflection of his own face under the guise of the Ruler of Kashmir. In one of the first passages describing Rubião's derangement, Machado uses the peculiar phrase "he was wearing bright blue laughter on his lips." Is this not reminiscent, perhaps, of *a mosca azul* of the poem in which the color blue seems to symbolize illusion? And in the novel, too, whether merely through coincidence or through further symbolism, one cannot be certain, the rose is again associated with the beginnings of hallucination; for one of Rubião's early visions of that imperial splendor that was soon to constitute the dream world into which he would drift more and more frequently, is inspired by two modest roses that were blooming in a corner of Sophia's garden.

And so, since the often cynical humor that involves the works of Machado de Assis is allied to the bitterness with which he contemplates the sorrows of mankind, he, like Erasmus, finds in the lunatic's gratification of the "pleasure principle" a theme

[3] Estabrooks, *op. cit.*

for ironical laughter. Yet his is a mockery that is not without compassion. Ridicule and pity blend, for they are closely akin. Indeed, in the eyes of Nature as Machado conceives it, wholly unconcerned with man's suffering, they are one and the same. The Southern Cross, he reminds us, is "too high in the heavens to distinguish between man's laughter and tears."

Philosopher or Dog?

Rubião was gazing at the bay—it was eight o'clock in the morning. Whoever might have seen him at the window of a large house in Botafogo, thumbs stuck through the cord of his dressing gown, would have believed that he was admiring that piece of quiet water; but I tell you that actually he was thinking of something else. He was comparing the past with the present. What was he a year ago? A teacher. What is he now? A capitalist. He looks at himself, at his slippers (some Tunisian slippers that a recently acquired friend, Christiano Palha gave him), at the house, at the garden, at the bay, at the hills, and at the sky; and he has the sensation that everything from slippers to sky, everything is his very own.

He is thinking: "See how God writes straight on crooked lines. Had Sister Piedade married Quincas Borba, I could have hoped only for a collateral inheritance. She did not marry him; both died, and now everything is mine; so that what seemed a misfortune—"

II

What an abyss there is between the mind and the heart! The ex-teacher's mind, displeased with that thought, recoiled, sought something else to think about, a small boat that was going by; the heart, however, allowed itself to beat joyously. What did it care about the boat, or the boatman, which Rubião's eyes were following in a wide open stare? It, the heart, was saying that since Sister Piedade had to die, it was well that she did not marry; there might have been a son or daughter. —A pretty boat! —It was better so! —How well the man bends to the oars! —One thing certain is that they are in Heaven!

III

A manservant brought him his coffee. Rubião took the cup, and while he put in some sugar he looked furtively at the tray, which was of wrought silver. Silver and gold were the metals that he dearly loved; he did not like bronze, but his friend Palha had told him that it was a highly valuable substance, and this explains the pair of figures that are here in the drawing room, a Mephistopheles and a Faust. If he had to choose, however, he would choose the silver tray—a perfect piece of silverware of fine and finished craftsmanship. The servant was waiting, stiff and unsmiling. He was a Spaniard, and it was not without resistance that Rubião had accepted him from the hands of Christiano. No matter how many times he had told him that he was accustomed to his Negroes from Minas and did not want foreign languages in the house, his friend insisted, pointing out to him the need of having white servants. Rubião had yielded with reluctance. His good houseboy, whom he had wanted to put in the drawing room as a sort of provincial piece, he had not even been able to leave in the kitchen. Jean, a Frenchman, held sway there; and the houseboy had been demoted.

"Is Quincas Borba very restless?" asked Rubião, drinking the last swallow of coffee and casting a final glance at the tray.

"*Me parece que si.*"

"I'll go and unleash him."

He did not go; he remained for awhile, looking at the furniture. Seeing the little English prints that were hanging on the wall over the two bronzes, Rubião thought of the beautiful Sophia, Palha's wife, took a few steps, and sat down on the ottoman in the center of the room, a faraway look in his eyes.

It was she who recommended those two little pictures to me when the three of us were looking for things to buy. She was so pretty. But what I like most about her are her shoulders, which I saw at the Colonel's ball. What shoulders! They look like wax, so smooth, so white! Her arms, too! Oh, her arms! How well shaped!

Rubião sighed, crossed his legs, and drummed on his knees with the tassels of his dressing gown. He felt that he was not entirely happy; but he felt, too, that he was not far from complete happiness. He was going over in his mind her manner toward him, her way of looking at him, little gestures of affection that could have no other explanation than that she was fond of him, very fond of him. He was not old; he would soon be forty-one, and, indeed, he looked younger. This observation was accompanied by a gesture; he rubbed his hand over his chin, which he shaved every day now. This was a thing he never used to do, for the sake of economy and because it was not necessary. A mere teacher! He used to wear whiskers (later he let a full beard grow), so soft that it was a pleasure to run one's fingers through them— And so it was that he recalled the first meeting, in the Vassouras railway station, where Sophia and her husband had entered the coach in which he was coming down from Minas; it was there that he encountered that pair of tender eyes which seemed to repeat the prophet's exhortation, "Ho, everyone that thirsteth, come ye to the waters." In truth, he did not have at the time any ideas that were adequate to the invitation; his head was filled with the inheritance, the will, the inventory, things that must first be explained in order that you may understand the present and the future. Let us leave Rubião, then, in his Botafogo drawing room, drumming on his knees with the tassels of his dressing gown and thinking of the beautiful Sophia. Come with me, reader; let us take a look at him, months before, at the bedside of Quincas Borba.

I V

This Quincas Borba, if perchance you were kind enough to read the "Epitaph of a Small Winner," is the same castaway that appears there as a beggar, unexpected heir, and creator of a philosophy. Now here he is in Barbacena.

From the moment of his arrival, he fell in love with a widow, a woman of humble station and modest means, but so retiring that her lover's sighs went unechoed. Her name was Maria da Piedade. A brother of hers, the present Rubião, did everything possible to bring about their marriage. But Piedade resisted, and an attack of pleurisy carried her off.

It was that brief interlude of romance that brought the two men together. Could Rubião have known that within Quincas Borba was that tiny grain of madness that a certain doctor had once supposed he had found in him? Surely not; he thought that he was merely an eccentric. And yet that tiny grain had not dislodged itself from Quincas Borba's brain either before or after the malady that slowly devoured him. Quincas Borba had had several relatives there, who had died *in* 1867; the last one was the uncle whose heir he had become. Rubião became the philosopher's only friend. At that time he was directing a boy's school, which he later closed in order to take care of the sick

6

man. Before he had become a teacher, he had turned his hand to several enterprises, all of which had failed.

His nurse's duty lasted five, nearly six months. Rubião, patient and smiling, was genuinely devoted. He attended to everything, listening to the doctor's orders, administering the remedies at the prescribed time, going out for a walk with his patient. And he forgot nothing, neither the household tasks nor the reading of the newspaper as soon as the mail arrived from the capital or from Ouro-Preto.

"You are good, Rubião," Quincas Borba would sigh.

"A noble achievement! As if you were bad!"

The doctor's ostensible opinion was that Quincas Borba's illness would slowly work itself out. One day, our Rubião, accompanying the doctor to the street door, asked him how his friend really was, and learned that he was doomed, utterly doomed, but that he, Rubião, should encourage him. Why make death harder by the certainty—

"No," interrupted Rubião, "for that matter, death is an easy business for him. You never read a book that he wrote years ago, some philosophy business."

"No, but philosophy is one thing, and actual dying is another. Good-day."

v

Rubião found a rival for Quincas Borba's heart—a dog, a pretty dog, medium-sized, with a lead-colored, black-spotted coat. Quincas Borba used to take him everywhere; they slept in the same room. In the morning it was the dog that awakened his master, climbing on to the bed, where they exchanged their first greetings. One of the master's eccentricities was to give the dog his own name, for which he offered two reasons, one doctrinary, the other private.

"Since Humanity, according to my doctrine, is the principle of life and resides everywhere, it is present in the dog, and thus the latter can receive a person's name, be it Christian or Mussulman—"

"Very well, but why didn't you give him, rather, the name Bernardo?" said Rubião, thinking of a local political rival.

"That's the private reason. If I die first, as I presume I shall, I'll survive through the name of my good dog. You're laughing, aren't you?" Rubião made a gesture of denial.

"Well, you should be laughing, my dear fellow. Because immortality is my lot, or my endowment, or whatever you will. I'll live on forever in my great book. However, those who can't read will call the dog Quincas Borba and—"

The dog, hearing his name, ran excitedly to Quincas Borba's bed and looked at Quincas Borba.

"My poor friend. My good friend! My only friend!"

"Only?"

"Forgive me, you are my friend, too. Well do I know it, and I am very grateful. But one must excuse a sick man. Perhaps my delirium is beginning. Let me see the mirror."

Rubião gave him the mirror. For several seconds the sick man contemplated his emaciated face, his fevered eyes, in which he discovered the outskirts of death through which he was traveling with slow but sure steps. Then, with a wan and ironical smile:

"Everything here on the outside corresponds to what I feel inside; I'm going to die, my dear Rubião— Don't gesticulate; I'm going to die. And what is death that one should be so terrified?"

"I know, I know that you have a certain philosophy—but let's talk about dinner; what's it to be today?"

Quincas Borba sat up in bed, dangling his legs. When they were not in trousers, one could see how thin they must be.

"What's it to be? What do you want?" said Rubião hastily.

"Nothing," replied the patient, smiling. "A certain philosophy! How disdainfully you say that! Go on, repeat it. I want to hear it again. A certain philosophy!"

"But it's not disdain— Am I capable of disdaining philosophy? I say merely that you can believe that death is of no consequence, because you probably have certain reasons, certain principles—"

Quincas Borba felt for his slippers with his feet and Rubião placed them near him. Then he put them on, and began to walk about to stretch his legs. He patted the dog, and lighted a cigarette. Rubião wanted him to bundle up, and brought him a cutaway coat, a vest, a dressing gown, and an overcoat to choose from. Quincas Borba waved them all away. He looked quite different now; his eyes, which had become introspective, were watching the workings of his brain. After much walking about, he stopped for a few seconds in front of Rubião.

VI

"If you want to know what life and death really are, I need only tell you how my grandmother died."

"How did she?"

"Sit down."

Rubião obeyed, assuming the most interested expression he could, while Quincas Borba continued to walk about.

"It was in Rio de Janeiro," he began, "in front of the Imperial Chapel, which was at that time the Royal Chapel, on an important fete day. My grandmother came out of the chapel and crossed the yard toward the litter that was waiting for her in the Palace Square. The people were like a swarm of ants; they all wanted to watch the great ladies enter in their fine attire. Just as my grandmother emerged from the churchyard on her way to the litter, which was nearby, it happened that one of the animals of a carriage took fright and started off in a dash. The other one followed; there was confusion, an uproar, my grandmother fell, and was run over by the mules and the carriage too. She was carried to an apothecary's shop on Direita Street; a bloodletter came, but it was too late. She had a great gash in her head, one leg and one shoulder were fractured, and she was covered with blood. She died a few minutes later."

"That was indeed a tragedy."

"No, it wasn't."

"No?"

"Listen to the rest. This is how it had happened. The owner of the carriage was in the churchyard, and he was hungry, very hungry, because he had breakfasted early and lightly. From where he was, he was able to signal the coachman and the latter, in answer to his master's summons, whipped the mules. In the middle of the road the carriage encountered an obstacle and ran it down; that obstacle was my grandmother. The first act of that series of acts was an impulse of preservation; Humanity was hungry. If, instead of my grandmother, it had been a rat or a dog, it is true that my grandmother would not have died, but it would still have been true that Humanity needed to eat. If, instead of a rat or a dog, it had been a poet, Byron or Gonçalves Dias, the matter would have been different in that it would have furnished material for many an obituary notice, but the fundamental fact would have remained the same. The universe has not yet come to an end for lack of a few poems that have died aflower in a man's head, be the man illustrious or obscure; but Humanity (and this, above all, is important), Humanity must eat."

Rubião was listening, with his soul in his eyes, sincerely wanting to understand; but he could not see that necessity to which his friend ascribed his grandmother's death. Surely, the owner of the carriage, however late he might have reached home, would not have died from hunger, while the good woman really did die, and forever. As best he could, he explained his doubts, and finally asked:

"And what is this Humanity that you're talking about?"

"Humanity is the principle. But no, I'll not say anything. You're not capable of understanding this, my dear Rubião. Let's talk about something else."

"Do go on."

Quincas Borba, who had not stopped his pacing, paused for a few moments.

"Do you wish to be my disciple?"

"I do."

"Very well, you'll gradually come to understand my philosophy; the day that you've penetrated it fully, ah! on that day life's greatest joy will be yours; for there is no wine so intoxicating as the truth. Believe me, Humanitism is the apogee of all things, and I, who formulated it, am the greatest man on earth. Look! See how my good Quincas Borba is looking at me? It isn't he, it's Humanity."

"What is that Humanity that you're talking about?"

"Humanity is the principle. In all things there is a certain hidden and identical substance, a principle, unique, universal, eternal, common, indivisible and indestructible—or to use the language of the great Camões:

'A veracity that in all things does exist,
That is to be found in the seen and the unseen.'

"Now that substance or veracity is what Humanity is. I call it that because it sums up the universe, and the universe is man. Are you beginning to understand?"

"A little; but even so, how is it that your grandmother's death—?"

"There is no death. The encounter of two expansions, or the expansion of two forms may determine the suppression of one of them; but, actually, there is no death; there is life, because the suppression of one is conditional upon the other's survival, and the destruction does not reach the universal and common principle. Hence, the preservative and beneficent nature of war. Suppose the existence of a potato field and two famished tribes. There are not enough potatoes to feed both tribes; so one of them gathers its forces to cross the mountain to the other slope where potatoes are abundant. If the two tribes were to divide the field of potatoes peacefully, there would not be enough for sufficient nourishment, and they would die from starvation. Peace, in that case, is destruction; war is preservation.

"One of the tribes exterminates the other and collects the spoils. Hence, the rejoicing in victory, the hymns, acclamations, public rewards, and all the other consequences of belligerence. If war were not that, there would not be such demonstrations, for the very real reason that man loves and commemorates only what is pleasing or advantageous to him, and for the rational reason that no one canonizes an act that virtually betrays him. To the vanquished, hatred or compassion; to the victor, the potatoes."

"But what about the opinion of those who are exterminated?"

"None is exterminated. The phenomenon disappears; the substance is the same. Have you never seen water boiling? You must remember that the bubbles are continually forming and breaking, and yet the water remains the same. Individuals are those transitory bubbles."

"Very well, then; what about the opinion of the bubbles?"

"A bubble doesn't have an opinion. Would it seem that there is anything sadder than one of those terrible plagues that devastate some part of the globe? And, yet, that supposed evil is a boon, not only because it eliminates the frail organisms, incapable of existence, but because it gives rise to observation, to the discovery of a curative drug. Hygiene is the child of age-old decay; we owe it to millions of individuals that have rotted away from disease and infection. Nothing is lost; everything is gained. Again, I say, the bubbles remain in the water. Do you see this book? It is Don Quixote. If I destroy my copy, I'll not eliminate the work itself, which will live on forever in the surviving copies and later editions. Eternal and beautiful, beautifully eternal, like this divine and more than divine world of ours."

VII

Quincas Borba stopped talking, exhausted, and sat down gasping. Rubião quickly brought some water, and begged him to lie down and rest; but after a few minutes the sick man replied that it was nothing. It was only that he had lost the habit of making speeches. And motioning to Rubião to move back so that he might look into his face without any effort on his part, he undertook a brilliant description of the world and its wonders. He so mingled ideas of his own and of others and images of all sorts, idyllic and epic, that Rubião wondered how a man near death could treat such matters so gallantly.

"Go rest a little while."

Quincas Borba reflected.

"No, I'm going to take a walk."

"Not now; you're too tired."

"No, no, it's over now."

He got up and placed his hands on Rubião's shoulders in a fatherly fashion.

"You are my friend?"

"What a question!"

"Tell me."

"As much as or more than this animal," answered Rubião, in an ecstasy of tender affection.

Quincas Borba squeezed his hands.

"Good."

VIII

Next day Quincas Borba awoke, resolved to go to Rio de Janeiro. He would return at the end of a month; he had certain business affairs—. Rubião was amazed. What about his sickness and the doctor? The invalid answered that the doctor was a quack, and that sickness as well as health required distraction. Sickness and health were two seeds of the same fruit, two states of Humanity.

"I'm going to attend to some personal affairs," he concluded, "and, besides that I have a plan, so sublime, that not even you will be able to understand it. Forgive my frankness, but I'd rather be frank with you than with anyone else."

Rubião trusted that in time this project would pass as had many others; but he was mistaken. What is more, the sick man seemed to be getting better. Instead of going to bed, he went out, and even did some writing. After a week, he called for a notary.

"A notary?" his friend repeated.

"Yes, I want to record my will. Or, we might go to the notary's, the two of us—"

Actually the three of them went, because the dog would not let his lord and master leave the house without going with him. Quincas Borba recorded his will with all due formality, and serenely went back home. Rubião felt his heart beating violently.

"Of course I'm not going to let you go to the capital alone," he said to his friend.

"You don't have to go with me. Besides, Quincas Borba isn't going, and I'll not entrust him to anyone but you. I'm leaving the house just as it is. I'll be back in a month. I'm going tomorrow, but I don't want the dog to see me leave. Take care of him, Rubião."

"Yes, I'll take care of him."

"Do you swear?"

"By this light that's shining on me. Am I a child not to be trusted?"

"Give him milk at the proper time; all his meals, as usual, and his baths. And when you go out walking with him, see that he doesn't run away. No, it'll be better if you don't go out— don't go out—."

"Don't worry."

Quincas Borba was crying over the other Quincas Borba. He did not want to see him when he left. Yes, he was really crying; tears of madness or of love, whatever they were, he was shedding them upon the good soil of Minas Gerais, like the last drops of sweat from an obscure soul about to topple into the abyss.

I X

Hours later Rubião had a horrible thought. People might believe that he, himself, had urged his friend to take the trip in

14

order to hasten his death and come into the legacy, if he really were included in the will. He felt remorse. Why had he not used every means to dissuade him from going? He saw Quincas Borba's corpse, pallid and foul, fixing a vengeful eye upon him, and he resolved that if, perchance, the end should come during the trip, he would relinquish the legacy.

The dog, for his part, went about sniffing and whining, and he kept trying to run away. He could not sleep quietly; he would get up many times at night, and wander over the house, going back to his corner finally. In the morning, Rubião would call him to his bed, and the dog would come running joyfully, thinking that it was his master. Then he would see that it was not, but none-the-less, he would accept Rubião's caresses and return them, as though he hoped they might be passed on to his master, or, even, that he might be taken to see him. He did not eat for the first days, but since he was less well able to endure thirst, Rubião succeeded in getting him to drink some milk. Afterwards he would lie for hours all quiet and sad, curled up, or stretched out with his head between his paws.

When the doctor came again, he was amazed at his patient's rashness. He should have been prevented from going; death was certain.

"Certain?"

"Sooner or later. Did he take the dog along?"

"No. He's with me. He asked me to take care of him, and when he did, he cried, he actually cried, as if he'd never stop. Of course," added Rubião, coming to the invalid's defense, "that dog really does deserve his master's esteem; he's just like a person."

The doctor took off his wide straw hat to adjust its ribbon band. He smiled. "A person? Like a person, you say?"

Rubião insisted. Then he explained that he was not just like an ordinary person, but that he did have feelings and even judgment. "Look, I was going to tell you—"

"No, not now, man, later, later— I'm on my way to an erysipelas patient. Look, if any letters come from him, and if they're not of a private nature, I'd like to see them. And my regards to the dog," he concluded as he was leaving.

Some people began to poke fun at Rubião and his singular responsibility of watching a dog instead of the dog's watching him. There was mockery and a shower of epithets. What was the teacher going to become? A dog's sentry? Rubião was afraid of public opinion. In fact, the whole thing seemed ridiculous to him; he shunned the eyes of strangers, regarded the dog with aversion, cursed himself, and cursed the day he was born. Had he not had the hope of a legacy, small as it might be— It just could not be that he would not be left some remembrance.

X

Seven weeks later, this letter, in Quincas Borba's writing and addressed from Rio de Janeiro came to Barbacena.

My dear friend,
   You have probably wondered at my silence. I haven't written you for certain particular reasons. I'll come back soon, but right now I wish to communicate to you a secret, very secret matter.
   Who am I, Rubião? I am Saint Augustine. I know that you'll smile, because you're an ignoramus, Rubião. Our intimacy would permit me to use a cruder word, but I'll make this concession, which is the last. Ignoramus!
   Listen, ignoramus. I am Saint Augustine. I found it out day before yesterday. Listen and say nothing.
   Everything in our lives coincides. The saint and I spent a part of our time in pleasures and heresy; for I consider heresy everything that does not pertain to my doctrine of Humanity; we both stole, he, as a little boy in Carthage, some pears, I, already a youth, a watch from my friend Braz Cubas. Our mothers were chaste and devout. Finally, he believed as I do, that everything that exists is good, and he demonstrates it in Chapter XVI, Book VII of his

Confessions, with the difference that for him, evil is a deviation of the will, an illusion peculiar to a backward age, a concession to error, whereas evil does not even exist, and only the first assertion is true; all things are good, *omnia boa,* and farewell.

Farewell, ignoramus. Don't tell anyone what I have just confided to you, if you don't wish to lose your ears; guard and be grateful for the good fortune of having a great man like me as a friend, even though you don't understand me. You will understand me. As soon as I return to Barbacena, I'll give you a true idea of what a great man is, in simple, explicit terms, adequate to the comprehension of an ass. Farewell; regards to my poor Quincas Borba. Don't forget to give him his milk; his milk and his baths. Farewell, farewell.

Your fond
Quincas Borba.

Rubião could scarcely hold the letter in his fingers. After a few seconds it occurred to him that his friend might be joking, and he reread the letter; but the second reading confirmed the first impression. There was no doubt about it; he was mad. Poor Quincas Borba! Thus, the eccentricities, the frequent changes of mood, the unreasoned impulses, the disproportionate affections, were merely the forerunners of the brain's total collapse. This was a kind of dying before death! He was so good! So happy! He was impertinent, of course, but the sickness accounted for that. Rubião dried his eyes, which were wet with emotion. Then he recalled the possible legacy, and that grieved him all the more, since it made him realize what a good friend he was going to lose.

He wanted to read the letter once again, slowly this time, analyzing the words, tearing them apart to perceive their meaning, and to discover whether this really were a philosopher's prank. He well knew this playful way of insulting him, but the rest confirmed his suspicion of disaster. When he had almost reached the end of the letter, he turned pale. If the testator's mental alienation were proved, would the will be nullified and the bequests be lost? Rubião suddenly felt dizzy. He was still holding the letter open in his hands when he saw the doctor making his appearance. He was coming for news of his patient; the mail clerk had told him that a letter had arrived. Was that the one?

"This is the one, but—"

"Does it contain some secret communication?"

"Right; it does contain a most secret communication; personal affairs— May I?"

And saying this, Rubião put the letter into his pocket. As soon as the doctor left, he drew a deep breath. He had escaped the danger of making public so grave a document through which Quincas Borba's mental state could be proved. A few minutes afterwards, he repented his action; he ought to have shown the letter. He felt so remorseful that he even thought of sending it to the doctor's house. He called a slave, but by the time the slave came, he had already changed his mind once again. That would be unwise, he thought; the sick man would be back shortly—in a few days—he might ask for the letter, accuse him of indiscretion, betrayal. Easy remorse, that endures but a moment.

"I don't want anything after all," he said to the slave. And again he turned his thoughts to the legacy. He calculated the amount. Surely it would not be less than ten contos. He would buy a piece of land, a house, exploit a gold mine. It wouldn't be so good if it were less, say, five contos— Five? That wasn't very much, but, after all, it might be more than that. Even if it were only five, that would be something, and something would be better than nothing. Five contos— It would be worse if the will were nullified. Well then, five contos!

XI

When, at the first of the following week he received the newspapers from the capital (to which Quincas Borba was still subscribing), Rubião read this notice in one of them:

Sr. Joaquim Borba dos Santos died yesterday after a singularly philosophical sufferance of his illness. He was a man of much wisdom, and he wore himself out struggling against that sickly, yellow pessimism that has yet to reach us here some day; it is an illness of the age. His last word was that pain is an illusion, and that Pangloss was not so stupid as Voltaire made him out— He was already delirious. He leaves considerable wealth. The will is in Barbacena.

XII

"His suffering is over," sighed Rubião.

Then, examining the notice, he saw that it spoke of a man who enjoyed esteem and consideration, and to whom a philosophical struggle was attributed. There was no allusion to madness. On the contrary, it said, in conclusion, that he had been delirious at the last, due to his illness. Good! Rubião reread the letter, and the hypothesis of a prank seemed again more likely. He knew well enough that he was a joker; surely he wanted to have some fun with him. He might as well have resorted to Saint Ambrosius or Saint Hilarius as to Saint Augustine. He wrote an enigmatic letter just to confuse him until such time as he, Quincas Borba, would return and laugh at his success. Poor friend—he was sane—sane and dead. Yes, he was no longer suffering now. Seeing the dog, he sighed:

"Poor Quincas Borba! If only he could know that his master had died—"

And, then, to himself:

"Now that I've fulfilled my obligation, I'll give him to my good friend Angelica."

The notice had circulated through the city; the vicar, the apothecary who served the house, the doctor had all sent to find out if it were true. The postal clerk, who had read it in the papers, delivered to Rubião personally a letter that had come in the mail for him. It might be from the deceased, though the handwriting on the envelope was not his.

"So the fellow finally turned up his toes?" he said while Rubião opened the letter, looked first at the signature, and read, "Braz Cubas." It was just a note:

> My poor friend Quincas Borba died yesterday at my house where he showed up some time ago, tattered and bedraggled as a result of his illness. Before he died, he asked me to write you and send you this notice in particular and also his deep gratitude. He said that the rest would be carried out through court procedure.

That part about gratitude made the teacher turn pale, but the part about court procedure sent the blood coursing through his veins again. Rubião folded the letter without a word. The clerk talked about one thing and another, and then he left. Rubião ordered a slave to take the dog as a gift to his good friend Angelica, and to tell her that since she liked animals here was one more. He was to ask her to treat him well as he was used to good treatment, and, finally, he was to tell her that the dog's name was the same as that of his deceased master, Quincas Borba.

When the will was opened, Rubião almost fell over. Guess why? He was named the testator's sole heir. Not five, nor ten, nor twenty contos, but everything, the entire capital, specified property, houses in the capital, one in Barbacena, slaves, policies, stock in the Bank of Brazil and other establishments, jewels, cash, books, in short, everything was becoming Rubião's, with no deviations, no bequests, no contributions to charity, no debts. There was only one condition stated in the will and that was that the heir, Rubião, keep the poor dog, Quincas Borba, whose master had given him his own name because of the great love that he bore him. The aforesaid Rubião was to treat the dog as if he still belonged to the testator. He was to deny him nothing that might be for his good; he was to see that he did not run away, and he was to protect him from sickness, theft, and death, which persons of evil intent might seek to inflict upon him. In short, he was to treat him as if he were not a dog, but a human being. Upon the dog's death, Rubião was to give him decent burial on his own property, which should be covered with flowers and aromatic shrubs. In due time, the bones of the aforesaid dog were to be disinterred and collected in an urn of precious wood to be put in the most honored place in the house.

XV

So read the clause. Rubião did not find it surprising, because, actually, he could think about nothing but the inheritance. He had had his eye on no more than a bequest, and here was the whole legacy coming to him. He simply could not believe it; he had to clench his fists hard—hard as when one is giving someone a congratulatory handshake—to convince himself that it was really true.

"Yes, sir, just figure it up," said the apothecary who had supplied Quincas Borba's medicines.

Just to be heir was a great deal; but sole heir— This word "sole" certainly inflated the inheritance. Heir to everything; not so much as one little spoon would be missing. And what comprised "everything?" he wondered. Houses, policies, stocks, slaves, clothing, china, pictures, (he probably had some in the capital, because he was a man of taste, a connoisseur of art). And books? He must have many books; he used to quote many. But how much would it all amount to? A hundred contos? Perhaps two hundred. That was quite possible. Even three hundred would not be surprising. Three hundred contos! Three hundred! And Rubião felt the impulse to execute a dance right out in the street. But then he calmed down. What if it were two hundred? Well, whatever it was, it was merely a dream that God was letting him have; but a long, unending dream.

At last, remembrance of the dog managed to stand up against the whirlwind of thoughts that were spinning through our Rubião's head. He was not surprised by the clause concerning the dog, but since he and the dog were friends, he did think it was unnecessary. Of course they would remain together, in memory of their friend, the deceased, author of their felicity. No doubt, there were some particulars in the clause, something about an urn, who knows what all— But it would all be complied with, though the heavens come tumbling down—no, rather, with the help of God, he amended. A good dog! An excellent dog!

Rubião was not forgetting that often he had tried to become rich through enterprises that had failed. At that time he had supposed himself to be an unlucky person, when the truth was that "he whom God helps is better off than he who rises early." It was not so impossible to become rich, for he was rich now.

"Impossible?" he exclaimed in a loud voice. "To say impossible is to sin against God. God does not fail those to whom he makes a promise."

Cogitating thus, and with his blood pulsating in his veins, Rubião went roaming aimlessly up and down the city streets, paying no heed to the houses. Suddenly, this grave problem occurred to him—would he go to live in Rio de Janeiro or would he stay in Barbacena? He was tempted to stay, to dazzle where he had been lost in obscurity, to outshine all those who never noticed him and chiefly those who had sneered at Quincas Borba's friendship. But then he visualized Rio de Janeiro, which he knew well, with its charm, its activity, theaters everywhere, pretty young women clad in French fashions, and he decided that would be better. He would be able to come up to his native city often.

"Quincas Borba! Quincas Borba! Oh, Quincas Borba!" he shouted, as he entered the house.

But there was no dog. Only then did he remember having sent it to his friend Angelica. He hastened to her house, which was at some distance, and on the way he thought of all the unpleasant things, and some fantastic ones, too, that might have happened. One unpleasant thought was that the dog might have run away. Another, this one fantastic, that some enemy, knowing about the clause and the gift, might have gone to Angelica's, stolen the dog, and concealed or killed it. In that case, the inheritance— A cloud passed before his eyes; then he began to see more clearly.

"I know nothing about law," he thought, "but it seems to me that I would have no concern with that. The clause supposes the dog to be alive or at home. But if it were to run away or die, a dog isn't to be created; therefore, the principal intention— My enemies, though, are quite capable of chicanery. If the clause is not fulfilled—"

At this point, our friend's forehead and the backs of his hands were wet with perspiration. Another cloud before his eyes (and his heart beat fast, very fast). The clause was beginning to seem extravagant. Rubião grasped at the saints, promised masses, ten masses. But there was Angelica's house. Rubião quickened his pace; he saw someone. Was it she? It was, it was she, leaning against the door and laughing.

"What are you trying to look like, Rubião? You look crazy, swinging your arms like that."

"Where's the dog, Angelica?" asked Rubião, with an assumed air of indifference, though his face was pale.

"Come in and sit down," she answered. "What dog?"

"What dog?" replied Rubião, becoming more and more pale. "The one that I sent you. Don't you remember that I sent you a dog so that it might stay here and rest for a few days, to see if—in short, a very valuable dog. He's not mine. I came to— But don't you remember?"

"Ah! Don't say anything to me about that creature," she answered, speaking rapidly.

She was small, and she shook all over at the least little thing. Whenever she became excited the veins in her neck would swell. She repeated that she did not want him to say anything to her about that "creature."

"But what has he done to you, Angelica?"

"What has he done to me? What would the poor animal do to me? He won't eat anything, he won't drink anything, he cries like a baby, and he's always trying to run away."

Rubião drew a breath of relief, while she continued to enumerate the dog's annoying habits. He said he was anxious to see him.

"He's out there in the back, in the large inclosure; he's alone so that the others won't fight with him. But are you coming to get him? They didn't tell me that. I understood that he was for me, that he was a gift."

"I'd give you five or six, if I could," replied Rubião. "This one I can't give you, as I am merely his depositary. But never mind, I promise you one of his pups. The message didn't come to you straight."

Rubião had already gotten up, and his friend, instead of leading the way, walked along with him. There was the dog, in the inclosure, lying at some distance from a dish of food. Dogs and birds were jumping all around outside. At one side, there was a hen house, a little farther away lay a sleepy cow

with two hens beside her that were pecking at her belly, removing ticks.

"Look at my peacock!" said Angelica.

But Rubião's eyes were on Quincas Borba, who was sniffing
impatiently, and who rushed at him the moment the Negro
boy opened the gate of the inclosure. There was a scene of wild
rejoicing; the dog returned Rubião's caresses, barking, leaping,
kissing his hands.

"Heavens! What a friendship!"

"You just can't imagine what good friends we are, Angelica.
Good-by. I promise you one of his pups."

XVIII

When Rubião and the dog entered the house, they seemed to
sense the presence and hear the voice of their deceased friend.
While the dog went about sniffing, Rubião sat down in the
chair in which he had been sitting when Quincas Borba, with
scientific explanations, had related his grandmother's death.
Though confusedly and with some loose ends, he put the philosopher's arguments together again, and for the first time he
considered carefully the allegory of the starving tribes, and
understood its conclusion. "To the victor, the potatoes!" Distinctly he heard the deceased's nasal voice expounding the
situation of the tribes, the conflict and the reason for the conflict, the extermination of one tribe, and the victory of the
other, and to himself he murmured, "To the victor, the potatoes!"

It was so simple, so clear! He looked down at his patched
suit and his frayed duck trousers and he realized that until
just a little while before he had been, so to speak, one of the
exterminated ones, a bubble, but that now he was a victor.
There was no doubt about it; potatoes were made for the tribe
that eliminates the other in order to cross over the mountains
and reach the potatoes on the other side. His own case pre-

cisely. He would go down from Barbacena to pull up and eat the potatoes that grew in the capital. It would behoove him to be hard and implacable; he would be powerful and strong. And suddenly overjoyed, he rose with uplifted arms and shouted: "To the victor the potatoes!"

The formula appealed to him; he thought it clever, succinct and eloquent besides being true and profound. He visualized the potatoes in their various forms and classified them according to flavor, appearance and nutritive value. In anticipation, he ate his fill at the banquet of life. It was high time to be done with the poor dry roots that merely deceived the stomach, and that had been the sorry fare of many long years. Now there would always be plenty of substantial food until death, and when death came, he would be lying under silken quilts, which is better than having it find one in rags. And once again he thought of the formula, and of his determination to be hard and implacable. He even went so far as to devise in his mind a seal for himself with the motto, "To the victor, the potatoes."

Rubião soon forgot all about the seal, but the formula lingered in his thoughts for a few days. "To the victor, the potatoes!" He probably had not understood it before the will; indeed, we have seen that he found it obscure and meaningless. For it is true as can be that the landscape depends upon one's point of view, and that the best way to appreciate a whip is to be holding its handle in one's hand.

XIX

I must not forget to tell that Rubião took it upon himself to have Mass said for the deceased, though he knew, or suspected, at least, that he was not a Catholic. Quincas Borba never joked about the priests nor did he discredit the Catholic doctrines. But he did not mention the church or its servants, and this, together with his devotion to Humanity made his heir doubt that Catholicism was his religion. He had Mass said, nonetheless, since he considered that it was not an act of will on the part of the dead man, but rather a prayer of the living, and since he thought, moreover, that it would be a scandal in the city if he who had been named heir by the deceased, failed to give his patron the suffrage that is not denied even the lowliest and most wretched.

If some people did not attend because they did not wish to see Rubião's triumph, many did go and they were not the rabble, either—and what they saw was the former schoolmaster's genuine humility.

x x

After attending to the preliminaries of the settlement, Rubião tried to get away to Rio de Janeiro, where he was going to establish himself as soon as everything was completed. There were affairs to be arranged in both cities, but matters promised to proceed quickly.

x x i

Sophia and her husband, Christiano de Almeida e Palha got on the train at the Vassouras station. Palha was a young man of thirty-two; his wife was between twenty-seven and twenty-eight. They sat down on the two seats opposite Rubião, arranged the small baskets and bundles of souvenirs that they were bringing from Vassouras, where they had spent a week, buttoned up their dusters, and exchanged a few words in an undertone.

After the train started, Palha noticed Rubião, who, amid so many sullen and bored-looking people, was the only one whose face expressed serenity and content. It was Christiano who opened the conversation with the remark that train travel was very tiring, to which Rubião replied that it was, indeed, and added that for one accustomed to donkey-back it was especially so, and wholly without charm. It was undeniable, though, that it marked progress.

"Of course," agreed Palha. "And great progress."

"Are you a farmer?"

"No, sir."

"Do you live in the city?"

"In Vassouras? No, we came here to spend a week. I live in the capital. I have no inclination to be a farmer, though I think it a fine, honorable position."

From farming they went on to cattle, slavery, and politics. Christiano Palha cursed the government, which had introduced into the royal speech a word concerning servile property; but to his great surprise Rubião did not share his indignation. It was his plan to sell the slaves that the testator had left him, except for a houseboy; if there were a loss it would be covered by the inheritance. Besides, the royal speech, which he, too, had read, ordered that present property be respected. What did he care about future slaves, if he were not going to buy any? The houseboy would be free, as soon as he came into possession of his belongings. Palha changed the conversation, and passed on to politics, the Chambers and the war with Paraguay, general subjects, all of them, to which Rubião gave only partial attention. Sophia scarcely listened; she merely turned her eyes, which she knew to be pretty, fixing them now upon her husband and now upon his interlocutor.

"Are you going to remain in the capital or are you returning to Barbacena?" asked Palha, after twenty minutes of conversation.

"It is my wish to remain, and I will remain," replied Rubião. "I'm tired of the provinces. I want to enjoy life. I may even go to Europe, but I don't know yet."

Palha's eyes suddenly shone.

"That's wonderful. I'd do the same if I could. I can't just now, though. You've probably been there already?"

"Never. That's why I got the idea of leaving Barbacena. So

here goes. One has to get that ennui out of one's system. I don't know when I'm going, but I'm—"

"You have the right idea. They say there are many fine things over there. No wonder, they're older than we are; and we have things that are equal to theirs and even superior. I don't say that our capital can compete with Paris or London, but it's attractive, you'll see.

"I've already seen it."

"Already?"

"Many years ago."

"You'll find it improved; there's been much progress in a short time. Then, when you go to Europe—"

"Have you been to Europe?" interrupted Rubião, addressing himself to Sophia.

"No."

"I forgot to introduce my wife to you," said Christiano. Rubião bowed respectfully, and, turning to the husband, he said, smiling:

"But won't you introduce yourself to me?"

Palha smiled, too. He realized that they did not know one another's names, and he hastened to tell his.

"Christiano de Almeida e Palha."

"Pedro Rubião de Alvarenga, but Rubião is what everyone calls me."

The exchange of names put them even more at their ease. Sophia did not enter into the conversation, but she gave free rein to her eyes, and they roved at will. Rubião talked good-humoredly, and listened attentively to Palha, grateful for the friendliness of a young man whom he had never seen before. He went so far as to suggest that some day they might go to Europe together.

"Oh, I'll not be able to go these first years," replied Palha.

"I didn't mean that; I'll not be going that soon myself. The desire I felt when I left Barbacena was a mere desire, without having any time set. There's no doubt that I'll go, but it will be at some time in the future, when it is God's will."

"And when I say that it won't be until years from now," said Palha hurriedly, "I must add that God's will may well

29

ordain the contrary. Who can see even a few months ahead? It's really Divine Providence that decides."

The gesture that accompanied these words was one of conviction and piety, but Sophia did not see it (she was looking at her feet), and Rubião did not even hear the last words. Our friend was dying to tell the reason for his going to the capital. His mouth was full of the confidence, eager to pour it into his traveling companion's ear, and only a remnant of already flabby scruples held it back. And, after all, if it were not a crime, if it were going to become public anyway, why hold it back?

"I have to attend to an inventory," he murmured finally.

"Your father?"

"No, a friend, who named me his sole heir."

"Ah!"

"Sole heir. Believe me, there are wonderful friends in this world, but few like him. He was priceless. And what a head! What intelligence! What learning! He was sick toward the end, and he became somewhat impudent, somewhat notional. You know how it is. Sick and wealthy, without any family, naturally he was somewhat demanding— But he was pure gold. When he esteemed someone, he esteemed him once and for all. We were friends, but he never said anything to me. Then one day, when he died, the will was opened, and I found myself with everything. That's true. Sole heir. There's not one bequest in the will for anyone else. He had no relatives. The only relative he would have had, would have been I, had he married a sister of mine, who died, poor thing. I was just a friend; but he knew how to be a friend, don't you think?"

"He certainly did," affirmed Palha.

The latter's eyes were no longer shining; they were lost in deep thought.

Rubião had entered a deep woodland where all the little birds of fortune were singing to him; he regaled himself talking about the inheritance; he confessed that he did not know the total amount, but he could calculate roughly—

"It's better not to calculate," interrupted Palha. "It won't be less than a hundred contos?"

"Make it more."

"If it's more, you should just wait and not say anything. And another thing—"

"I think it won't be less than three hundred."

"Another thing. Don't tell your affairs to strangers. I thank you for the confidence that I merited; but don't talk to the first person you meet. Discretion and kind faces don't always go together."

XXII

When they reached the station in the capital, they took leave of one another almost as if they were old friends. Palha offered the hospitality of his house in Santa Theresa, but the former teacher was going to the Union Hostelry. They parted with the promise that they would see one another again.

XXIII

The very next day, Rubião wanted to be with this new friend whom he had met on the train, and he decided to go to Santa Theresa in the afternoon; but already in the morning Palha came to wish him good day and to find out if he were comfortable where he was, or whether he would prefer his house, which was up on the hill. Rubião did not accept the offer of hospitality, but he did accept the lawyer (a distant relative of Palha's) whom Palha recommended, despite his youth, as one of the best.

"You can take advantage of him before he starts making his clients pay for his name."

Rubião took him for lunch, and then, in spite of protests from the dog, who wanted to go along, accompanied him to the lawyer's office where all arrangements were completed.

"Come and have dinner with me soon, in Santa Theresa," said Palha, as he took his leave. "You needn't hesitate; I'll be expecting you," he concluded, as he withdrew.

XXIV

Since he did not know how to act with women, Rubião felt some constraint because of Sophia. Fortunately, however, he remembered the promise he had made to himself to be strong and implacable. And so he went to dinner! Blessed resolve! Where else could he have spent such happy hours? Sophia appeared to much better advantage in the home than in the train. In the train, though, to be sure, her eyes were uncovered, she was wearing a cape. Here at home, both eyes and body were visible, the latter sheathed in a cambric gown that revealed her pretty hands, and a bit of arm. Besides, here she was mistress of the house. She was more talkative, and she made every effort to be gracious. Rubião went down from the hill with his head in a whirl.

XXV

He dined there often. He was timid and shy. Frequency attenuated the impression of the first days, but there still burned uneasily a certain peculiar fire that he could not extinguish. During the inventory, and especially during the denunciation that was brought forward by someone who alleged that, since he had obviously not been of sound mind, Quincas Borba could not make a will, Rubião was preoccupied. But the denunciation was nullified, and the inventory proceeded rapidly to its conclusion. Palha celebrated the occasion with a dinner, at which, besides the three of them, the lawyer was present, and also the procurator and the court clerk. That day Sophia's eyes were the most beautiful eyes on earth.

XXVI

She must buy them in some mysterious factory, thought Rubião, as he went down the hill. I never saw them so beautiful as they were today.

The next thing he did was to move into the house at Botafogo, one of his inheritances; it had to be furnished, and here again friend Palha generously lent his services, guiding Rubião's taste, advising him as to the advertisements and going with him to shops and auctions. Sometimes, as we already know, the three of them would go together; because "there are certain things," said Sophia, charmingly, "that only a woman can select." Rubião accepted gratefully, and lingered over his purchases as long as he could, with much purposeless consultation and much pretense of needing things that he really did not need at all, just so that he could have the young woman beside him a little longer. And, as for her, she would make no move to leave; but would go right on talking and explaining and demonstrating.

XXVII

All this was running through Rubião's head, after his morning cup of coffee, in the very spot where we left him sitting and gazing off into the distance. He was still drumming with the tassels of his dressing gown. Finally he remembered to go and see Quincas Borba and unleash him. That was his daily duty. He got up and went out to the back garden.

But what sort of sinful thought is this that keeps pursuing me? he thought, as he was on his way out. She's married; she gets along well with her husband, her husband is my friend, he has more confidence in me than anyone else— What kind of temptation is this?

He stopped, for a moment, and, thereupon, the temptation stopped, too. He, a lay Saint Anthony, differed from the anchorite in that he liked the devil's promptings, once they really persisted. Hence, the alternating monologues:

She's so pretty! And she seems to like me so much! If her manner doesn't indicate that she's fond of me, I don't know what "being fond of" means. She clasps my hand with such pleasure and so warmly—I just can't tear myself away from those people even if they leave me alone. I can't resist.

Quincas Borba heard his footsteps and began to bark. Rubião hurried to unleash him, because it meant that for a few moments he could unleash himself from what was pursuing him.

"Quincas Borba!" he cried, opening the gate.

The dog sprang forward. Such joy! Such excitement! Such a leaping about his master! He's so happy that he even licks his hand, but Rubião gives him a painful tap. Mournfully the dog recoils a little, his tail between his legs; then, at a snap of his master's fingers, here he is back again, joyful as ever.

"Quiet! Quiet!"

Quincas Borba follows him out through the garden and around the house, walking sedately one moment and wildly jumping the next. He is relishing his freedom, but he won't lose sight of his master! He sniffs here, he pauses there to scratch an ear, a little farther on, he catches a flea on his stomach, but with one bound he leaps over the space and time lost, and again follows close upon his master's heels. He is convinced that Rubião is walking around like this for his sake, so that he, too, will get a walk and make up for all the time that was lost when he was kept in. When Rubião stops, he looks up at him expectantly. Of course his master is thinking of him and making some plan; perhaps it's that they'll go out together or something pleasant like that. The possibility of a kick or a tap doesn't even occur to him. He has a trustful nature, and if ever he is struck, it is soon forgotten. Caresses, on the other hand, no matter how absent-mindedly they may be given, make a lasting impression. He likes to be loved, and he gratifies himself with the belief that this is so.

His life there is neither wholly good nor wholly bad. There is a Negro boy who gives him a bath in cold water every day, a confounded procedure that he can't get used to. Then there's Jean, the cook, who likes him, and the Spanish servant, who doesn't like him at all. Rubião spends many hours away from home, but he doesn't treat him badly. He lets him go up to the house, be present at lunch time and dinner time, go with him into the living room or study. Sometimes he plays with him and gets him to jump. But if formal visitors come, he has him taken away. Then, very gently at first, the Spaniard removes Quincas Borba; but he soon takes revenge upon the dog's steady resistance, dragging him along by an ear or leg, hurling him far from the house and closing all means of entrance.

"Perro del infierno!"

Smarting, and separated from his master, Quincas Borba goes and lies down in a corner, where he will stay quietly for a long time. He stirs about a little until he finds the position that is just right, and then he closes his eyes. He does not sleep, though; he collects his thoughts. He recalls and merges certain images; perhaps, far, far, away, the face of his dead friend drifts by vaguely and fragmentarily, and then blends with the face of his present friend until they appear to be a single person. Then there are other thoughts—

By now there have been many thoughts—too many thoughts; at any rate, they are a dog's thoughts, the mere dust of thoughts —perhaps less than dust, the reader will say. And yet the truth is that that eye that keeps opening every little while to gaze so expressively into space seems to translate something that shines inside, very deep inside, something else that is not—

I don't quite know what words to use when referring to a dog's body—the tail, perhaps, or the ears. Man's poor, inadequate language!

At last he falls asleep. Then images, some of them vague, others of recent occurrence, begin to play about inside of him in the form of dreams, a scrap here, a patch there. When he awakens, he forgets all that was unpleasant; however, he looks —well, not to annoy the reader—I'll not say melancholy. One may say of a landscape that it's melancholy, but one does not say that of a dog, for the reason, no doubt, that the melancholy of the landscape lies within ourselves, whereas if we attribute it to a dog, we externalize it. Be that as it may, Quincas Borba's expression is not the joyful one of a little while before. But let a whistle come from the cook or a gesture from his master, and it will disappear, his eyes will shine, his nose wrinkle with pleasure, and his legs fly like wings.

XXIX

Rubião spent the rest of the morning pleasurably. It was Sunday. Two friends had come to have lunch with him, a young man of twenty-four, who was nibbling the first peelings of his mother's wealth and a man of forty-four or forty-six, who no longer had anything left to gnaw.

Carlos Maria was the name of the former; Freitas, that of the latter. Rubião liked them both, but each in a different way. It was not solely Freitas' age that brought him closer to him, but the man's disposition as well. Freitas had a special courteous word of praise for everything, greeted each dish, each wine individually, and always went away with his pockets crammed with cigars, proving thus that he preferred them to any others. Rubião had been introduced to him in a certain store on Municipal Street where they once dined together. Rubião had heard about the man; heard, though not in detail, about his good and bad fortune, and had turned up his nose, thinking that this was evidently some castaway, whose companionship would bring him neither personal pleasure nor public esteem. Freitas, however, soon modified that first impression; he was alert, interesting, full of anecdotes, cheerful as a man with an income of fifty contos. As Rubião spoke of the pretty roses that he grew, he asked permission to go and see them; he was mad about flowers. Not many days later, he showed up at the house and said that he had come for just a few minutes to see the roses and that if Rubião were busy he should not be disturbed. Rubião, however, was glad to see that the man had not forgotten their conversation. He went down to the garden, where his visitor had remained waiting, and went with him to show him the roses.

Freitas thought them admirable, and he examined them so attentively that it was necessary to pull him away from one rosebush in order to move him on to the next. He knew the names of them all, and he mentioned casually many species with which even Rubião was not familiar. He continued to mention various kinds, and to describe this and that about them (to indicate their size, for instance, he would open and round his thumb and forefinger) and he named the people who had had the best specimens. Rubião's, however, were the best species; this one was rare, that one also, etc. The gardener listened in amazement. After they had all been inspected, Rubião said:

"Come in and have something. What shall it be?"

Freitas said that anything would be quite all right. When they reached the house, he expressed admiration for its furnishings. He inspected the bronzes, the pictures, the furniture, and he looked out toward the sea.

"Yes, indeed," he said. "You live like a nobleman."

Rubião smiled; "nobleman," even in a comparison, is a word that is good to hear. The Spanish servant came with the silver tray, glasses and various liquors; it was a happy moment for Rubião. He, himself, suggested this liquor or that; finally he recommended one that had been rated as superior to anything of its kind that would be available in the market. Freitas smiled incredulously.

"That may be exaggeration," he said.

He took the first swallow and savoured it; then a second and then a third. Finally he confessed in astonishment that it was perfect, and asked Rubião where he had bought it. Rubião replied that a friend, owner of a large winery, had presented him with a bottle, but that he liked it so well that already he had ordered three dozen.

Their friendship soon became closer, and now Freitas goes there for lunch or dinner often—oftener, indeed, than he should, or even wants to—because it is hard to resist a man who is so gracious and who so likes to see friendly faces.

XXX

Rubião asked him once.

"Tell me, Mr. Freitas, if I should take it into my head to go to Europe, would you go with me?"

"No."

"Why not?"

"Because now I'm free to come and go; but if we were to take a trip together, we might have disagreements."

"Well, I'm sorry, because you're such a cheerful person."

"Ah, but you're wrong. I wear this smiling mask, but, actually, I'm a mournful person. I'm an architect of ruins. I'd go first of all to the ruins of Athens; then I'd go to the theater to see *O Pobre das Ruinas*, a tearful play, and then to the courts of bankruptcy where ruined men—"

Rubião laughed; he liked that frankness and lack of restraint.

XXXI

Do you wish the reverse of this, curious reader? Well, take a look at this other luncheon guest, Carlos Maria. If Freitas is "frank and unrestrained" in a laudatory sense—it is obvious that Maria is quite the opposite. It will not be hard for you, then, to imagine his slow entry into the room, and the cold, superior way in which he acknowledges the introduction to Freitas, who, though he has been cursing him cordially for his delay (it is near midday) greets him now with effusive courtesy and much inward rejoicing.

You will also be able to see for yourself that if our Rubião likes Freitas better, he holds the other in higher esteem. He has been waiting for him patiently, and he would be willing to wait for him until tomorrow. As for Carlos Maria, he holds neither of the two men in esteem. Take a good look at him. He's an elegant youth with large, placid eyes, very much master of himself, and even more so of others. He looks at you down his nose, and his laugh is mocking rather than jovial. Now as he sits down at the table, it is evident in the way that he picks up the silverware and opens his napkin, in fact, in everything that he does, that he is conferring a great favor on his host—perhaps two favors, that of eating lunch and that of not calling him an imbecile.

And, yet, despite this disparity in temperaments, the luncheon was agreeable. Freitas ate ravenously, with a pause now and then, to be sure, and confessing to himself that, had the lunch been on time (eleven o'clock), it might not have tasted so good. He was judging by the first mouthfuls, which were such as might alleviate the hunger of a castaway. After about ten minutes, he was able to talk, and with much laughter and a diffusion of gestures and expressive glances, recited a rosary of pointed sayings and picturesque anecdotes. To humiliate him, Carlos Maria listened to most of them without the flicker of a smile, so that Rubião, who really found Freitas amusing, did not dare to laugh. Toward the end of the lunch, Carlos Maria loosened up and recounted several amorous adventures that had befallen others. Freitas, wishing to flatter him, asked him for one or two of his own. Carlos Maria burst out laughing.

"What sort of a person do you take me for?"

Freitas explained that it was facts he was asking for, not an apology; yes, it was facts he was asking for; there was nothing wrong in that; no one would suppose—

"You like living here in Botafogo?" interposed Carlos Maria, addressing himself to his host.

Freitas, interrupted, bit his lips, and for the second time, cursed the fellow. He leaned back stiffly in his chair and stared unsmilingly at a picture on the wall. Rubião replied that he liked living in Botafogo very much, and that the beach was beautiful.

"The view is pretty, but I never could stand the bad smell that's here at certain times," said Carlos Maria. "What do you think of it?" he continued, turning to Freitas.

Freitas leaned forward and expatiated on the subject. He thought that they could both be right, but he insisted that in spite of everything, the beach was magnificent. He spoke without resentment or vexation, and even had the courtesy to call Carlos Maria's attention to a bit of fruit that had clung to the tip of his mustache.

They came to the end of the luncheon. It was a little after one o'clock. Rubião was quietly going over it in his mind, dish by dish, and looking contentedly at the glasses with their residue of wine, at the scattered crumbs, and at the table, which appeared in its final stage, with only the coffee still to be served. Now and again he would steal a glance at the servant's coat. He succeeded in catching Carlos Maria's face in flagrant pleasure as he was drawing the first puffs on one of the cigars that had been passed around. At this moment, the servant entered with a small basket, covered with a cambric handkerchief, and a letter, both of which had just been delivered.

XXXII

"Who's sending this?" asked Rubião.

"Dona Sophia."

Rubião did not recognize the writing; it was the first time that she had written him. What could it be? His excitement was visible in his face and fingers. Freitas familiarly uncovered the little basket; there were strawberries in it. Tremulously, Rubião read these lines:

> I am sending you this fruit for lunch, if it arrives in time; and by order of Christiano you are summoned to dine with us today without fail.
>
> Your true friend,
> Sophia

"What kind of fruit is it?" asked Rubião, folding the letter. "Strawberries."

"They came too late. Strawberries?" he repeated, without knowing what he was saying.

"You needn't blush, my dear fellow," laughed Freitas, as soon as the servant went out. "These things happen to one who's in love—"

"In love?" repeated Rubião, actually blushing. "But here, you may read the letter. See—"

He was on the point of showing it, but drew back and put it into his pocket. He was really beside himself with mingled confusion and joy, and Carlos Maria took delight in telling him that he could not conceal that the gift was from some inamorata. He assured him, though, that there was nothing reprehensible in that, since love was a universal law. If she were a married woman, he would praise his discretion.

"But by the love of Heaven!" interrupted his Amphytrion.

"A widow? Then we're in the same situation," continued Carlos Maria, "and discretion is truly a merit. The greatest sin, after the initial sin, is its publication. If I were a legislator, I'd propose the burning of every man convicted of indiscretion in such matters and like those condemned by the Inquisition, they would all have to go to the stake, only, instead of a hood of green and yellow baize, they would wear a cap of parrot feathers."

Freitas could not contain himself for laughter, and he banged on the table as if in applause. Rubião, slightly pale, hastened to say that the woman was neither married, nor a widow.

"A spinster, then?" replied the young man. "Will there be wedding bells before long? It's high time. Here are strawberries for the wedding party," he continued, picking up a few between his fingers. "They smack of the maiden's bedchamber and of the priest's Latin."

Rubião no longer knew what to say. Finally, he started all over again, and explained that she was the wife of a very special friend. Carlos Maria winked, and Freitas intervened to say that everything was explained now. In the beginning, the mysteriousness of it all, the way the little basket had been sent, the look of the strawberries themselves—adulterous strawberries— he said, laughing, all that made the affair appear immoral and guilty, but that was over now.

They drank their coffee in silence, and then went into the living room. Rubião put himself out to be gracious, but he was preoccupied. After a few minutes' reflection, the initial supposition of his two guests, that of an adulterous love affair, appealed to him, and he even thought that he had defended himself too ardently. So long as he had not told anyone's name, he could have admitted that it was, indeed, an intimate affair. But, then, too, the very ardour of his denial may have left some doubt, some suspicion, in the minds of the two. At this point in his thoughts, he felt consoled, and smiled.

Carlos Maria consulted his watch; it was two o'clock and he made ready to leave. Rubião thanked him very effusively for coming, and asked him to come again. They could spend some Sunday afternoons like that in friendly talk.

"Hear, hear!" shouted Freitas, as he joined them.

He had put half a dozen cigars into his pockets, and, as he left, he whispered into Rubião's ear:

"Here goes my usual souvenir; six days of pleasure, a pleasure for each day."

"Take more."

"No. I'll get them another time."

Rubião accompanied them to the iron gate. The moment Quincas Borba heard voices, he ran from the back of the garden, and came to greet them, with a special greeting for his master. He made a demonstration over Carlos Maria and tried to lick his hand, but the young man drew away with repugnance. Rubião gave the dog a kick that made him yelp and run off. Finally, the three friends said good-bye.

"Where are you going?" Carlos Maria asked Freitas.

Freitas supposed that Maria was probably going to make a call in the direction of São Clemente, and, as he wanted to accompany him, he said, "I'm going to the end of the beach."

"I'm turning back," the other man replied.

XXXIII

Rubião watched them go, and then went in, ensconsed himself in the living room, and once again read Sophia's note. Each word on that unexpected page was a mystery in itself; the signature, a capitulation. Just Sophia; no other name, family or married. "True friend" was evidently a metaphor. As for the first words, "I'm sending you this fruit for lunch," they breathed the candor of a good and generous soul. Through the mere force of instinct Rubião saw the whole thing clearly, sensed its meaning and grasped its import. He found himself kissing the paper —or rather, kissing the name, the name given at the baptismal font, repeated by the mother, entrusted to the husband as part of the wedding document, and now removed from all these sources and ownerships to be sent to him at the bottom of a sheet of paper— Sophia! Sophia! Sophia!

XXXIV

"Why have you come so late?" Sophia asked, when he appeared at the garden gate in Santa Theresa.

"After lunch, which was over at two o'clock, I was arranging some papers. But it isn't so late," continued Rubião, looking at his watch. "It's half past four."

"It's always late where friends are concerned," replied Sophia, reproachfully.

Rubião realized his error, but he did not have time to amend it. In front of him, sitting silently on iron benches beside the house, were four women, who were looking at him with curiosity. They were callers who had been awaiting the arrival of a certain capitalist, Rubião. Three of them were married women, one, a spinster, or shall we say an old maid? She was thirty-nine years old, and had black eyes that were weary of waiting. She was the daughter of a Major Siqueira, who, himself came into the garden a few minutes later.

"Our Palha has already spoken of you," said the Major, after his introduction to Rubião. "I assure you that he's a real friend of yours. He told me about the chance meeting that brought you together. Generally the best friendships are like that. In the thirties, just before the Majority, I had a friend, my very best friend at the time, whom I met by chance in that way, in the Bernardes apothecary's shop. His nickname was João, Padded-Legs. I think he padded the calves of his legs when he was a youth between 1801 and 1812, and the nickname had always clung. The apothecary's shop was at the intersection of São José and Misericordia Streets. João Padded Legs—the padding filled out his legs, you see. Bernardes was his real name, João Alves Bernardes— He had the apothecary's shop on São José Street. Afternoons and evenings, groups often used to gather together there for conversation. The men would wear their cloaks and carry their canes and some carried a lantern. I didn't— I only wore my cloak. It was the fashion to wear a cloak. Bernardes— João Alves Bernardes was his full name—was a native of Marica, but he was brought up here in Rio de Janeiro— João Padded-Legs was his nickname. They said that he padded his calves as a young man and that he was one of the dandies about town. I've never forgotten João Padded-Legs— that day it was the fashion to wear a cloak—"

Rubião's spirit was flinging its arms about, groping for an escape from this shower of words, but it was in a blind alley. Walls everywhere. No open door anywhere, no corridor, and the rain was falling. Had he been able to look over toward the

44

women, he would have seen, at least, that he was the object of their curiosity. They were all curious about him, especially the Major's daughter, Dona Tonica. But he could not; he was listening, and the Major continued to pour. It was Palha who brought him an umbrella. Sophia had gone to tell her husband that Rubião had just arrived, and in no time Palha was in the garden, greeting his friend and saying that he had come late. The Major, who was once again explaining the apothecary's nickname, abandoned his prey, and went over to the ladies. Later, he left.

X X X V

The married women were pretty; even the spinster had probably not been unattractive at twenty-five; but Sophia stood out among them all.

This is saying a great deal, though our friend probably was even more impressed by her beauty. She was that type of woman whom time, like a deliberate sculptor, does not complete all at once, but polishes and repolishes over a long period. Such sculptures, which evolve gradually, are marvelous. Though Sophia was creeping up on twenty-eight, she was more beautiful than at twenty-seven, and it would seem that not until she was thirty would the sculptor give the finishing touches, if, indeed, he might not wish to prolong the work for two or three years more.

The eyes, for instance, are not those of the train, when our Rubião was talking with Palha, and they, the eyes, were underlining the conversation. Now they seem blacker, and they no longer underline anything. They compose by themselves, in a full, showy handwriting, not one line or two, but entire chapters. The mouth looks fresher. Shoulders, arms, and hands are better, and she shows them to advantage in well-chosen poses and gestures. Even the excessively heavy eyebrows, one feature that their possessor had never been able to tolerate, and that Rubião himself had at first found out of harmony with the rest of the face, though they are still heavy as ever, seem to impart a very distinguished appearance.

She dresses well; she nips in her waist, and moulds her bust in a simple chestnut colored bodice of fine wool, and wears two genuine pearl earrings—an Easter gift from our Rubião.

The lovely lady is the daughter of an old public official. At the age of twenty she married this Christiano de Almeida e Palha, a broker, who was twenty-five. Her husband was successful, clever and enterprising, and he had a flair for doing business and for sensing situations. In 1864, though he had not held his position long at that time, he had a foreboding— one cannot call it anything else—he had a foreboding of the bank failures.

"Something's going to happen one of these days. The situation is very precarious; the least cry of alarm will set it off."

The worst part of it was that he spent all that he made and more. He liked good living; frequent parties, expensive gowns and jewels for his wife, ornaments for the house, particularly if they were novelties, took all his earnings, present and future. Except for food, he was parsimonious with himself. Often when he went to the theater he did not care for it and at dances he enjoyed himself only moderately—but after all, he went less for himself than to accompany his wife's eyes and bosom. In order to reveal his personal good fortune to others, he had the peculiar vanity of dressing his wife in low-cut gowns whenever it was possible, and even where it was not. Thus, he was a sort of King Candaules, exhibiting less, to be sure, but to a larger public.

And at this point let us do justice to our lady. Though at first she yielded to her husband's wishes with indifference, so great was the admiration garnered, and to such an extent does habit accommodate one to circumstances, that finally she came to enjoy being shown, very much shown, for the pleasure and provocation of others. Let us not make her out to be any more or less saintly than she was. Her eyes sufficed to pay for her vanity; they were laughing eyes, restless and inviting, but only inviting. We can compare them to the lantern of an inn in which there were no rooms for the guests. Because its color was so pretty and its emblems so original, the lantern made everyone stop. Everyone would stop, look and continue on his way. Why open the windows? In the end, she did open them; but the door, if we may so call the heart, remained doubly barred.

XXXVI

Good Lord, how pretty she is! I feel capable of starting a scandal, thought Rubião that evening, as he sat in a window embrasure, facing the room and gazing at Sophia.

One of the women was singing. The three husbands, who were there now, interrupted their game of *voltarete* in another room, and came into the drawing room for a few moments to listen to the singer, who was the wife of one of them. Palha, who was accompanying her at the piano, did not see that his wife and the capitalist were gazing at each other. I do not know whether anyone saw them. But, yes, I do know that one did, the Major's daughter, Dona Tonica.

Good Lord, how pretty she is! I feel capable of starting a scandal, Rubião continued thinking to himself, as he sat leaning against the window, his eyes lost in contemplation of the lovely lady, who in her turn was gazing at him.

XXXVII

It is quite understandable that Dona Tonica should observe this mutual contemplation. Since the moment of Rubião's arrival, her one thought had been to attract him. Her poor thirty-nine year old eyes, that were without equal, and that were on the point of slipping wearily into despair, found that they still had a few sparks. She was an old hand at moving them languidly and turning them this way and that. It would not be at all hard for her to arm them against Rubião. Something told her that this wealthy man from Minas Gerais was destined by Heaven to solve her marriage problem. He was even wealthier than she wanted; she did not want wealth; she wanted a husband. All her campaigns had been waged without any pecuniary consideration. Lately she had been coming down, down, down; the last one had been against a poor young student— But who knows whether Heaven might not be destining a wealthy man for her? Dona Tonica had faith in her patroness, Our Lady of the Immaculate Conception, and she attacked the fortress with great skill and courage.

All the other women are married, she thought.

Soon she perceived that Rubião's glances and Sophia's were traveling toward one another; she noticed, however, that Sophia's were less frequent and less lingering, a phenomenon that could be explained, she thought, by the caution required under the circumstances. It could be that they were in love— This suspicion disquieted her, but thereupon, desire and hope pointed out that even after one or two love affairs a man might well marry in the end. The question was to catch him; the prospect of marrying and having a family might put an end to any other inclination on his part, if, indeed, he had any.

She redoubled her forces. All her charms were summoned to their posts, and, though withered, they obeyed. Gesturings with her fan, a parting of her lips, sidewise glances, walking up and down to show the elegance of her figure and the slenderness of her waist, it was all used. It was the old collection of formulas in action; up until now, it had not brought any returns, but the lottery is just the same; suddenly a ticket comes along that redeems all the losses.

Right now, however, this evening, during the singing at the piano, Dona Tonica saw their mutual infatuation. She no longer had any doubt; these were not brief, casual glances, as before; this was an absorption that eliminated the rest of the room, and Dona Tonica heard the cawing of the old crow of despair— Quoth the Raven: Never More.

Even so, she continued the struggle; she succeeded in getting Rubião to sit down beside her for a few minutes, and she tried to say something pleasant, phrases remembered from novels, phrases quite different from those that the melancholy of the present circumstances would have inspired. Rubião listened, and answered, but he was perturbed when Sophia left the room, and no less so when she returned. At one moment he was particularly absent-minded. Dona Tonica was confessing that she would very much like to see Minas and especially, Barbacena, and she asked: "How is the climate?"

"The climate," Rubião repeated mechanically.

He was looking at Sophia, who was standing with her back toward him, talking to two women, who were seated. Once again he was admiring her figure, her well-sculptured bust, which tapered down to emerge from ample hips like a great armful of leaves coming out from a vase. To carry out that comparison, one might say, then, that her head was like a single, uplifted magnolia blossom fastened to the center of the cluster. It was this that Rubião was gazing at when Dona Tonica asked him about the climate in Barbacena, and he repeated the word without even giving it its interrogatory inflection.

XXXVIII

Rubião was determined. Never before had Sophia's spirit seemed so insistently to invite his to fly away in unison with it to that clandestine land whence, in general, spirits come back old and weary. Some do not come back at all. Others stop midway. A great many never get past the eaves of the house.

The moon was magnificent. There on the hill, between the sky and the level terrain below, the least audacious spirit could have faced a hostile army and destroyed it. Witness what this timorous spirit could not do with an amicable army. Sophia had slipped her arm through Rubião's to go to see the moon. She had asked Dona Tonica to go along, but the poor woman replied that her foot was asleep, and that she wouldn't go just then, and she did not go.

The two remained quiet for awhile. Through the open windows, one could see the others, who were conversing, and even the men who had stopped playing voltarete. The garden was small; but the human voice has a full range, and the two might have recited poetry without anyone's hearing them.

Rubião remembered an antiquated comparison, picked up goodness knows where—perhaps from some stanza of 1850 or some prose passage of any period. He called Sophia's eyes terrestrial stars, and he called the stars celestial eyes. All this in a very low, tremulous voice.

Sophia was dumbfounded. Suddenly she straightened her body, which until that moment had been leaning on Rubião's arm. She was so used to the man's timidity— Stars? Eyes? She wanted to tell him not to tease her, but she did not know how to put it without either rejecting a conviction that was also hers, or else encouraging him to go on. Hence, a long silence.

"With one difference," continued Rubião. "The stars are even less beautiful than your eyes, and, after all, I really don't know what the stars look like. God put them so high that they can't be seen from near by without losing much of their beauty; whereas that's not true of your eyes; they're right here beside me, luminous, more luminous than the sky—

Rubião did not stop there. Fearless and loquacious, he seemed totally different from his usual self. He went right on talking, though he kept within the same circle of ideas. He did not have many, and despite the man's sudden change, the situation tended to restrict the few he did have rather than inspire new ones. Sophia did not know what to do. She thought she had been holding a gentle, quiet little dove in her arms, and it was turning out to be a hawk—a hawk, with hooked beak and ravenous eye.

She must answer him, make him stop, tell him that he was headed in a direction that she did not wish to take, and all that without making him angry or driving him away. Sophia sought some way out, but she could not find it, because she came up against the insoluble question of whether it would be better to let him see that she understood or let him think that she did not understand. Then she remembered what her own manner had been, the soft little words, the special attentions, and she concluded that, under the circumstances, she could not pretend not to know the meaning of the man's compliments. But the delicate point was to confess that she did understand and not to dismiss him from the house.

X L

Up above, the stars seemed to be laughing at the inextricable situation.

It was quite all right, of course, for the moon to see them. The moon does not know how to sneer. No doubt the poets, who find her provocative of yearning and a mood of nostalgia, know that long ago she was in love with some wandering star that left her after many centuries. Perhaps her eclipses (pardon the astronomy) are merely amorous trysts. The myth of Diana's coming down to meet Endymion may well be true. To come down, though, is too much. What harm is there in the two meeting right up there in the sky just as the crickets do among the leaves down here? Charitable Mother Night takes it upon herself to watch over all her creatures.

And the moon is alone. Solitude makes a person serious. The stars, in their great multitude, are like young girls between fifteen and twenty, gay, full of chatter, laughing and talking all at once about everything and everyone.

I do not deny that they are chaste; but so much the worse—then, probably they have laughed at what they do not understand. Chaste stars! That is what the terrible Othello calls them and the jovial Tristram Shandy. On one point those extremes of heart and mind agree: the stars are chaste. And they (chaste stars!) heard everything that Rubião's reckless mouth was pouring into Sophia's astounded soul. He, who for so many months had been modest and prudent, was now (chaste stars!) no less than a libertine. You would almost think that the Devil (Devil Rubião) had set out to deceive the young woman by the two great archangel's wings that God had placed on him; because, suddenly, he put them into his pocket and took off his hat, revealing the two malefic projections affixed to his forehead. And, laughing with the crooked laughter of evil creatures, he proposed not only to buy the soul, but the soul and the body— Chaste stars!

XLI

"Let's go in," murmured Sophia.

She tried to pull her arm away, but he held it firmly. No, why should they go in? It was very nice where they were. What could be better? Or, perhaps, he was boring her? She hastened to reply that, indeed, he was not, but that she must be hostess for her guests— They had been out there so long!

"It isn't ten minutes," said Rubião. "What is ten minutes?"

"But they may have noticed our absence—"

Rubião trembled at this possessive, *our* absence. He found in it a beginning of complicity. He agreed that they might have noticed our absence. She was right, they ought to separate; he would only ask one thing of her; no, two things. The first was that she should never forget that sublime ten minutes and the second that she should look at the Southern Cross every night. He would look at it, too, and their thoughts would join there in intimacy between God and men.

The request was poetic, but only the request. Rubião was
devouring the young woman with fiery eyes, and he was holding
one of her hands tight lest it get away from him. There was
nothing poetic about the eyes nor the gesture. Sophia was
about to say something harsh, but she quickly swallowed it,
remembering that he was a good friend of the household. She
tried to laugh, but she could not. Then she assumed an air of
annoyance, then resignation, and finally, supplication, entreat-
ing in the name of his mother who must be in Heaven— At
the moment Rubião did not know what she meant by Heaven
or his mother, or anything. The look on his face seemed to
say, what was she talking about? His mother? Heaven?

"Ouch! You're breaking my fingers!" sighed the young woman
in a whisper.

Then he began to come back to his senses; he loosened his
grasp, though he did not let go of the fingers.

"Go," he said, "but first—"

He was bending down to kiss the hand, when a voice not
far away woke him up completely.

XLII

"Hello! Are you enjoying the moon? It is really delightful. It's
a night for lovers. Yes, delightful. I haven't seen a night like
this for a long time. Just look at the gas lights down below—
Delightful for lovers! —Lovers always like the moon. In my
day, in Icarahy—"

It was Siqueira, the terrible Major. Rubião did not know
what to say; Sophia, after the first few moments, recovered her
self-possession. She replied that the night was indeed beautiful, and then she told that Rubião persisted in saying that
Rio's nights could not be compared with those of Barbacena,
and that, apropos of this, he had recounted an anecdote about
a certain Father Mendes—wasn't it Mendes?"

"Mendes, yes, Father Mendes," murmured Rubião.

The Major could scarcely contain his surprise. He had seen

the two clasped hands, Rubião's half-bent head, the quick start of both when he came into the garden, and now from all this came a Father Mendes. He looked at Sophia and found her smiling, serene, inscrutable. No fear, no embarrassment, and she talked so easily that the Major thought that he must not have seen aright. But Rubião spoiled everything. Glumly silent, he did nothing but pull his watch from his pocket to see the time. He held it to his ear as if he thought it were not running and then wiped it slowly with his handkerchief without looking at either of them.

"Well, you two talk together," said Sophia. "I'm going in with the women. They mustn't be left alone. Have the men finished their confounded *voltarete*?"

"Yes," answered the Major, looking at Sophia curiously. "And they've been asking for this gentleman. That's why I came to see if I could find him in the garden. Have you been here long?"

"We just came out," said Sophia.

Then, tapping the Major's shoulder affectionately, she went into the house. But instead of entering through the drawing room door, she went in through that of the dining room, so that when she reached the drawing room, it might appear that she had just been giving orders for tea.

Though by now Rubião had come to, he still found nothing to say, and, yet, it was urgent that he say something. The anecdote about Father Mendes had been a good idea; only the worst part of it was that he was incapable of inventing anything himself.

"Father Mendes! Very funny, Father Mendes!"

"I knew him," said the Major, smiling. "Father Mendes? knew him. He died a canon. Was he in Minas for awhile?"

"I believe he was," the other murmured, in amazement.

"He was a native son of Saquarema. He was lacking the eye," continued the Major, raising his finger to his left eye. " knew him very well, if it's the same one. It may be another one."

"May be."

"He died a canon. He was a man of good habits, but he liked to see pretty young women. It's like admiring the painting of

54

master, and what master is greater than God? For instance, he never saw this Dona Sophia on the street but what he'd say to me, 'I saw that pretty wife of Palha today.' He died a canon; he was a native son of Saquarema— And, for a fact, he had good taste. Our Palha's wife is really perfect—fine face and figure. I think she's handsome rather than pretty. What do you think?"

"I think so."

"She's a good woman, an excellent housekeeper," the Major continued, lighting a cigar.

The light from the match gave the Major's face a look of mockery, or, if it was not quite mockery, it was something no less hostile. Rubião felt a chill run along his spine. Could he have heard, seen, guessed? Was this fellow a tattler, a meddler? You couldn't tell that by the man's face; in any case it was safer to believe the worst! And now we find our hero just like someone who, after having sailed close to shore for many years, finds himself one day out on the high seas. Fortunately, fear is also a purveyor of ideas, and it provided one now, that of flattering his interlocutor. He hastened to tell him that he thought him charming and interesting, and that his house on the beach at Botafogo, number so and so, was at his disposal. He would feel highly honored in acquiring his friendship. He had few friends here: Palha, to whom he was indebted for many courtesies, Dona Sophia, who was an unusually serious-minded woman, and three or four others. He lived alone; he might even go back to Minas.

"Right away?"

"Not right away, no, but it may be before too long. You know it's very hard for a person who's lived all his life in one place to become accustomed to another."

"That depends."

"Yes, it depends. But it's the general rule."

"It's probably the rule, but you're going to be an exception. The capital is a devil of a place; you catch an infatuation for it just as you'd catch a cold. A little air, through a crack, and you're done for. Look, I wager that you'll be married in six months—"

"He didn't see anything," thought Rubião.

And then, gaily:

"Maybe, but there are marriages in Minas too. Nor are priests lacking."

"Father Mendes is," laughed the Major.

Rubião smiled with constraint, not knowing whether the remark was innocent or malicious. The Major then gathered up the reins of the subject, and spoke of other things, of the weather, the city, the ministry, the war, and Marshal Lopez. And see what a contrast with that first shower! This one, though heavier, seemed like a ray of sunshine to our Rubião. Basking in the warmth of this infinite discourse, he whisked the dust from his soul. Whenever he could he would interject a little word, all the while nodding his head in approval. And once again the thought came to him that he, the Major, hadn't seen anything.

"Papa! Papa! Are you out there?" said a voice at the door that opened into the garden.

It was Dona Tonica, coming to ask her father to take her home. Yes, she knew that tea was served, but she couldn't wait any longer, because she had a headache, she whispered to the Major. Then she held out her fingers to Rubião. He begged her to stay a few minutes longer. "The estimable Major—"

"You're wasting your time," interrupted the Major. "She's the one who gives me my orders."

Rubião offered him the hospitality of his house with insistence; he even wanted him to indicate a day of that very week, but the Major said that he could never be certain of any particular day, that he would go as soon as he could. His life was very busy; he had all the arsenal duties, which were many, and others—"

"Papa! Let's go."

"Well now! You see? I can't converse a minute. Have you said your good-byes? Where's my hat?"

On the way down the hill, Dona Tonica heard the rest of her father's discourse, which changed its theme without changing its diffuse and rambling style. She heard without understanding, though, completely absorbed within herself, mulling over the evening, recalling Sophia's and Rubião's glances.

When they came to their house on Senado Street, the father went to bed at once, but the daughter sat up for awhile in a little chair beside her commode, where she had an image of the Virgin. And the thoughts that she was thinking were not serene, pure thoughts. Though she knew nothing of love, she had heard of adultery, and Sophia seemed to her to be depraved. She saw her now as a monster, half human, half serpent; she felt that she abhorred her, and that she, herself, might go so far as to seek an exemplary revenge by telling everything to Sophia's husband.

"I'll tell him everything," she thought, "either in person or in a letter. No, not in a letter. I'll tell him everything someday, in private."

And, imagining the colloquy, she foresaw first the man's surprise, then his anger, and finally his abuse, the harsh words that he would address to his wife, wretched, vile, unworthy— All these epithets sounded sweet to the ears of her desire; she deflected the course of her own anger to flow through them and to the point of satiety she indulged in the woman's degradation —making her less than the dust beneath her husband's feet, since she could not trample upon her herself. Vile, unworthy, wretched!

That outburst of inner fury lasted a long time—nearly twenty minutes. But the spirit grew weary, and became itself again; and the imagination, exhausted, turned its attention to near-by reality. It cast a glance around, and looked at the spinster's room, an artful little arrangement—devised with that ingenious art that makes silk out of chintz, a ribbon out of an old patch, that covers, ties together, brightens up the bareness of things as best it can, adorns the forlorn walls, embellishes the few humble pieces of furniture. Everything there appeared to have been contrived for the reception of a cherished lover.

Where have I read that, according to an old tradition, during a certain night of the year an Israelite virgin awaited a divine conception? Wherever it may have been, let us compare her to this other virgin, who differs only in having no fixed night. It is every night, every, every night— Never has the wind that whistles outside brought the man she has been waiting for, nor has that white maiden, the dawn, told her in what part of the land he dwells. All she has been able to do is wait and wait—.

Now, with imagination and resentment appeased, she looks about the lonely room again and again, and she recalls her most intimate girl friends, family and school friends, all of whom are married. The last to marry married a naval officer when she was thirty. This had invigorated her spinster friend's hopes; though, despite the fact that the aspirant's uniform was the first thing that had enticed her eyes at fifteen, Dona Tonica did not expect so much. But where had those hopes gone? Now five years had passed, she had had her thirty-ninth birthday, and the fortieth would not be long in coming. A woman in her forties, a spinster! Dona Tonica shuddered. She looked around again, all her recent thoughts rushed through her head, and she flung herself on the bed, weeping—.

XLIV

Do not believe, however, that the lady's grief was more genuine than her anger. They were equal, but their effects were different. Her anger could not manifest itself, whereas her humiliation found expression in legitimate tears. And yet she would have liked to strangle Sophia, crush her under-foot, and tear out her heart bit by bit, all the while shouting into her face those cruel epithets which she had imagined her husband using. These were all just imaginings, of course. Believe me, intention can make a tyrant. Who knows? For the moment, the lady's soul harbored a tenuous fiber of Caligula.

X L V

And while one weeps, another laughs. That is the law of the world, my fine reader, and it makes for universal perfection. All weeping would be monotonous, all laughing, tiresome. A good distribution of tears and polkas, sobs and sarabands, finally brings to the world's spirit the variety that it needs, and the balance of life is contrived.

The one who is laughing at this moment is Rubião's soul, with which he is going down the hill, saying the most intimate things to the stars, a sort of rhapsody composed in a language that has never been alphabetized since it would be impossible to find a sign to express its words. Down below, the deserted streets seem to him to be filled, the silence is a tumult, and feminine figures lean out from every window, pretty faces and heavy eyebrows, just so many Sophias that all merge into one single Sophia. Sometimes Rubião thinks that he has been rash, indiscreet. He recalls the garden episode, the young woman's resistance and annoyance, and he is repentant. Then he has chills, and he is terrified by the thought that they may shut the door in his face and cut off all relations, all just because he precipitated events! Yes, he should have waited; it was not the right occasion, what with the guests, and lights everywhere; of what had he been thinking, to have become so indiscreetly, shamelessly amorous? He thought that she had been right; she had done well to send him away.

"I was crazy!" he said aloud.

He did not give a thought to the dinner, which was sumptuous, nor to the wines, which were generous, nor to the lighting, which was such as is required by a roomful of elegant ladies; he was thinking of himself, and he thought that he had been crazy, utterly crazy.

But right after, the soul that had been accusing itself, defended itself. Sophia seemed to have encouraged him to do what he did; her frequent glances (finally she didn't take her eyes off him), her courtesies, her singling him out to sit beside her at the dinner table, to be the sole recipient of her attentions, her sweet murmuring of little pleasantries—what was all this if not exhortations and solicitations? Then the good soul went on to explain the young woman's contradictory behavior in the garden; it was the first time that she had heard such words from anyone other than her husband, and, naturally, with everyone around, she must have been startled. Besides, he had been too effusive, he had rushed headlong without any gradual approach. He should have proceeded cautiously, and he should not have held her hands so tightly that he hurt her. In conclusion, he thought that he had been crude. The fear that they might shut the door in his face returned; but, then he went back once more to the consolation of hope, to an analysis of the young woman's actions and to her invention of Father Mendes, a falsehood of complicity. He thought, too, of her husband's esteem for him. And this made him tremble. Not only did her husband trust him completely, but he owed him a sum of money and three bills of exchange that Rubião had accepted for him.

"I can't, I mustn't," he kept saying to himself. "It's not right to go on. Of course, actually, I'm not the one who started it; she's the one who's been challenging me for a long time now. Well, let her challenge! I must resist! I lent the money almost without being asked for it, because he needed it very much and I was indebted to him for kindnesses; it's true that he asked me to sign the bills of exchange, but he's never asked for anything else. I know he's honest and works hard; it's his confounded wife who's to blame, thrusting herself between us with her pretty eyes and that figure— Good Lord, what an admirable figure. It was divine today! When her arm brushed against mine at the table, in spite of my sleeve—

Thus, you see, all confused and uncertain, he was musing upon the loyalty he owed his friend, his conscience cleft in two, one part severely reprimanding the other, the other explaining itself, and both parts completely disoriented.

Finally he found himself in Constitution Square. He had been walking at random. He considered going to the theater, but it was late; so he went to São Francisco Square to get a tilbury for Botafogo. He found three that came to him immediately, offering their services, each driver having particular praise for his horse, "a good horse"—"an excellent animal".

XLVI

The sound of the voices and of the vehicles awakened a beggar, who was asleep on the church steps. The poor fellow sat up, saw what it was, then lay down again, awake now, lying on his back, with his eyes staring up into the sky. The sky was staring at him, too, impassive as he, but without the beggar's wrinkles or his torn shoes or his rags; a bright, starry, tranquil, Olympian sky, just such a one as presided over Jacob's wedding and Lucretia's suicide. They continued staring at each other, the sky and the beggar, as if they were playing a sort of game to see which one of the two could, with sober face, outstare the other. They appeared to be vying with each other to maintain a quiet gravity, without arrogance, without humility, as though the beggar were saying to the sky, "After all, you're not going to fall on top of me," and the sky to the beggar, "nor are you going to climb up to me."

XLVII

Rubião was not a philosopher: the comparison that he made between his own anxieties and the ragamuffin's brought only a shade of envy to his heart. "That vagabond isn't thinking about anything," he said to himself, "he'll soon be asleep, while I—"

"Get in, sir. This is a good animal. We'll be there in fifteen minutes."

The other two drivers said the same thing in almost the exact words.

"Come over here, sir, and see—"

"Please, it's a thirteen-minute trip; we'll be there in thirteen minutes."

After some further hesitation, Rubião found himself in the nearest tilbury, and ordered it to set out for Botafogo. Then he recalled an old experience that he had long forgotten. It may have been without his being aware of it that the experience was now providing a solution to his problem. However it was, Rubião so guided his train of thought as to escape the immediate sensations of the evening.

It had happened many years ago, when he was very young and poor. One day, at eight o'clock in the morning he left his house on Cano (Sete de Setembro) Street, entered São Francisco de Paula Square and from there went down Ouvidor Street. He was somewhat worried, because he was staying at the house of a friend, who was beginning to treat him as though he were a three-day guest; and he had already been there four weeks. They say that three-day guests are putrid; corpses are long before that, at least in hot climates—. Well, our Rubião, simple as a good Mineiran, but suspicious as a Paulista, certainly was worried and decided that he must move from his friend's house as soon as possible. You may be sure that from the time he had left the house, entered São Francisco Square and gone down Ourives Street, he had neither seen nor heard anything.

At the corner of Ourives Street, he was stopped by a crowd and a strange procession. A man in judicial attire was reading aloud a sentence from a paper. Besides the judge, there were a priest, soldiers and idlers. But the chief figures were two Negroes. One of them, light-colored, thin, of medium height, kept his eyes lowered. His hands were tied behind his back and around his neck was wound a rope, the ends of which were fastened to the other Negro, a very black fellow who was looking straight ahead, confronting the crowd's curiosity bravely. After the paper had been read the procession continued on through Ourives Street; it had come from the jail and was going to Moura Square.

Rubião, naturally, was impressed. He spent a few minutes, as just now, in selecting a tilbury, as it were, with conflicting inner forces vying with one another in offering their horses; some suggesting that he turn back and go on to work, others suggesting that he go to see the Negro hanged. "It's so unusual to see a hanging. It'll be over in twenty minutes, sir."—"Oh, sir, let's attend to business." And our man shut his eyes and let himself be led by chance. Chance, instead of taking him down Ouvidor Street to Quitanda Street, deflected his route by way of Ourives Street, following the procession. He wouldn't see the execution, he thought; it was just to see the march of the culprit, the face of the executioner, the ceremonies— He didn't want to see the execution. Every little while the procession would stop, people would come to doors and windows, and the officer of the law would reread the sentence. Then the line would start up again as solemnly as before. The idlers who were hanging on kept recounting the crime to one another—a murder in Mata-porcos. The murderer was described as a brutal, ruthless fellow. Knowledge of the man's nature helped Rubião; it gave him strength to look into the face of the culprit without any feeling of faintness inspired by pity. However, it was no longer the face of a criminal; terror had concealed its depravity. Suddenly, without realizing how he got there, he found himself in the execution square. A number of people were there already; and together with those who were coming they formed a dense throng.

"Let's go back," he said to himself.

The condemned man had not mounted the gallows yet, and he would not be put to death immediately; there was still time to get away. And if he should stay, why not close his eyes as a certain Alypius did before the spectacle of the Circus? Note well that Rubião knew nothing about that ancient youth; not only did he not know that he had closed his eyes, but also he did not know that he had opened them right away again, slowly and curiously—.

Now the condemned man mounts the gallows. A shudder ran through the crowd. The executioner began his work. It was at this point that Rubião's right foot described an outward turn, in obedience to an impulse to go back; but the left foot, seized by a contrary impulse, stood still. They struggled for a few moments— "Look at my horse." "See what a fine animal." "Don't be cruel!" "Don't be timid!" And Rubião stood thus for a few seconds, just long enough for the fatal moment to arrive. All eyes were fixed upon the same point—his, too. Rubião did not know what creature was gnawing his vitals, nor what hands of iron were clutching his spirit, holding it there. The fatal instant was really just an instant; the culprit convulsively thrashed about with his legs, then he shrank together; and the executioner bestrode him gaily and with much skill. A great murmur ran through the multitude; Rubião uttered a cry, and saw nothing more.

XLVIII

"You must have seen, sir, that the little horse is good—"

Rubião opened half-shut eyes and saw that the driver was lightly shaking the tip of the lash to quicken the animal's pace. Inwardly, he was angry with the man for having evoked old memories. They were not pleasant, but they were old—old, and yes, they were healing, too; for they supplied a tonic that seemed to cure him completely of the present. So let the driver jolt him and wake him up. They were going up Lopa Street, and the horse was eating up the distance as if they were going down.

"You'd not believe what a friend of mine this horse is," continued the driver. "I could tell extraordinary tales. Some people say that I make them all up, but that's not so, sir. Who doesn't know that horses and dogs are the animals that are most fond of people? I think that a dog is even more so—."

The word "dog" made Rubião think of Quincas Borba, who, no doubt, was anxiously waiting for him at home. Rubião was not forgetting the condition stipulated by the will, and he had sworn to fulfill it to the letter. It must be said that along with Rubião's fear that the dog might run away went the apprehension that he might lose his inheritance. The lawyer's assurances made no difference. The letter had told him that, since there was no reversible clause in the will, even if the dog did run away, the property could not get out of his hands. Why did he care if he ran away? It would be better. He'd have less bother. Rubião accepted the explanation apparently, but he was still dubious. He knew what long lawsuits could mean, how judges often could not agree on a matter, what harm an envious or unfriendly person could do, and he dreaded (and this was really the substance of it all), he dreaded being left without a penny. Hence, the great precautions he took to keep the dog in, and, hence, too, the remorse he felt for having spent the afternoon and evening without even once thinking of Quincas Borba.

"I'm an ingrate," he said to himself.

Then he corrected himself; he was more of an ingrate not to have thought of the other Quincas Borba, who had left him everything. Especially if, as it occurred to him, the two Quincas Borbas might now be one and the same, supposing that the dead man, less to purge his sins than to keep watch over the new master, had transferred his soul to the dog's body? It was a Negress from João d'El Rey who had suggested this idea of transmigration to him when he was a child. She said that the soul, full of sin, entered an animal's body; she even swore that she had known a notary who had become a *gambá*.

"Don't forget to tell me where the house is, sir," the driver said suddenly.

"Stop here."

XLIX

The dog barked from inside the grounds, but, as soon as Rubião entered, he received him joyfully, and no matter how annoying it may have been, Rubião made a great fuss over him. He was shivering at the thought that the testator might be present. Together the two went up the stone steps to the house, and stood for awhile at the top, under the light of the lamp that

Rubião had asked to be left lighted. Rubião was more credulous than any sectarian; he had no reason to attack or defend anything, eternally virgin soil ready for any planting. From living in the capital, however, he had developed one peculiarity—among incredulous people, he was becoming incredulous.

He looked at the dog while he was waiting for the door to be opened. The dog looked at him, too, and in such a way that the deceased Quincas Borba seemed to be right there inside of him; the dog was looking with the same contemplative gaze with which the philosopher used to examine human affairs—. Another shiver, but Rubião's fear, though great, was not so great that it tied his hands. He spread them out over the animal's head, scratching his ears and his neck.

"Poor Quincas Borba! You like your master, don't you? Rubião's a very good friend of Quincas Borba."

And the dog slowly moved his head from left to right, helping to distribute the caresses to the two drooping ears. Then he lifted his tail so that his master would scratch underneath, and the master obeyed the dog's eyes, half-closed in delight, looking all the while like the philosopher's when he lay in bed, telling Rubião things of which he, Rubião, understood little or nothing. Rubião closed his own eyes. Then the door opened, and he left the dog outside, with as great a show of affection, though, as if he were letting him in. The Spanish servant took him down into the garden again.

"Don't strike him," Rubião admonished.

He did not strike him, but the descent itself was painful, and the friendly dog moaned in the garden for some time. Rubião went into the house, undressed, and went to bed. Ah! he had lived a day full of diverse and contrary sensations, from the morning's recollections to the lunch with his two friends until that most recent thought of transmigration. In between there had been the remembrance of the hanging and a declaration of love not accepted, yet scarcely rejected, guessed, perhaps, by others—. He mixed everything up; his mind bounced back and forth like a rubber ball in the hands of children. And, yet, the most important sensation was that of love. Rubião was astounded at himself, and he was repentant. His repentance, however, was the work of his conscience; whereas his imagination would not relinquish the lovely Sophia's figure at any price— One o'clock, two o'clock, three o'clock— Elusive sleep— Where had the three hours gone? Half-past three— At last, after all this thinking, sleep appeared, squeezed the classical poppies, and, after that, it was just a moment. Rubião was asleep before four·

L

No, my lady, this very long day is still not over. We don't know yet what went on between Sophia and Palha after everyone left. It may even be that it will leave a better taste in your mouth than the affair of the hanged man.

Have patience; you'll have to come to Santa Thereza once again. The living room is still lighted, but by only one gas jet; the others have been extinguished, and this last one was about to be, when Palha asked the servant to wait a moment. Sophia was leaving the room, but he detained her. She trembled.

"Our party was nice," he said.

"Yes, it was."

"Siqueira's a bore, but never mind; he's a jolly fellow. His daughter didn't look bad. Did you see how Remos gobbled up everything that was put on his plate? You'll see him swallow his wife one day."

"His wife?" said Sophia, smiling.

"She's fat, I'll agree; but the first one was much fatter, and I don't believe she died; he swallowed her, for sure."

Sophia, reclining on the couch, laughed at her husband's jokes. They went over several incidents that had occurred that afternoon and evening, and then, as she was stroking her husband's hair, Sophia said suddenly:

"And you still don't know the best thing that happened tonight."

"What was it?"

"Guess."

Palha said nothing for awhile, looking at his wife to see if he could guess what the best thing that had happened that night had been. He could not; he thought of this or that, but, no, Sophia would shake her head.

"Well, what was it then?"

"I don't know; you guess."

"I can't. Tell me."

"Under one condition," she said. "I don't want any anger or commotion—"

Palha was becoming serious. Anger? Commotion? What the deuce could it be? he thought. He was no longer laughing; he had no more than the remnant of a forced smile of resignation. He looked straight at his wife, and he asked her what it had been.

"You promise what I said?"

"Yes, what was it?'

"Well, know then, that I heard a declaration of love, no less."

Palha turned pale. He had not promised not to turn pale. He was fond of his wife, so fond of her, that, as we know, he liked to show her off, and he could not listen to this announcement dispassionately. Sophia saw his pallor, and she was pleased with his displeasure. That she might relish it fully, she leaned forward, loosened her hair, which was slightly uncomfortable, gathered the pins in a handkerchief, then shook her head, breathed deeply, and reached up to squeeze her husband's hands. He had remained standing.

"It's true, my dear. Someone made love to your wife!"

"But who was the scoundrel?" he said, impatiently.

"If you ask like that, I'll not say anything. Who was it? You want to know who it was? Then you must listen calmly. It was Rubião."

"Rubião?"

"I never dreamed of such a thing; he seemed shy and respectful. Certainly appearances can be deceptive. I've never heard the least little word from all the men who come here. They look at me, naturally, because I'm not ugly— Why are you pacing up and down like that? Stand still; I don't want to raise my voice— Well, let's come to the point. He didn't make a positive declaration—"

"Ah! No?" interrupted her husband, eagerly.

"No, but it amounted to the same thing."

And, after telling what had taken place in the garden from the time the two of them had gone into it until the Major came along, she concluded, "That's all it was, but it's enough to see that if he didn't pronounce the word 'love,' it's because it didn't come to his lips. It came to his hand, though, which squeezed my fingers—. That's all, but we'll have to make a break either all at once, or gradually. I'd prefer it right away, but anything's all right as far as I'm concerned. What do you think?"

Biting his lower lip, Palha stood staring at her like an idiot. Then he sat down on the couch, without a word, turning the affair over in his mind. He found it natural that his wife's charms should captivate a man, and it might be Rubião as well as another. It was only that he so trusted Rubião; it was he, indeed, who composed the note that Sophia sent along with the strawberries; his wife had merely copied, signed and sent it. It had never occurred to him that his friend would ever make a declaration of love to anyone, much less Sophia. But had it really been a declaration of love? — Maybe it had just been the banter of an intimate friend? Rubião looked at her a great deal, it's true, and, Sophia seemed to return his glances, sometimes— Merely the concessions of an attractive young woman! After all, if her eyes remained his, some of their sparkle could go elsewhere. He musn't be jealous of the optic nerve, he thought.

Sophia got up, put her handkerchief with the pins on top of the piano, and glanced at the mirror to see herself with her hair down. When she went back to the couch, her husband seized her hand, and laughed.

"I think that you've become more upset than the affair justifies. After all, a young woman's eyes may be compared to the stars, and the stars may be compared to eyes in plain view of everybody, in the midst of one's family, or in prose or verse that is for publication. The fault lies with the one who has the beautiful eyes. Besides, in spite of what you tell me, you know that he's still just a country bumpkin—"

"Then the Devil's a country bumpkin, too, because he was the very Devil. What about his asking me to look at the Southern Cross at a certain time so that our souls might meet?"

"Yes, that does smack of love-making," agreed Palha, "but you see, it's the request of a pure soul. That's the way fifteen-year-old girls talk and simpletons of all ages, and poets, too. Well, he's neither a girl nor a poet."

"I should say not! But what about his taking hold of my hands to keep me in the garden?"

Palha shivered; the thought of the contact of hands and the effort to detain his wife is what mortified him most. Frankly, if he could have, he would have gone right up to the fellow and grabbed him by the neck. Other thoughts came crowding along, however, and dispelled the effect of the first one. Sophia thought she had aroused his anger when she saw him shrug his shoulders scornfully, with the reply that that had, indeed, been the act of a boor.

"But Sophia, why ever did you ask him to go and see the moon? Will you tell me that?"

"I called Dona Tonica to go with us."

"But when Dona Tonica refused, you should have found ways and means of staying away from the garden. Some things happen quickly. It's you who provided the occasion."

Sophia looked at him, puckering her heavy eyebrows. She was on the point of making a retort, but she kept still. Palha went on in the same vein; it was her own fault, she ought not to have provided the occasion—

"But haven't you, yourself, told me that we are to treat him with special consideration? Surely, I'd not have gone into the garden could I have foreseen what took place. I didn't dream that such a meek man, a man so— Oh, I don't know how to describe him! —would withdraw from his own thoughts to say queer things to me—"

"Well, hereafter, avoid the moon and the garden," said her husband, making an effort to smile.

"But, Christiano, how do you expect me to speak to him the first time he comes here? I haven't the courage; the best thing is to break off."

Palha crossed one leg over the other, and began to drum on his shoe. For a few moments, they said nothing. Palha was considering the proposal to break off, not that he wanted to accept it; but he did not know how to answer his wife, who manifested such resentment and was comporting herself with such dignity. He must neither disapprove nor accept the proposal, and he could not think of anything. He got up, put his hands into his trousers' pockets and, after taking a few steps, stopped in front of Sophia.

"Maybe we're being upset by what was merely the result of too much wine. He certainly didn't send his share to the vicar; a weak head, a little commotion, and what was inside of it spilled out— Yes, I can't deny that you may have made a certain impression on him, as so many other women do. He went to a ball in Cattete a few days ago, and he came back enchanted by the women whom he had seen there, by one in particular, the Widow Mendes—"

Sophia interrupted:

"Why didn't he ask that beauty to look at the Southern Cross?"

"Because he didn't dine at her house, of course, and there was neither a garden nor a moon. What I mean is that *our friend* could not have been himself. Perhaps at this very moment, he repents what he did, and is ashamed, not knowing how he's going to explain or whether he will explain at all— It's quite possible, even, that he'll stay away—"

"It would be better."

"—if we don't call him," concluded Palha.

"But why call him?"

"Sophia," said her husband, sitting down beside her. "I don't wish to go into details; I'll say only that I'd not allow anyone to be disrespectful toward you—"

There was a slight pause. Sophia was looking at him and waiting.

"I'd not allow it; woe upon him who would be, or upon you, were you to consent! You know that I'm adamant in that respect, and that it's the certainty of your love and esteem that puts my mind at ease. Nothing can shake my faith in Rubião either. Be assured that he is our friend. I am indebted to him."

"A few gifts, a few jewels, box seats at the theater, are not sufficient reasons for me to look at the Southern Cross with him."

"Would to God that's all it were," sighed the broker.

"What more is there?"

"Let's not go into details— There are other things— We'll talk about it later— But be assured that nothing would make me desist, if there were really anything serious in what you have told me. There's nothing, though. The man's a booby—"

"No, he isn't."

"Isn't he?"

Sophia got up. She did not care to go into details either. Her husband took her hand; she remained standing silently. Palha, with his head resting against the back of the sofa, looked at her smilingly, but he found nothing to say. After a few minutes, he observed that it was late, and that he'd have the lights put out.

"Well," he said, after a brief silence. "I'll write him tomorrow not to set foot here again."

He looked at his wife, hoping for some protest. Sophia was scratching her eyebrows and made no reply. Palha repeated the solution, and this time, perhaps, with sincerity.

"Now, Christiano," said his wife, with apparent displeasure. "Who's asking you for letters? I told you about a discourtesy, and said that it would be better to break off—gradually, or all at once."

"But how are we to break off all at once?"

"Forbid him the house; but I don't say that we need go that far; we can proceed gradually, if you wish—"

It was a concession, and Palha accepted it. Immediately, however, he became serious, and released his wife's hand with a gesture of despair. Then, seizing her by the waist, he said in a louder voice than he had been using:

"But my love, I owe him a great deal of money."

Sophia clapped her hand over his mouth and looked toward the corridor with alarm.

"Very well," she said, "let's be done with this. I'll see how he behaves, and I'll try to be more distant— In that case, you mustn't change, so that it'll not appear that you know what happened. I'll see what I can do."

"You know, pressure of business, a few needs—one must stop up a hole here, another one there—it's the devil! That's why— But, never mind, my love, it's nothing. You know I trust you."

"Come, it's late."

"Come," repeated Palha, kissing her cheek.

"I have a very bad headache," she murmured. "I think it's from the night dew, or else that business— I have a very bad headache."

L I

Bathed, shaven, and partly dressed, Palha was reading the newspapers before breakfast, when he saw his wife enter the study. She was somewhat pale.

"Are you worse?"

Sophia answered with a movement of the lips that was neither a denial nor an affirmation. Palha said he believed the indisposition would pass as the day went on. Then he asked her permission to finish reading about a certain business deal— a dispute between two businessmen regarding some drafts; one had written in the evening paper; now today, came the other's reply. A complete reply, he remarked, as he read the rest of it. And he explained the matter of the drafts to his wife at great length, the mechanism of the operation, the position of the two adversaries, the rumors of the exchange, all in technical vocabulary. Sophia listened and sighed, but against professional despotism neither a woman's sighs nor a man's courtesy avail. Happily, breakfast was served.

After she was alone, our friend, who had taken nothing but some broth, went into the garden around two o'clock, and sat down beside the door. Naturally, her thoughts went back to the occurrence of the evening before. She was at sixes and sevens.

She regretted having told her husband about the incident; at the same time, she was annoyed with his attempts to explain it. In the midst of her reflections, she heard quite distinctly the Major's words, "Hello! Are you enjoying the moon?" as if the leaves had held them and were repeating them now that they were beginning to be stirred by the breeze. Sophia shivered. Siqueira was indiscreet—indiscreet in sniffing out and investigating the affairs of others; would he go so far as to make them public? And since Sophia realized that already she might be the object of suspicion or calumny, she made plans. She would not go to see anyone nor would she go away to Nuevo Friburgo or farther. Her husband's insistence that she receive Rubião as before was really asking too much, especially for the reason he gave. As she did not wish to obey or disobey, she would leave the city under some pretext or other.

"It was my fault!" she sighed to herself.

The fault lay in the special attentions she had lavished on the man, all the little courtesies and affabilities, and, then, the evening before there had been those long, lingering glances. Had it not been for that— And she drifted off into a long train of reflections. All her immediate surroundings impressed her disagreeably; everything, plants, furniture, a cicada that was singing, the sound of voices in the street, and a clatter of dishes in the house, the coming and going of the slaves as they attended to their tasks, even a poor old Negro, who was toiling up a little hill in front of her house. The deliberateness with which the Negro was making his way set her nerves aquiver.

LII

Then a tall young man passed by. He greeted her smilingly, and lingered over his greeting. Sophia greeted him, too, somewhat struck by his appearance and manner.

"Who is this fellow?" she thought.

And she began to ponder where she had met him, because

neither his face with its large, placid eyes nor his manner were unfamiliar to her. Where could she have seen him? She went through several houses without coming upon the right one; finally she remembered a certain ball—of the preceding month —at the home of a lawyer who was celebrating his birthday. That was it; she had seen him there, and they had danced a quadrille. It had been pure condescension on his part, because he never danced. She recalled that he had said many flattering things about feminine beauty. It lay, mainly, he had said, in the eyes and the shoulders. Hers, as we know, were magnificent. He scarcely spoke of anything else—shoulders and eyes. Apropos of both, he recounted various experiences he had had. Some of them were not interesting; but then, he spoke so well! And the subject was so suitable to her! Yes, she remembered now that right after he had left her, Palha had come over and sat down beside her and told her the young man's name, because she had not heard well the person who had introduced him to her. It was Carlos Maria—none other than Rubião's luncheon guest.

"He's the most important person in the room," said her husband, proud to see that he had spent so much time with her.

"Among the men, you mean."

"Among the women, you are the most important," he said, looking with pride at his wife's bosom, and then sweeping the room with a look of masterful possessiveness that Sophia knew and liked.

By the time she had recalled everything, the young man was, doubtless, already a long way past the house. Well, at least, it had been a break in the series of troubles that were besetting her. She had a pain in her back which had subsided for a few moments. Now, here it was again, stubborn and unpleasant! Sophia leaned back in her chair and closed her eyes. She tried to go to sleep, but could not. Her thoughts were as stubborn as the pain, and even more unpleasant. Now and again a rapid beating of wings broke the silence; it was the doves of a neighboring house that were returning to the dovecot. At first, Sophia opened her eyes once or twice; then, becoming used to the sound, she kept them closed to see whether she could fall asleep. After awhile she heard footsteps in the street, and raised her head, supposing that it was Carlos Maria on his way back. It was a mailman who was bringing her a letter from the country. He handed it to her, and as he was leaving the garden, he stumbled over the foot of a bench and fell headlong, scattering the letters all over the ground. Sophia burst out laughing.

LIII

Forgive her that laughter. I know, of course, that her anxiety, her bad night, her fear of public opinion, are all in startling contrast to that inopportune laughter. But, dear reader, perhaps you've never seen a mailman fall. Homer's gods—and they really were gods—were contending seriously and even angrily once on Olympus. The haughty Juno, jealous of Thetis' and Jupiter's colloquies in behalf of Achilles, interrupted the son of Saturn. Jupiter thundered and threatened, his wife shook with fury. The others moaned and groaned. But when Vulcan picked up the jar of nectar and started hobbling around to serve them all, there burst forth on Olympus an enormous, inextinguishable guffaw. Why? My dear lady, you've surely never seen a mailman fall.

Sometimes, he does not even have to fall; other times, he does not even have to exist. It suffices to imagine him or remember him. If the mere shadow of the shadow of a grotesque memory projects itself into the midst of the most grievous sorrow, a smile—however faint, perhaps, a mere trace of a smile—may rise to the surface. So let us leave Sophia for awhile, laughing and reading her letter from the country.

One day, a fortnight later, when Rubião was at home, Sophia's husband came to see him. He said he had come to inquire what had become of him, where had he hidden himself, if he had been ill, or if he had lost interest in the poor? Rubião, meanwhile, was ruminating his words, without succeeding in putting a single phrase together. Suddenly Palha saw there was a man in the room looking at the pictures, and he lowered his voice.

"Pardon me, I didn't see that you had a visitor," he said.

"You don't have to ask pardon; he's a friend like yourself. Doctor, this is my friend Christiano de Almeida e Palha. I believe I've already spoken to you of him. This is my friend Doctor Camacho— João de Souza Camacho."

Camacho nodded, said a word or two, and made ready to leave. But Rubião insisted that he stay; they were both friends, and the moon would soon be shining over the lovely bay of Botafogo.

The moon—the moon again—and that phrase, "I believe I've already spoken to you of him," so befuddled Palha that for some time he could not utter a word. It's well to add, too, that his host did not know what to say, either. The three of them were seated, Rubião on the couch, and Palha and Camacho in chairs facing each other. Camacho, who had kept his cane in his hand, placed it vertically on his knees, tapping his nose and staring at the ceiling. Outside, there was the sound of carriages, the clatter of horses' hooves and some shouting. It was half-past seven in the evening, or rather, nearly eight. The silence inside was lasting longer than the occasion permitted, but neither Rubião nor Palha noticed it. It was Camacho, who, finally becoming bored, went over to the window and called back to the two:

"The moonlight's coming!"

Rubião and Palha each made a move. But how different were their moves! Rubião's was to betake himself to the window, Palha's was to grab the former by the throat. However, rather because of his recollection of the violence with which Rubião had seized his wife's hands to draw her to him than because of the thought that the affair might be divulged, Palha desisted. In fact, both men contained themselves; a moment after, Rubião crossed his left leg over his right, turned to Palha and asked:

"Do you know that I'm leaving you?"

Palha was expecting anything but this. Hence, the amazement into which his anger dissolved; hence, too, a little shade of regret, which is what the reader is least expecting. He was going to leave them? Of course, then, he was going away from Rio de Janeiro; that was the punishment he was imposing upon himself for his misbehavior at Santa Thereza; he was ashamed and repentant. He did not have the courage to face his friend's wife. Such was Palha's first conclusion; however, other hypotheses followed. For instance, his passion might be enduring and his departure would get him away from the loved one. It might be, too, that some marriage plan entered into it.

The final hypothesis brought a new element to Palha's face, which I don't know how to describe. Disappointment? The elegant Garret found no other term for such sensations, and, Englishman that he was, did not disdain it. Very well, disappointment then. If one adds to this, regret over the coming separation, if one does not forget the anger that thundered softly in the beginning, surely someone is going to say that this man's soul is a patchwork quilt. It may be. Spiritually speaking, quilts of one piece are so rare! The main thing is that even if they cannot be symmetrical, their colors must not clash. At first glance, he appeared to be a hodgepodge, but if you looked closely, you saw that, completely different as the shades might be, the spiritual unity was there.

But why was Rubião going to leave them? What was the reason?

The day after the Santa Thereza affair, he awoke depressed. He ate only a little for breakfast; he put on his African slippers listlessly; he did not look at the beautiful or merely costly adornments that filled his house. He could not endure the dog's show of affection for more than two minutes; no sooner had he let him into the drawing room than he had him taken away. The dog, however, deceived the servants and returned to the drawing room. But such was the cuff that he received on the ear that he did not repeat his caresses. He stretched out on the floor, with his eyes on his friend.

Rubião was contrite, annoyed, ashamed. In Chapter X of his book, it was written that this man's remorse came easily but that it did not last long; it was not explained what kind of acts might make it brief or protracted. There, it was a question of that letter written by the deceased Quincas Borba, so expressive of the writer's mental state, and which he, Rubião, since it could be of use to science or the law, concealed from the doctor. Had he shown the letter, he would not have had remorse—or, perhaps, any legacy, either—not even the small legacy that he was at that time expecting from the sick man. In the present instance, it was an attempt at adultery. Of course, he had been amorous and had had inner temptations for a long time, but it was only the young woman's indiscreet vivacity and the excitement of the moment itself that prompted him to make the rejected declaration. With the clouds of that first night dispelled from his mind, he felt not only annoyance, but remorse. Sins are many, but there is only one moral code.

Let us skip over all that he felt and thought during the first days. He even hoped for something on Sunday, a note like that of the preceding Sunday—with strawberries or without them. On Monday, he was determined to go to Minas for two months; he needed to restore his soul in the air of Barbacena. He was not counting on Doctor Camacho.

"You're going to leave us?" Palha asked, finally.

"I think so; I'm going to Minas."

Camacho, coming back from the window, sat down in the chair in which he had been sitting before.

"What's this about Minas?" he said, smiling. "Forget Minas for the present. You'll go there when you have to, and you'll not stay very long."

Palha was no less astonished by this man's words than by the other's. Where had this man, with his domineering attitude toward Rubião, suddenly come from? He looked at him; he was a person of medium stature, narrow face, sparse beard, long chin and wide open pavilion ears. That was all he could see in a rapid glance. Well, he did see, too, that without being luxurious, his clothing was good and that his feet were not ill shod. He did not examine his eyes, nor his hands, nor his mannerisms; he did not at first notice his bald spot nor his thin, heavy hands.

LVII

Camacho was a politician. Upon receiving his law degree from the school of Recife in 1844, he had returned to his native province where he began to practice. At the academy he had already written a political journal which was not affiliated with any definite party, but which contained many ideas gathered from here and there and set forth in a style at once thin and turgid. Someone who collected those first fruits of Camacho made an index of his principles and aspirations—order through liberty, liberty through order—authority cannot abuse the law without slapping itself—principles are the spiritual necessity of young nations as well as of old; —give me good politics and I'll give you good finances (Barão Louis); —let us plunge into the constitutional Jordan; —make way for the valiant, men of power, they will be your supporters, etc., etc.

In his native province, that order of ideas had to give way to others, and the same may be said of his style. He founded a journal there, but since local politics were less abstract, Camacho clipped his wings and descended to the nominations of delegates, to provincial enterprises, bonuses, contention with the opposition's publication, and the use of epithets proper and improper. Indeed, the use of adjectives demanded great nicety. Ill-omened, wasteful, shameful, perverse, were the terms required when he attacked the government, but, if, through a change in president, he went over to its defense, the attributes changed too; now it was forceful, enlightened, just, faithful to principles, a veritable triumph of the administration, etc., etc. Such gunfire went on for three years, and by that time, a passion for politics had taken hold of the young bachelor's soul.

A member of the provincial assembly, then of the Chamber of Deputies, president of a second-rate province, where, through the natural shifting of fate he read in the opposition's publications all the epithets that he, himself, had written formerly, ill-omened, wasteful, shameful, perverse, Camacho had his ups and downs, was in and out of the Chamber, and was speaking, writing, and fighting constantly. Finally he came to live in the capital of the empire. While he was deputy for the conciliation of the parties, the Marquis of Paraná was in power. Camacho advised several nominations, and he was listened to. Whether the marquis really sought his advice and confided his plans to him, no one can affirm, because, where he, himself, was concerned, Camacho falsified easily.

What one can believe is that he wanted to be minister, and that he worked for it. He joined various groups when he considered it wise; in the Chamber he spoke at length on administrative matters, accumulated figures, articles of legislation, fragments of reports, and passages from French writers (though these were poorly translated). But between the spike of flowers and the hand is the wall of which the poet speaks, and try as our man might to reach forth the hand of his desire to pluck it, the spike of flowers remained on the other side, to be snatched by other hands, only slightly greedy, or even indifferent.

There are political bachelors, and Camacho was entering that category in which all dreams of matrimony evaporate eventually. But he was incapable of rising above it. No one who organized a cabinet dared to give him a position even if he wanted to. Camacho felt himself slipping; to simulate influence, he treated those currently in power with familiarity and he recounted his visits to the ministers and other dignitaries of state in a loud voice.

He had enough to eat. His family was small, a wife, a daughter going on eighteen, and a nine-year old godson, and his law practice sufficed to take care of them. But politics was in his blood; he neither read nor thought of anything else. He had absolutely no interest in literature, the natural sciences, history, philosophy, or the arts. He did not know a great deal about law either; he retained a little of what the academy had taught him, in addition to subsequent legislation and practice in the courts. However, making use of what he did know, he presented his cases, and always won.

LVIII

Some days before, when he had gone to spend the evening at a counsellor's, he had seen Rubião there. The talk had turned to the Conservatives' summons to power and the dissolution of the Chamber. Rubião had attended the session in which Minister Itaborahy had asked for the budget. He still shook with emotion when he told his impressions and described the Chamber, the courts, the galleries, so crammed that there would not have been room for a pin, the speech of José Bonifacio, the motion, the voting. Of course, it was all told from the viewpoint of a simple man, but his disordered gestures and vehement manner of speaking bore the eloquence of sincerity. Camacho listened attentively, and later he managed to draw him over to a window embrasure and make certain grave observations regarding the situation, to which Rubião responded with occasional nods and words of approbation.

"The Conservatives won't stay in power," Camacho said, finally.

"They won't?"

"No; they don't want war and they'll be forced out. Remember how successful I was with the policy I advocated in my publication?"

"What publication was that?"

"We'll talk about it another time."

The next day they had lunch at the Hotel de la Bourse at Camacho's invitation, and he told Rubião how, some months before, he had started a paper for the sole purpose of advocating the continuance of the war at all costs. As there was much dissension among the Liberals, he thought that the best way to serve his own party was to furnish them with an issue at once neutral and national.

"And it is now proving to be in our favor," he concluded, "because the government is leaning toward peace. As a matter of fact, a furious article of mine is coming out tomorrow."

Rubião listened almost without taking his eyes off the other man, eating rapidly during the intervals when Camacho himself bent his head over his plate. He was enjoying his role as political confidant, and to tell the truth, the idea of participating in a struggle in order to acquire some prize in the end, a seat in the Chamber, perhaps, removed the dust from the golden wings in our friend's brain. Camacho did not talk any more that day; he looked for Rubião the next day, and did not find him. Now, shortly after Camacho's arrival, Palha came and interrupted them.

LIX

"But I must go to Minas," persisted Rubião.

"Why?" asked Camacho.

Palha asked the same question. Why go to Minas except for a very short time? Or was he already tired of the capital?

"No, I'm not tired of it; on the contrary—"

On the contrary, he liked it very much; but however unattractive it may be, if it's only a poor, most ordinary spot, the place of one's birth makes one homesick, and all the more so if one has come away from it as a grown man. Rubião wanted to see Barbacena. Barbacena was the most important, the most wonderful place on earth. For a few minutes, since, for the moment, his native land was within himself, he succeeded in getting away from his companions. Ambition, vanity, passing pleasures, everything gave way to the Mineiran's nostalgic longing for his province. If at times, he was shrewd and listened to the voice of self-interest, now he was just a simple man repenting his pleasure and unaccustomed to his own wealth.

Palha and Camacho looked at each other— Oh! that look was like a calling card exchanged between two consciences. Neither conscience told its secret, but they saw their names on the card, and they greeted each other. Yes, Rubião must be prevented from going away; Minas might keep him. They agreed that he might go later—a few months later—and Palha might go, too. He had never seen Minas; it would be an excellent opportunity.

"You'll go?" asked Rubião.

"Yes; for a long time I've been wanting to see Minas and São Paulo. Look, more than a year ago, we considered going —Sophia is a good companion for such trips. Do you remember when we met in the railway station? We were coming from Vassouras. We've never given up the plan to go to Minas, though; the three of us will go."

Rubião snatched at the forthcoming elections, but here Camacho intervened, asserting that that was not necessary, that the serpent should be crushed right there in the capital, and that there would be plenty of time afterwards to allay his homesickness and receive the reward. Rubião squirmed on the couch. The reward would surely be the title of deputy. A magnificent vision, an ambition he had never had when he was a poor devil— an ambition that has laid a hold upon him now, whetting his appetite for greatness and glory. Meanwhile, he still insisted that he must go for a few days, and, to be exact, I am compelled to make it clear that he did it without any wish that they accept his proposal.

The moon was bright now; the bay seen through the windows, presented that enchanting aspect that no carioca believes can exist anywhere else in the world. Away off in the distance, Sophia's figure passed along the slope of the hill and vanished into the moonlight; the last tumultuous session of the Chamber resounded in Rubião's ears— Camacho went over to the window and came right back.

"How many days?" he asked.

"I don't know, but not many."

"In any case, we'll talk about it tomorrow."

Camacho took his leave, and Palha stayed a few minutes longer to say that it would be strange if he went to Minas without settling their accounts— Rubião broke in, "Accounts?" Who was asking him for accounts?

"It's evident that you're not a businessman," retorted Christiano.

"No, I'm not; that's true. But one pays one's accounts when one can. It's always been that way between us. Or, who knows? Be frank. Do you need some money?"

"No, I don't need any, thanks. I have a business deal to propose, but it will have to be when there's more time. I just came to see if you were here so that I'd not have to put an announcement in the papers, 'A friend of mine, Rubião by name, who has a dog, has disappeared—.' "

Rubião liked the joke. Palha left, and he accompanied him to the corner of Marquez de Abrantes Street. When they parted, he promised to go to see him at Santa Thereza before leaving for Minas.

L X

Poor Minas! Rubião slowly returned home alone, pondering over how he could get out of going there now. And the words of his two friends went darting about in his brain like little goldfishes in a glass bowl, up and down and all aglitter. *"The head of the serpent should be crushed right here." "Sophia is a good companion for such trips."* Poor Minas!

The next day he received a paper that he had never seen before, the *Atalaia*. The editorial inveighed against the ministry, though its conclusion was expanded to include all the parties and the whole nation: *Let us plunge into the constitutional Jordan.* Rubião thought it excellent, and looked to see where the sheet was printed so that he might subscribe to it. It was in Ajuda Street, and he went there first of all when he left the house. There he learned that Doctor Camacho was the editor. At once he hurried to the latter's office, but, as he reached the street on which it was located, he heard a woman's voice calling frantically from the door of a mattress shop:

"Deolindo! Deolindo!"

Rubião heard the cry, turned around, and saw what was happening. A carriage was coming down the street and a three- or four-year-old child was crossing in front of it. The horses were almost on top of the child, despite the driver's efforts to keep them in check. Rubião lunged toward the animals, and snatched the child from peril. When the mother took him from Rubião, she was pale and trembling and unable to speak. Several people began to dispute with the driver, but a bald-headed man, who was inside, ordered the driver to go on. The driver obeyed and when the child's father, who had been in the mattress shop, came out, the carriage was already turning the corner of São José Street.

"He was nearly killed," said the mother. "Had it not been for this gentleman, I don't know what would have become of my poor boy."

It was an event in the block. Neighbors came in to see what had happened to the child; out on the street white children and little Negro boys were looking on with astonishment. Actually, the child had only a scratch on the left shoulder from the fall.

"It was nothing," said Rubião. "In any case, don't let that little boy go out into the street; he's too small."

"Thank you," said the father. "But where is your hat?"

Rubião noticed that he had lost his hat and that a ragged boy, who had picked it up, was in the door of the mattress shop, awaiting an opportunity to return it. Rubião gave him a few coppers as a reward, which the boy had not expected when he ent to pick up the hat. However, he accepted them gladly; it may have been they that first gave him the notion of venality.

"But wait," said the mattress maker. "Did you hurt yourself?"

Indeed, there was blood on our friend's hand from a wound n the palm, not a big one; only then was he beginning to feel it. Though Rubião said that it was nothing, and that she should ot bother, the child's mother ran to get a basin and towel. Then she brought water, and while she was bathing the hand, he mattress maker hurried to the nearest pharmacy, and rought back a little arnica. Rubião took it and tied his handkerchief around his hand; the mattress maker's wife brushed is hat, and as he left they both thanked him very much for aving saved their son. When he went out he was flanked on oth sides by the people in the doorway and on the sidewalk.

LXI

What's wrong with your hand?" inquired Camacho, when Rubião entered his office.

Rubião recounted the incident that had occurred in Ajuda treet. The lawyer asked a great many questions about the hild, the parents, the number of the house, but Rubião cut his nswers short.

"Don't you at least know the child's name?"

"I heard the mother calling 'Deolindo.' But let's get on to omething important. I've come to subscribe to your paper; received an issue, and I want to contribute—"

Camacho quickly assured him that he did not need subscriptions. As far as subscriptions were concerned, the paper was oing well. What he did need was typographic material and xpansion of the contents, more news items, more miscellaneous eatures, port and commercial activities, the translation of a ovel, etc. He had advertising, as Rubião had seen.

"Yes."

"I have almost all the subscriptions for the capital. Ten people are enough, and there are eight already; myself and seven
others. We need two. With two more people, the capital will be
complete."

I wonder how much it is? thought Rubião.

Camacho was tapping the edge of his small desk with a pen-
knife, and peering at Rubião furtively. Rubião looked around
the room, at the few pieces of furniture, some documents on a
stool beside the lawyer, a case with books, Lobão, Pereira e
Souza, Dalloz, *Ordenacões do Reino*, a portrait on the wall in
front of the small desk.

"Do you recognize him?" said Camacho, pointing to the
portrait.

"No, I don't."

"See if you don't."

"I don't know who it is. Nunes Machado?"

"No," said the former deputy, assuming an unhappy expression. "I haven't been able to get a good portrait of him. They're
selling some lithographs here that I think aren't good. No
that's the marquis."

"Of Barbacena?"

"No, of Paraná. He's the great marquis, my special friend
He tried to conciliate the parties, and that's why I was with him
He died young, however, and his work could not go on. If he
wanted it today, he'd have me against him. No! no conciliation
today; war unto death. We must destroy them; read the *Atalaia*
my good comrade in battle; you're going to get it at the
house—"

"No."

"Why not?"

Rubião lowered his eyes before Camacho's inquiring nose

"No; I'm adamant; I wish to help my friends. To get the
paper for nothing—"

"But I told you that we're doing well without subscriptions,"
retorted Camacho.

"Yes, but didn't you say, too, that two more people are
needed for the capital?"

"Two, yes; we have eight."

"What is the capital?"

"The capital is fifty contos; five per person."

"Well, I'll come in with five."

Camacho thanked him in the name of what the paper stood or. He had intended to ask him to go in with them; it was a privilege that his new friend's convictions and loyalty and concern for public affairs well deserved. Now that he had joined of his own accord, he, Camacho, begged him to forgive him for not having asked him sooner. Then he showed him the list of other names. Camacho's was at the head; it was he who took charge of the paper, what equipment they had, the subscriptions and the Herculean work— He considered changing the expression, but then he repeated bravely, "the Herculean work." One could truly say that it was Herculean. As a boy he had strangled snakes, and it was still a vice, this love of violent struggle; he would die in it, wrapped in the flag—.

LXII

Rubião made his departure. In the hall a tall, black-gowned woman passed him with the sound of silk and glass-bead embroidery. As he was about to descend the stairway, he heard Camacho's voice raised in greeting:

"Oh, Baroness!"

On the first step he paused. The lady's silvery voice began to speak; the first words concerned a lawsuit. Baroness! And our Rubião continued on down the stairs falteringly and quietly so as not to seem to have been listening. The air sent up his nose a rare, delicate perfume, a thing to make you giddy, the perfume that the lady had left behind. Baroness! He reached the street door and saw a *coupé* waiting; the lackey was standing on the sidewalk and the driver sitting on the cushion, looking out, both in livery. What could be so new and startling in all that? —Nothing. A lady of title, sweet-smelling and rich, engaged in a lawsuit, for no other reason, perhaps, than to have something to do. But the fact is that Rubião, without knowing why, and despite his own wealth, felt as though he were again the teacher of Barbacena.—

LXIII

On the street he met Sophia with a young woman and an elderly one. He did not have eyes to see clearly the features of these women, because all his faculties together were too few for Sophia. They spoke together for only two minutes, in a constrained manner, and then continued on their way. A little farther on, Rubião stopped, and looked back but the three women were walking along without turning their heads. After dinner, he said to himself:

"Shall I go there today?"

He pondered over it for some time without reaching any conclusion. One moment he thought he would go and the next that he would not. He had thought she had acted queerly; but he recalled that she had smiled, not much, but she had smiled. He decided to leave the question to chance. If the first carriage that passed came from the right, he would go; if it came from the left, he would not. So he sat down on the ottoman in the drawing room and watched. Before long a tilbury came from the left. It was settled; he would not go to Santa Thereza. But at this point, his conscience reacted; it wanted the precise terms of the proposition, a carriage. It should be what is commonly called a carriage, an open or closed calash, or even a victoria. A tilbury was not a carriage. In a little while a number of calashes that were returning from a funeral came from the right. He went.

Sophia gave him her hand graciously without the least of ill-will. The two women who had been walking with her were with her now, in house dresses, and she introduced them. The young woman was a cousin, the elderly one an aunt—that aunt from the country, writer of the letter that Sophia received in the garden from the hands of the mailman, who fell down immediately afterward. The aunt's name was Dona Maria Augusta; she had a small farm, a few slaves, and debts, which her husband had left her, along with her grief. The daughter's name was Maria Benedicta, a name that displeased her, because it was an old woman's name, she said. To this her mother answered that old women had once been young, and that names adequate to the person were the imaginings of poets and story-tellers. Maria Benedicta was the name of her grandmother, god-daughter of Luiz de Vasconcellos, the viceroy. What more did she want?

They told this to Rubião, but Maria Benedicta did not mind. To make light of the matter or for some other reason, Sophia added that the ugliest names could be made pretty by their possessors. Maria Benedicta was very pretty.

"Don't you think so?" she concluded, turning to Rubião.

"Stop teasing, cousin," laughed Maria Benedicta.

We may believe that neither the old lady nor Rubião heard what was said—the old lady because she was dozing off, Rubião because he was fondling a little dog that he had given Sophia, a playful, slender, black-eyed creature, with a bell at its neck. But, as his hostess insisted that he answer, he said, "Yes," without knowing why. Maria Benedicta made a grimace. In truth, she was not a beauty; she did not have eyes that fascinate, nor one of those mouths that, though still, always seem to be whispering a secret; she was natural, without any rustic shyness, and she had a peculiar grace that made up for the lack of elegance in her dress!

She had been born at Iguassú, not far out in the country, and she liked the place. Occasionally she came to the city to spend a few days, but at the end of the first two days she was always anxious to return home. Her schooling was slight; reading, writing, doctrine, some needle work. Lately (she was nineteen) Sophia had urged her to study piano, her aunt had consented, and she had come to her cousin's house. She stayed there for about eighteen days, but she could not stand it any longer. She was homesick for her mother; so she went back to the country, to the consternation of her teacher, who had maintained from the beginning that she had great musical talent.

"Oh, unquestionably, a great talent!"

Maria Benedicta laughed when her cousin told her, and after that she could never look at the man with a serious face. Sometimes she would burst out laughing right in the middle of a lesson; then Sophia would frown by way of reproach, and the poor man would ask why the girl was laughing or would himself explain that she must have recalled something, and the lesson would continue. She had not studied French either, and this was another lacuna that Sophia found it hard to excuse. Dona Maria Augusta could not understand her niece's dismay. Why French? Her niece told her that it was indispensable for conversing, going to the shops, reading a novel—.

"I've always been happy without French," answered the old lady. "And the colored people with their gibberish are just the same; they don't get along any worse than the rest."

One day she added:

"Nor will you lack suitors because of that. You may get married; I've already told you that you may get married whenever you wish; I, too, married; you may even leave me all alone in the country to die like a worn out animal—"

"Mama!"

"Don't be sorry. All that's needed now is for the suitor to show up, and when he does, you go with him and let me stay here. You see what Maria José did to me? She's living in Ceará now."

"But her husband's a judge," observed Sophia.

"And a squint-eyed one for all I care. It doesn't matter to me The old woman is cast off like a rag. Get married, Maria Benedicta, get married quickly; I'll die with God. I'll not have any children, but I'll have Our Lady, who is the Mother of all. Get married, go on, get married!"

All that grumbling was calculated to arouse the girl's fear and pity, and make her desist from marriage, or, at least, defer it. I don't believe that the old woman revealed that sin to the confessor, nor that she even understood it. It was the product of an old and sensitive egotism. Dona Maria Augusta had long been the recipient of much love; her mother had been mad about her and her husband's love for her was as great on the day of his death as it had ever been. Now that both were dead, her filial and wifely affections were placed on the heads of her two daughters. One of them had already married, and left home. Threatened by solitude, if the other one married too, Dona Maria Augusta was doing all she could to avoid the disaster.

LXV

Rubião's call was short. At nine o'clock he rose discreetly, hoping for some word from Sophia, a request that he stay a little longer, or that he wait for her husband, who would be coming soon, or an expression of surprise that he was leaving. "Already?" But there was none of that. Sophia merely held out her hand, from such a distance that he could barely touch it. However, throughout the call, the young woman had seemed so natural, so without any bitterness— Of course, there were not the long, loquacious glances as before— It almost seemed as though it had all never been, neither the good nor the bad, the strawberries nor the moon. Rubião was shaking, and could find no words; Sophia found all that she wanted, and if she had to look at him, did so calmly and directly.

"My regards to our Palha," he murmured, hat and cane in hand.

"Thank you. He went to make a call. I think I hear footsteps. It must be he."

It was not he. It was Carlos Maria. Rubião was surprised to see him there, but then, he thought that the presence of the country woman and her daughter might explain everything; perhaps they were even related.

Rubião waited until Carlos Maria sat down beside Dona Maria Augusta, and then he said:

"I was just leaving when you came in."

"Ah!" replied the other man, looking at Sophia's portrait.

Sophia went to the door to say good-night to Rubião; she said that her husband would be sorry not to have been at home, but his call was an important one. Business— He would apologize.

"Apologize?" said Rubião.

He appeared to wish to say something more, but Sophia's handclasp and her curtsy gave him the signal to depart. He bowed, and crossed the garden, hearing Carlos Maria's voice in the drawing room.

"I'm going to denounce your husband, madam; he's a man of very poor taste."

Rubião stopped.

"Why?" said Sophia.

"He has this portrait of you in the drawing room, and you are much more beautiful, infinitely more beautiful than the painting. Just compare, ladies."

L X V I

How naturally and easily he said that, thought Rubião, after he was home, remembering Carlos Maria's words. What an idea to belittle the portrait merely to praise the original! And it is really a very good likeness.

In the morning, in bed, he had a start. The first paper he opened was the *Atalaia*. He read the editorial, a letter, and some new items. Suddenly he came upon his own name.

"What's this?"

It was his own name in glaring print, repeated a number of times, because it was no less than an account of the Ajuda Street incident. After the surprise, he felt annoyance. What was the confounded idea to print an incident that had been told in confidence? He did not want to read any of it; as soon as he saw what it was, he put the sheet on the floor and picked up another. Unfortunately, he had lost his serenity, and now read superficially, skipping over some lines, not understanding others, or finding himself at the end of a column without knowing how he had slid down that far.

When he got up, he sat down in the armchair beside the bed, and picked up the *Atalaia*. He glanced at the item; it was more than a column. A column and over for such a little thing! he thought to himself. And finally, just to see how Camacho had filled in the space, he read it all, a little hastily, vexed by the adjectives and the dramatic description.

"It serves me right!" he said aloud. "Why did I have to be such a gabber?"

He went into the bathroom and dressed and combed his hair, without for a moment forgetting that meddlesome sheet, embarrassed by the publication of an incident that he considered trivial, and even more by the writer's exaggeration, as if it were a question of political praise or blame. At breakfast he picked up the page again to read of other things, government nominations, a murder in Garanhuns, something about meteorology, until his eyes fell, unhappily, upon the item. This time he read it slowly, and at this point admitted that one could, indeed, believe in the writer's sincerity. The latter's eloquence of expression could be explained by the impression that the fact had left upon him; so great had it been that it had not permitted more restraint. That was it, of course. Rubião recalled his entrance into Camacho's office, and the way he had spoken, and from there he went back to the incident itself. Stretched out in his study, he evoked the scene; the child, the carriage, the horses, the cry, the leap that he had taken, moved by an irresistible impulse— Even now, he was unable to explain the business; it was as though a shadow had passed before his eyes. He had plunged toward the child and the horses, blind and deaf, without giving any heed to his own risk— And he might have fallen under the animals, been crushed by the wheels, killed or wounded. Had he been wounded, might he or might he not—? It was impossible to deny that the situation was serious. The proof of it was that the parents and neighbors—

Rubião interrupted his reflections to read the account again. There was no doubt that it was well written. There were passages that he re-read with great satisfaction. The confounded man seemed to have witnessed the scene himself. What narration! What a lively style! A few points were added through a confusion in memory—but the addition was not bad. And was that a certain pride that he noted in the repetition of his name, "Our friend, our most distinguished friend, our valiant friend—"?

By lunch time he was laughing at himself. He really had allowed himself to become too upset. What was wrong if Camacho gave his readers a news account that was true, interesting, dramatic—and, surely—not common-place? When he went out he received some compliments. Freitas called him Saint Vincent de Paul. And our friend smiled, thanked him, and made light of the matter. It had been nothing—

"Nothing?" someone retorted. "Give me plenty of that kind of nothing. Saving a child at the risk of one's own life—"

And so it went, Rubião listening, agreeing, smiling, recounting the scene to several curious people who wanted it straight from the lips of the protagonist. Certain listeners responded with their own exploits—one, who had once saved a man, another, a little girl who had almost drowned while bathing in the mouth of the Passage. Some told also about suicides they had prevented by taking the pistol away from the poor devil and making him swear— Every little shining deed that had been hidden away was pecking at its shell and sticking out its head to flock featherless but with open eyes, around Rubião's supremely shining one. There were the envious ones, too, some who knew him only through having heard him loudly praised. Rubião went to thank Camacho, not without some reproach, to be sure, but a very mild reproach, and then he went to buy some copies of the paper for his friends in Barbacena. No other paper copied the item, but at the advice of Freitas, he had it reprinted, with double spacing, in the *Trade Journal* among the items published at the reader's request.

LXVIII

Maria Benedicta finally consented to study French and the piano. For four days her cousin kept insisting, so artfully and in such a way, that the girl's mother resolved to hasten the return to the farm lest her daughter accept finally. But the girl resisted; she said that French and piano-playing were superfluities and that a country girl does not need city talents. One night, however, when Carlos Maria was there, he asked her to play something, and Maria Benedicta blushed crimson. Sophia came to the rescue with a falsehood:

"Don't ask her; she hasn't played since she came. She says that she plays only for the farmers, now."

"Then pretend that we're farmers," insisted the young man.

However, he went right on to something else, the ball of the Baroness do Piauhy (the very one whom our friend Rubião met in Camacho's office) "a magnificent ball!" "Oh, magnificent!" The baroness thought very highly of him, he said. The next day Maria Benedicta declared to her cousin that she was ready to study the piano and French, the violin, and even Russian if she wanted her to. The difficulty would be to win over her mother. When the latter heard of her daughter's resolution, she put her hands to her head. "French? Piano?" And she shouted that she should not study them, or, if she did, she should no longer consider herself her daughter; oh, she could stay there, if she wanted, and play and sing and speak the African language— Cabinda—or the Devil's own language, and they could all go to the Devil. It was Palha who persuaded her finally; he told her that however superfluous those talents might seem to her, they were the minimum accomplishments of a drawing room education.

"But I brought my daughter up in the country and for the country," interrupted Sophia's aunt.

"For the country? Who knows what he's bringing his children up for? My father wanted me to be a priest; that's why I have a smattering of Latin. You're not going to live forever, and your business affairs aren't going so well. Maria Benedicta may be left all alone— No, I'll not say alone, because so long as we're living we're all one family. But isn't it better to look to the future? It might even be that, if we're all gone, she could live well only by teaching French and the piano. Just knowing them will put her in a better position. She's pretty, just as you were in your time, and she has rare moral qualities. She may find a rich husband. You know, I already have someone in mind, a worthy person."

"Indeed? Then she's going to learn French, the piano, and lovemaking?"

"What do you mean, lovemaking? I am referring to a seriously considered thought, to a plan that seems to me to be adequate to her happiness and that of her mother. Well, I had— Oh, come now, Aunt Augusta!"

Palha looked so perturbed that the aunt modified the asperity of her tone. She still held out, but the night gave her good counsel. The state of her business affairs and the possibility of a well-to-do son-in-law were more effective than any other arguments. The best sons-in-law out in the country were allying themselves with other farms and families of influence and assured means. Two days later, then, they found a *modus vivendi*. Maria Benedicta would stay with her cousin; from time to time they would go to the country, and the aunt, too, would come to the capital to see them. Palha even said that as soon as the exchange permitted, he would find a way to liquidate her affairs, and then she could live with them. But this the good woman refused.

Let it not be thought that all was so easy as it appears here on the written page. Actually, there were obstacles, the languishing of Maria Benedicta, her homesickness and her rebelliousness. Eighteen days after her mother's return to the farm, she wanted to go and visit her, and her cousin went along; they were there a week. Two months after, the mother came to spend a few days with them. Sophia cleverly accustomed her cousin to the distractions of the city: theaters, calls, drives, household gatherings, new dresses, pretty hats, jewelry. Maria Benedicta was a woman, but a strange woman; she liked such things, and yet she was convinced that, whenever she wished, she could break all those bonds, and go to the country. Sometimes, the country came to her, in a dream, or merely through a whim of fancy. When she was returning home from her first two evening parties, it was not the impressions of the evening that filled her mind, but her longing for Iguassú. This longing increased at certain hours of the day when the house and street were completely still. Then her mind would wing its way back to the veranda of the old house, where she used to drink coffee with her mother; she would think of the slaves, the old furniture, the pretty slippers that her godfather, a rich farmer of São João d'El-Rey, had sent her, and that had been left at the house because Sophia had not allowed her to take them with her.

The French and piano instructors were men who knew their business. Sophia found a way to tell them privately that her cousin was ashamed to be learning so late in life, and asked them never to speak of her as a student. They promised that they would not; the piano instructor merely told the request to several colleagues, who thought it amusing, and told some stories about their own clientele. It is certainly true that Maria Benedicta was learning remarkably easily, and that she was studying so diligently almost all the time that even her cousin judged it wise to interrupt her.

"Good heavens, girl! Rest a while!"

"Let me recover lost time," Maria Benedicta would reply, laughingly.

Then Sophia would invent random walks to make her rest. Now one quarter of the city, now another. Certain streets were not a waste of time for Maria Benedicta. She would read the French advertisements, and ask for new commodities that sometimes her cousin could not name, so strictly limited was her vocabulary to the matters of dress, the drawing room, and gallantry.

But it was not only in these disciplines that Maria Benedicta was making rapid progress. She had adjusted herself to her environment more quickly than her natural inclination and her life in the country would have led one to expect. Already she was competing with her aunt, although the latter had an elegance and an indefinable air all her own, which made colorful, as it were, every contour and gesture. Despite that difference, Maria Benedicta was, in truth, so much noticed that Sophia, though she did not disparage her, no longer sang her praises everywhere as she had at first but listened now in silence to the others' expressions of admiration. She spoke well; —but when she was quiet, it was for long periods, and then she said she was in the "dumps." She danced the quadrille languidly, which is the way it should be danced, and she very much liked to watch polkas and waltzes. Sophia, thinking that it was because of timidity that her cousin neither waltzed nor polkaed, wanted to give her lessons at home alone, with her husband at the piano, but the girl always refused.

"That's still a little bit of country rind," Sophia said to her, once.

Maria Benedicta smiled in so peculiar a way that the other did not insist. It was not a smile of humiliation or displeasure, or contempt. Contempt? Why should it be? And yet it is true that the smile appeared to be supercilious. No less true is it that Sophia waltzed and polkaed with vivacity, and no one clung more gracefully to her partner's shoulders than she. Carlos Maria, who seldom danced, waltzed only with Sophia—two or three whirls, he would say. Maria Benedicta counted fifteen minutes one evening.

The fifteen minutes were counted on Rubião's watch. He was beside Maria Benedicta, and twice she asked him what time it was, at the beginning and at the end of the waltz. The girl herself leaned over to see the minute hand.

"Are you sleepy?" asked Rubião.

Maria Benedicta looked at him askance. She saw that his face was serene, without design or laughter.

"No," she answered. "I'm even afraid that Cousin Sophia may want to go home early."

"She won't go early. She no longer has the excuse that she had at Santa Thereza because of the hill. The house is near here."

In fact, they were living on Flamengo Beach now, and the ball was in Arcos Street.

You must know that eight months had elapsed since the beginning of the preceding chapter, and there had been many changes. Rubião was in partnership with Sophia's husband in an importing house on Alfandega Street, under the name of Palha and Company. That was the business deal that Palha had been going to propose the evening that he found Doctor Camacho at the house in Botafogo. Despite his naivete, Rubião had hesitated for some time. They wanted a goodly sum of money, he did not understand business, had no inclination for it. Besides, his personal expenses were already considerable; his capital needed a diet of good interest and some economy to see if it could recover its original weight and complexion. However, the diet that was being indicated was not clear; Rubião was unable to understand Palha's figures, his calculations of profit, price lists, custom duties, in fact, he was unable to understand anything at all. But the spoken word supplemented the written. Palha said some remarkable things, and advised his friend to put his money into circulation and increase it. Of course, if he were afraid, that was different; he, Palha, would negotiate with John Roberts, former partner of the Wilkinson House, founded in 1844, whose head returned to England and was now a member of Parliament.

Rubião did not yield immediately; he asked for a period of five days. When he was alone he was more free, but this time his freedom served only to bewilder him. He computed his expenditures, evaluated the incursions made upon the funds that the philosopher left him. Quincas Borba, who was lying in the study with him, casually raised his head, and looked at him. Rubião shuddered; the supposition that within that Quincas Borba might be the soul of the other was never entirely dispelled from his mind. This time, he even saw a reproachful look in the eyes; he laughed; that was nonsense; a dog could not be a man. Unconsciously, though, he put down his hand and scratched the animal's ears by way of cajolery.

The reasons for refusal were followed by contradictory ones. What if the business were profitable? What if it really would increase what he had? Then, too, the position was honorable and might be advantageous to him in the election if, like the former head of Wilkinson House, he were to run for Parliament. Another, even stronger, reason, was the fear of hurting Palha, of appearing not to trust him with the money, when, actually, two days before, he had received part of the old debt, and the remaining part was to be returned within two months.

No one of these reasons formed the pretext of any other; they came of their own accord. Only at the very end did Sophia appear, though, actually, she had been there from the beginning as a latent, subconscious idea, one of the ultimate causes of the act, and the only one dissimulated. Rubião shook his head to expel her, and got up. Sophia (astute woman!), respectful of his moral freedom, took refuge in the man's subconscious, and let him decide for himself that he would enter into partnership with her husband, with certain security clauses. Thus it was that the business association was formed, and thus it was that Rubião legalized the assiduity of his social calls.

"Mr. Rubião," said Maria Benedicta, after a few moments silence, "don't you think that my cousin is very pretty?"

"With no disparagement to you, I do."

"Pretty and with an attractive figure."

Rubião accepted the compliment. They both watched the waltzers going down the room. Sophia was magnificent. She was wearing dark blue, very low-necked—for the reasons stated in Chapter XXXV; her plump bare arms of a pale golden tint formed a graceful line with her back and bosom, so used to being seen in the gas-light. She was wearing also a diadem of artificial pearls so well finished that they matched the real pearls that adorned her ears, and that Rubião had given her one day.

At her side, Carlos Maria did not cut a bad figure. He was an elegant young man, as we know, and his eyes were placid, just as upon the occasion of Rubião's luncheon. His were not the abrupt manners of some youths, nor the bowings and scrapings of others; he expressed himself with the grace of a benevolent king. And yet, if at first glance he appeared to be merely granting the lady a favor, it is nonetheless true that he was proud to have at his side the most slender lady of the evening. Nor were the two sentiments contradictory, since both were based upon the young man's self-adoration. Thus, contact with Sophia was, in his eyes, the prostration of a devotee. Nothing surprised him. Were he to awaken emperor one day, he would merely wonder at the ministry's delay in presenting its compliments.

"I'm going to rest a little," said Sophia.

"Are you tired or—bored?" he asked, offering her his arm.

"Ah, merely tired!"

Carlos Maria, regretting having supposed the other hypothesis, hastened to eliminate it.

"Yes, of course. Why should you be bored? I think you'll even give me a little more time. Five minutes?"

"Five minutes."

"Not one more? As for me, I'd spend eternity."

Sophia bent her head.

"With you, that is, of course."

Sophia walked along, guided by his arm, her eyes on the floor, and she did not answer, nor concur, nor even thank him for what he was saying. It might have been no more than gallantry, and it is customary to thank for gallantries. Already before, she had heard similar words ascribing supremacy to her over all women, but for six months she had not heard them—the four that Carlos Maria spent in Petropolis and two during which he had not come to the house. Recently, he had started coming again and paying her compliments, sometimes when they were alone, other times in everyone's presence. Now she let herself be led along; and they both walked without a word, until he broke the silence with the remark that, the evening before, the sea had been beating violently in front of her house.

"Did you pass by?" asked Sophia.

"I was there; I was going through Cattete quite late and I decided to go down to Flamengo Beach. It was a clear night; I stood for nearly an hour between the sea and your house. I'll wager you weren't even thinking of me, whereas I could almost hear your breathing."

Sophia made an effort to smile; he continued:

"The sea was beating violently; to be sure, but my heart was beating even more wildly—only the sea is stupid, and doesn't know why it beats, and my heart knew that it was beating for you."

"Oh!" murmured Sophia.

Was it an "Oh!" of amazement? Of indignation? Of fear? That is a number of questions all at once, and I suspect that the lady herself could not have answered precisely, so overwhelmed was she by the young man's declaration. In any case, it was not an "Oh!" of incredulity; and that is all that I can say, except that the exclamation was so faint, so muffled, that Carlos Maria could barely hear it. For his part, Carlos Maria disguised his feelings well from the roomful of eyes; neither before nor during, nor after his words, did his face betray the slightest agitation; it even bore the trace of a caustic laugh, a laugh that was usual with him when he made sport of someone; so he gave the appearance of having just recited an epigram. And yet more than one feminine eye was secretly observing Sophia's heart and studying the young woman's somewhat reserved manner and her obstinately lowered eyelids.

"You're disturbed," he said. "Hide your face with your fan."

Mechanically, Sophia began to fan herself, and she raised her eyes. She saw that many eyes were staring at her, and she turned pale. The minutes were elapsing like so many years; the first five and the second five were long past; it was now the thirteenth, and the wings of another were coming into view. Sophia told her escort that she wanted to sit down.

"I'll leave you and withdraw."

"No, don't," she said, quickly.

Then she emended:

"The ball is very pleasant."

"Yes, it is, but I wish to carry away the best remembrance of the evening. Anything that I may hear now will be like the croaking of frogs after the singing of a lovely bird, one of the birds in your house. Where do you wish me to leave you?"

"Beside my cousin."

L X X

Rubião gave up his chair and accompanied Carlos Maria, who crossed the drawing room and went to the vestibule where the overcoats were and where about ten men were conversing. Just as the young man was about to enter the vestibule, Rubião took him familiarly by the arm as if to ask him something or other, but, really, to detain him and sound him out. He was beginning to believe that an idea that had tormented him for days might be a possibility or even an actuality, and now the long conversation and her manner—

Carlos Maria knew nothing of the Mineiran's passion, long repressed and held in secret since he dared not confess it to anyone; he did not know how Rubião had been waiting for fortuitous favors, contenting himself with little, the mere sight of his beloved; not sleeping well nights, financing the commercial operations— For he, Rubião, was not jealous of the husband. The couple's intimacy had never aroused anger against the legitimate master. For many months now, his feelings had remained unchanged, and his hope undiminished. But the possibility of an outside rival stunned him; jealousy bit into our friend and bit so deeply that it drew blood.

"What is it?" asked Carlos Maria, turning around.

At the same time, he entered the vestibule, where the ten men were discussing politics, because this ball—I was forgetting to tell—was given at the residence of Camacho, upon the occasion of his wife's birthday. When Carlos Maria and Rubião went in, the conversation was general. All the men were talking at once —a whirlwind of words and assertions and divergent opinions—. One, who was a partisan of Liberalism, succeeded in getting the floor, and, for a few minutes, the others smoked in silence.

"They can do anything," said the Liberal, "but moral retribution is certain. The party's debts are paid unto the last coin and unto the last generation. Principles do not die; parties that forget that come to an ignominious end."

Another man, partly bald, did not believe in moral retribution, and he told why. But a third person referred to the dismissal of some collectors, and the adherents of the faction, half drunk with partisan feeling, immediately seized on this point. The collectors were guilty of nothing but holding their own views; and their dismissal could not be defended on the basis of the value of the replacements. One of these had gone through bankruptcy; another was the brother-in-law of a man by the name of Marques who had shot a government official in São José dos Campos with a pistol— And the new lieutenant colonels? Why! Regular criminals, with police records.

"Are you leaving already?" Rubião asked the young man when he saw him remove his overcoat from among the others.

"Yes, I'm sleepy. Help me into this sleeve. I'm sleepy."

"But it's still early. Stay awhile. Our friend Camacho does not like to have the young men leave; who'll dance with the young women?"

Carlos Maria answered smilingly that he was little given to dancing, that he had waltzed with Dona Sophia because she was such a good dancer, otherwise he would not even have done that. He was sleepy. He preferred his bed to the orchestra. Graciously he held out his hand; Rubião clasped it rather dubiously.

He did not know what to think. Maybe it was wrong for him to go away and leave her at the ball instead of waiting to accompany her to her carriage as he had done other times. And he recalled the evening at Santa Thereza, when he had dared to declare his feelings to the young woman, seizing her lovely, delicate hand. The Major had interrupted them; but why had he not persisted later? She had not reprimanded him, nor had her husband noticed anything— Then he thought again of the possible rival; to be sure, he had become sleepy and left, but her manner— Rubião went over to the salon door to see Sophia; then, restless and bored, he moved about, going to the *voltarete* table or retiring into a corner.

LXXI

At home, while she was taking her hair down, Sophia spoke of the party as though it had been tiresome. She kept yawning and she said that her legs ached. Palha disagreed; it was just that she was in a bad humor. If her legs ached, it was because she had danced too much. To which his wife retorted that had she not danced, she would have been bored to death. She went on taking out the pins, putting them into a crystal container, and gradually her hair fell down about her shoulders, which were only partly concealed by her cambric nightgown. Palha, who was standing behind her, commented that Carlos Maria waltzed very well. Sophia trembled; she looked at him in the mirror; his face was serene. She agreed that he did not waltz badly.

"No! rather he waltzes very well."

"You praise others because you know that no one can excel you. Come now, my conceited fellow, I know you."

Palha, putting out his hand and grasping her by the chin compelled her to look at him. Why conceited fellow? Why was he a conceited fellow?

"Ouch!" moaned Sophia, "don't hurt me."

Palha kissed her shoulder-blade, and she smiled. This night she was not weary. She did not have a headache. It was all quite different from that night at Santa Thereza when she told her husband of Rubião's temerity. It must be that hills are un-healthful and beaches salubrious.

The next day Sophia awakened early to the warbling of the birds in the house. It seemed to bring her a message from someone. She lingered in bed, and closed her eyes in order to see better.

To see what better? No, surely hills are unhealthful. The beach is another matter. At the window half an hour later, Sophia was contemplating the waves that were subsiding in front of the house, and those in the distance that were rising and breaking on the bar. The imaginative lady was wondering whether they might be waltzing, and for awhile she let herself drift down that stream of thought with neither sails nor oars. Finally she found herself gazing at the street beside the sea, as if seeking the distinguishing features of the man who had been there in the dead of night two nights before. I'll not swear it, but I believe that she found the features. At least it is true that she fitted her find to the text of the conversation:

"It was a clear night; I stood for nearly an hour between the sea and your house. I'll wager you weren't even thinking of me, whereas I could almost hear your breathing. The sea was beat-ing violently, to be sure, but my heart was beating even more wildly—only the sea is stupid, and doesn't know why it beats, and my heart knows that it was beating for you."

Sophia shivered; she tried to forget the text, but it kept repeating itself. "It was a clear night—"

LXXII

Between two phrases, she felt someone lay a hand on her shoul-der; it was her husband, who had just had breakfast and was leaving for town. They said good-by affectionately. Christiano suggested that she look after Maria Benedicta, who had awak-ened most unhappy.

"Up already!" exclaimed Sophia.

"When I came down I found her in the dining room. She's determined to go to the country. She had some dream or other—"

"It's the dumps!" concluded Sophia.

And with nimble, adroit fingers, she arranged her husband's cravat and brought forward the collar of his cutaway coat. Once again they said good-by. Palha went out. Sophia lingered at the window. Before he went around the corner, Palha turned his head, and as was their custom, they waved good-by.

LXXIII

"It was a clear night; I stood for nearly an hour between the sea and your house. I'll wager you—"

When Sophia was finally able to tear herself away from the window, the downstairs clock was striking nine. Angry, contrite, she solemnly swore to herself to think no more of the episode. She considered that it had really been nothing; only she should not have allowed the young man to finish his bold speech. And yet, by doing as she had, she had avoided a scandal, because he would have been quite capable of accompanying her to her chair and saying the rest of what he had to say right there before everyone. And, once again, the rest repeated itself in her mind, like a persistent melodic passage, with the same words and the same voice: "It was a clear night; I stood for nearly an hour . . ."

LXXIV

While she was repeating the declaration of the evening before, Carlos Maria was opening his eyes and stretching his arms and legs; and before going to the bathroom to dress for a canter, he reconstructed the previous evening in his mind. It was a habit of his; he always found something in the preceding day's happenings, some word, some note that was to his credit. That is where his mind would tarry; those were the inns along the highway, where he would dismount and slowly drink a draft of cool water. Even if there had not been any such happenings or had they been only adverse, he would not feel disconsolate. All he needed was the savor of some word that he himself had uttered, of some gesture that he had made, the contemplation of himself, the joy of having felt alive, for the previous evening not to have been a wasted one.

Sophia had played an important part the evening before. Indeed, she was the main part of the reconstruction, the facade of the spacious and magnificent edifice. Carlos relished the evening's conversation in retrospect; but when he recalled the confession of love, his reaction was at once pleasant and unpleasant. It was a compromise, a hindrance, an obligation, and although its advantages offset its disadvantages, the young man was torn between the two conflicting sensations. When he remembered that he had told her he had gone to Flamengo Beach the other evening, he could not help but laugh, because it was not true. The idea had sprung from the conversation; but the truth was that he had not gone there, nor had he even thought of going. Finally, he restrained his laughter and even began to regret what he had said; the fact of having falsified induced a feeling of inferiority, which humbled him. He went so far as to think that the first time he was with Sophia he would rectify what he had said, but then he realized that the correction would be worse than the sonnet and that, after all, there are false sonnets that are beautiful.

Quickly his spirits rose. He saw in memory the drawing room, the men and women, the impatient fans, the bristling whiskers, and he luxuriated in a bath of envy and admiration. The envy of others, of course; he lacked that vulgar sentiment. The envy and admiration of others, however, gave him profound delight. After all, the princess of the ball had devoted herself to him; it was thus that he defined Sophia's superiority. And yet he did recognize one capital defect in her—want of breeding. He had the impression that the young woman's polished manners, which he considered merely imitative, had been acquired only after or shortly before her marriage; and that, even so, they did not rise much above the milieu in which she lived.

Other women came to his mind—those who preferred his companionship and the admiration of his eyes to that of other men. Did he make love to them all? We don't know. Some, no doubt; we do know that he took delight in them all. Some there were, so virtuous, that they enjoyed having him near them, just for the pleasure of a handsome man's company, without the actuality or the danger of guilt—like the spectator who revels in Othello's passion, yet leaves the theatre with hands unsullied by Desdemona's death.

Now they all came, and formed a circle around his bed, each weaving him a garland identical to the one that all the others were weaving. They were probably not all young women, but distinction made up for youth. Carlos Maria received them as an ancient god, immobilized in marble, would receive his lovely devotees and their offerings. In the general murmur, he distinguished the voices of all, not all at once, but three or four at a time.

The last one was that of Sophia of recent memory; he listened to it, enamored still, but without the initial rapture, since the recollection of the other women, persons of quality, was lessening her importance. And yet, he could not deny that she was very attractive, and that she waltzed divinely. Would he ever be very much in love with her? Again he remembered the lie about the beach, and he got up from bed with annoyance.

"What the devil made me say such a thing?"

Again he felt the desire to restore truth, more seriously this time than before. Lying, he thought, was for lackeys and their ilk.

A half hour later he was mounting his horse and leaving the

house, which was on Invalidos Street. On the way to Cattete, it occurred to him that Sophia's house was at Flamengo Beach; nothing would be more natural than to shift his reins, go down one of the perpendicular streets, leading to the sea, and pass by the waltzer's door. He would find her at the window, perhaps; he would see her blush and greet him. All this passed through the young man's head in just a few seconds; he gave a turn to the reins, but his spirit—not the horse—his spirit reared! That was going after her too soon. He gave another turn to the reins, and continued his ride.

LXXVI

He rode well. No one who passed by or who was in a doorway could get his fill of looking at the young man's elegant posture, the royal composure with which he moved. Carlos Maria—and this was the point on which he yielded to the multitude—accepted all admiration, however slight. In adoring him, all men formed a part of humanity.

LXXVII

"Up already!" repeated Sophia, seeing her cousin reading the newspaper.

Maria Benedicta gave a start, but she regained her composure immediately; she had slept badly and awakened early. She did not like those all-night revelries, she said; but Sophia replied that one must become used to them, that life in Rio de Janeiro was not the same as in the country, where one went to bed with the chickens and awoke at cock's crow. Then she asked her what she had thought of the ball; Maria Benedicta shrugged her shoulders with indifference, but her verbal answer was that she thought it had been all right. She said little, and her words were listless. Sophia, meanwhile, observed that she had danced a great deal, everything but polkas and waltzes. And why had she not polkaed and waltzed too? Her cousin shot her a resentful glance.

"I don't like those dances."

"What do you mean, you don't like them? You're afraid of them."

"Afraid?"

"Not used to them," explained Sophia.

"I don't like to have a man hold my body close to his and go around with me like that in front of everybody. It makes me ashamed."

Sophia became serious; she did not defend herself or persist, she spoke of the country, asked if what Christiano had said were true, that she wanted to go home. Then her cousin, who was looking through the papers idly, replied animatedly that it was true, that she could not live without her mother.

"But why? Weren't you happy with us?"

Maria Benedicta said nothing; all atremble and nervously biting her lips, she ran her eyes over one of the papers as if seeking some piece of news. Sophia insisted upon finding out the cause of that sudden change. She touched her hands and found them cold.

"You must get married," she said, finally. "I have a fiancé for you already."

It was Rubião. Palha wanted to put the finishing touches by marrying his partner to his cousin; then everything would remain in the family, he told his wife. She had taken it upon herself to guide the affair, and now she remembered her promise. She had a fiancé all ready.

"Who is it?"

"Someone."

Will you believe it, future generations, Sophia could not utter Rubião's name? Once already she had told her husband that she had proposed it, but that time it had not been true. Now that she was really going to propose it, the name would not come from her lips. Jealousy? It would be strange if this woman, who had no love for that man, should not be willing to give him to her cousin as a fiancé; yet, Nature is capable of everything. It created the jealousy of Othello and that of the noble Desgrieux, and it might create this other kind, that of a person who wishes neither to relinquish nor to possess.

"But who is it?" repeated Maria Benedicta.

"I'll tell you later; let me arrange matters," Sophia answered, and changed the subject.

Maria Benedicta's expression was transformed; her mouth filled with laughter, joyous, hopeful laughter. Her eyes expressed their gratitude for the promise, and uttered words that no one could hear nor understand, obscure words:

"He (or was it she?) likes to dance, that's certain."

Who likes to dance? Probably she. Indeed, Sophia had danced so much with Carlos Maria the evening before that it might well have been a pretext. Maria Benedicta concluded now that that had been the real and the only reason. It was true that they had talked a great deal during the intermissions, but, naturally, it was of her that they were speaking, since her cousin had her heart set upon marrying her, and only asked her to let her arrange matters. Perhaps he thought her indifferent and without charm. However, once her cousin wanted to arrange matters— That is what the girl's happy eyes were saying.

LXXVIII

Rubião did not lose his suspicions so easily. He considered questioning Carlos Maria, and even went to Invalidos Street three times the next day. Not finding him in, he changed his mind and stayed behind closed doors for three days. It was Major Sigueira, who, having gone to inform him that he had moved to Dous de Dezembro Street, drew him out of his solitude. The Major very much liked our friend's house; its decorations, its drapes, all its little accessories, and he discoursed long upon the subject, recalling some of the furnishings of an earlier day.

Suddenly he paused to say that Rubião seemed bored in the house, and that that was only natural, since he was without a complement.

"You are happy, but there is something you need. You need a wife. You must get married. Marry, and tell me whether I'm wrong."

Rubião remembered Santa Thereza—that famous evening of conversation with Sophia—and he felt a shiver run along his spine; yet so little was the Major's voice inspired by self-interest that it bore no traces of sarcasm. His daughter was still as we left her in Chapter XLIII, except that her fortieth birthday had come and gone. A forty-year-old spinster! Early on the morning of her birthday, she commiserated with herself over the years and her status. She put neither ribbon nor rose in her hair and there was no party—only a speech from her father at lunch, reminding her of her childhood, anecdotes about her mother and grandmother, something about a domino at a masked ball, baptism in 1848, a necklace belonging to a Colonel Clodomiro, various things like that all mixed together to pass the time. Dona Tonica could scarcely listen. Absorbed within herself, she was munching the bread of spiritual solitude, and repenting her most recent efforts to seek a husband. Forty years old; it was time to stop. However, the Major had nothing of this in mind at the moment. To him it seemed that Rubião's house had no soul. And when he took his leave, he repeated:

"Marry, and tell me whether I'm wrong."

LXXIX

"And why not?" asked a voice, after the Major left.

Frightened, Rubião looked around; he saw only the dog looking at him. It was so absurd to think that the question might come from Quincas Borba, or rather the other Quincas Borba, whose spirit might be within this one's body, that our friend smiled scornfully, but at the same time executing a gesture we have seen in Chapter XLIX, he put out his hand and fondly scratched the animal's ears and neck, an act calculated to please the spirit of the deceased that might be within.

Thus it was that our friend acted, with only himself for an audience.

L X X X

But the voice repeated: "And why not?" Yes, why not marry reasoned Rubião. It would put an end to the passion that, without hope or consolation, was slowly devouring him. Besides, it was the entrance to a mystery. Yes, marry. Marry well, and right away.

When this idea began to bud, he was at his outer gate from there he went inside, mounting the stone steps and opening the door, completely unaware of what he was doing. As he closed the door, a bound from Quincas Borba who had come with him, brought him to. Where was the Major? He was about to go down to see, but he realized in time that he had just accompanied him to the street. His legs had done everything; it was they that, lucid and unfaltering, had propelled him all by themselves, so that his head might have only the task of thinking. Good legs! Friendly legs! Natural crutches of the mind! Blessed legs! They propelled him as far as the couch, and there slowly stretched out with him, while his mind all the while was belaboring the idea of marriage. It would be a way to escape from Sophia; it might even be something more.

Yes, it might be, too, a way to restore to his life the unity that it had lost with the change of fortune; but this consideration was not the child of his mind nor of his legs, but of something else, which he, like the spider, was unable to distinguish clearly. What does the spider know about Mozart? Nothing. And yet it listens with pleasure to one of the master's sonatas. The cat though it has never read Kant, is, perhaps, a metaphysical animal. Yes, in truth, marriage might be the cord that would tie his lost unity together. Rubião had a feeling of instability; even his friends, whom he loved so much and who did so much for him, since they were only transitory, gave his life the aspect of a journey during which the languages kept changing along with the cities, now Spanish, now Turkish. Sophia also contributed to that feeling; she was so variable, now this way, now that, that the days were passing by without either definite accord or perpetual disillusion.

Rubião had nothing to do. To while away the long, empty days, he would attend jury sessions, the Chamber of Deputies, and the change of the guard; he would take long walks, and in the evening he would make unnecessary calls or go to the theater, which he did not enjoy. Yet the house, with its bright luxury and the dreams that drifted about in its atmosphere, was restful to his spirit.

Recently he had been reading a great deal; he read novels, but only the historical ones of Dumas père, or the contemporary ones of Feuillet, the latter with difficulty, as he did not know very well the language in which they were written. Of the former, there were many translations. Occasionally he would risk another novel, if he found that it concerned an aristocratic and royal society, which was what constituted the other's chief appeal for him. Those scenes of the French court invented by the marvelous Dumas, his noble swordsmen and adventurers, Feuillet's countesses and dukes, who moved about in luxurious hothouses with considered and courteous speech, exalted and elegant, passed the time quickly for him. Almost always when he read, his book would fall to the floor finally, and he would remain staring thoughtfully into space. Perhaps some long deceased marquis was telling him tales of other days.

LXXXI

Before thinking about the bride, he thought about the wedding; he imagined all the ceremonial. There would be elegant old-fashioned coaches—if there still existed any of the sort that he saw pictured in old books. Oh! Great, proud coaches! How he liked to go on gala days and wait for the Emperor at the gate of the city palace to see the arrival of the imperial cortege, especially the coach of His Majesty, with its fine old paintings, its huge proportions and strong springs, and its four or five pairs of horses, driven by a grave and decorous coachman. It would be followed by others, smaller in size, but large enough even so to fill the eye.

One of these, or even a still smaller one, would do for his wedding, if all society were not leveled by the vulgar *coupé*. But after all, he would go in a *coupé*; he fancied it magnificently lined—with what? With a material that would not be common, which he, himself, could not make out for the moment, but which gave the vehicle the air of distinction it lacked without it. A fine pair of horses. A coachman in livery of gold. Oh! But a gold never seen before! Guests of the highest rank, generals, diplomats, senators, a minister or two, many of the most prominent people in business. And the ladies, the great ladies? Rubião named them over in his mind; he saw them enter, he at the top of the palace stairway—they crossing the lobby, lightly mounting the stairs with their short little satin slippers— Only a few were there at first, then more and more and still more. Carriage after carriage— There came the Count and Countess of So and So, he, a dashing man, she, a singular woman. "Here we are, my dear friend," the Count would say at the top, and, later, the Countess: "Mr. Rubião, the affair is brilliant—"

All of a sudden, the internuncio— Yes, he had forgotten that the internuncio would marry them; he would be there with his monsignor's purple socks and his large, Neapolitan eyes, conversing with the Minister from Russia. Gold and crystal chandeliers shining upon the city's loveliest necks, full-dress coats, some erect, others bending over to listen to the opening and closing of fans, epaulets and coronets, the orchestra giving a signal for the waltz. Then the black arms, crooked at an angle, went to seek the bare arms, gloved to the elbow, and off they went, whirling around the room, five, seven, ten, twelve, twenty couples. A brilliant supper. Bohemian glass, Hungarian china,

Sèvres glasses, nimble servants in livery, with Rubião's initials on their collars.

Those dreams came and went. What mysterious Prospero was thus transforming a banal island into a sublime masquerade? "Go, Ariel, bring the rabble, here, to this place; for I must bestow upon the eyes of this young couple some vanity of mine art."

The words would be the same as those of the play; the island and the masquerade were different. The former was our friend's head, and the latter was composed, not of goddesses and verse but of human folk and drawing-room prose. But it was elegant. Let us not forget that Shakespeare's Prospero was a Duke of Milan; perhaps that's how he got to our friend's island.

And, to be sure, the brides that appeared at Rubião's side in those wedding fantasies of his were always ladies of title. The names were the most sonorous and facile of our nobility, and here is the explanation; a few weeks before, Rubião had picked up a *Laemmert Almanac*, and in turning its pages, he had come to the chapter on persons of title. If he knew of some, he was far from being familiar with them all. He bought an almanac, and read it over and over, letting his eyes run down the page from the marquis to the barons and back again, repeating the fine names and learning many by heart. Occasionally he would take up his pen and a sheet of paper, select a title, new or old, and write it again and again, as if it were his and he were signing something:

Marquis of Barbacena

Marquis of Barbacena

Marquis of Barbacena

Marquis of Barbacena

Marquis of Barbacena

Marquis of Barbacena

And so on to the bottom of the page, varying the handwriting, making it now large, now small, with a backward slant or straight up and down, all styles. When he filled in the sheet, he picked it up and compared the signatures. Then he put it down, and became lost in dreams. Hence the hierarchy of brides. The worst part of it was that they all had Sophia's face; during the first moments they might resemble some neighbor or some young woman whom he had greeted on the street in the afternoon; they might start out very thin or very fat;—but before long they would change their appearance. The body would plump up or slim down, and the face of the beautiful Sophia would come shining out on top. Was there no escape in marrying? Rubião went so far as to think of the possibility of Palha's death; that was on a certain day as he was leaving the latter's house after having heard a number of vague, sweet words from Sophia. Though he rejected the idea immediately as an ill omen, it brought a deep sense of good fortune. Some days later, Sophia's manner being changed, he returned to his plans. More than once, it was Palha himself who incited those conjugal dreams.

"Do you have anywhere to go this evening?"

"No."

"Take this ticket for the Lyric Theater, box number eight, first row to the left."

Rubião would get there earlier than the others; he would wait for them, and give Sophia his arm. If she were in a good mood, the evening would be perfect; if not, it was martyrdom, to repeat what he, himself, said to his dog, one day.

"I suffered martyrdom yesterday, my poor friend."

"Marry and tell me whether I'm wrong," barked Quincas Borba.

"Yes, my poor friend," Rubião said, picking up Quincas Borba's forepaws and putting them on his knees. "You are right; you need a good feminine friend to give you a care that I cannot or do not know how to give. Quincas Borba, do you remember our Quincas Borba? A good friend of mine, a great friend of mine. I, too, was a friend of his; we were both great friends. If he were alive, he would be the godfather of my marriage, he would propose the toasts—at least the one to the bride and bridegroom—and it would be from a goblet of gold and diamonds, which I should order just for the occasion—Great Quincas Borba!"

Rubião's mind was hovering above the abyss.

LXXXIII

One day, as he had left the house earlier than usual, and did not know where to spend the first hour, he went to the warehouse. For a week he had not gone to Flamengo Beach, since Sophia had entered upon one of her periods of being cold and distant. He found Palha in mourning; his wife's aunt, Dona Maria Augusta, had died at the farm; the news had come two days before, in the afternoon.

"That young girl's mother?"

"Yes."

Palha spoke very highly of the deceased; then he spoke of Maria Benedicta's grief, which, he said, was pathetic. He asked Rubião if he would not go to Flamengo Beach that evening and help them to take her mind off her sorrow. Rubião promised to go.

"Good, you'll be doing us a favor. She's such a fine girl, poor thing! You've no idea how many excellent qualities she has! Good breeding and very strict; and as for the social graces, if she didn't have them as a child, she's made up for lost time remarkably fast. Sophia is her teacher. And her housekeeping? Well, my friend, I don't know anyone her age so proficient as she. She's staying with us now. She has a sister, Maria José, married to a judge in Ceará; she also has a godfather in São João d'El-Rey. The deceased used to praise him highly; I don't think he'll send for Maria Benedicta but even if he does, I'll not let her go. She's ours now. We're not going to let her go just for what her godfather may leave her in his will. She'll stay here," he concluded, flicking a bit of dust from Rubião's collar.

Rubião thanked him. Then, as they were in the back office,

he looked through the grating and saw that some cloth was coming into the warehouse. He asked what was being brought in.

"It's English shirting."

"Oh, English shirting," repeated Rubião. Actually, he had not the slightest interest.

"By the way, do you know that the firm Moraes and Cumba is paying all its creditors in full?"

Rubião did not know; he did not even know of the firm's existence, or whether they were its creditors. He received the information, said he was glad, and prepared to leave. But his partner detained him a few moments. Palha was quite cheerful now, just as though no one of his family had died. He spoke of Maria Benedicta once again. He intended to see that she married well; for she was not a silly, scatterbrained girl who would waste her time in idle chatter with a fop; she was a sensible girl who deserved a good, steady husband.

"Yes," said Rubião.

"Look," his partner murmured suddenly. "Don't be startled by what I'm going to say. I think you're the man to marry her."

"I?" Rubião shot back in astonishment. "No indeed." And then, to soften the effect of his refusal. "I don't deny that she's a fine girl; but—for the moment—I'm not thinking of getting married—"

"No one is telling you to get married tomorrow or the next day; marriage is not a thing to be entered into hastily. I'm merely telling you that I have a hunch. There is such a thing as a hunch, you know. Did Sophia never tell you about this one of mine?"

"Never."

"That's strange; she told me that she had spoken to you once or twice, I don't remember for certain."

"Maybe; I'm very absent-minded. About your wanting me to marry the girl, you mean?"

"No, about my hunch. But never mind. Let's leave it to time."

"Good-by."

"Good-by. Come over early."

So Sophia wanted to marry him off? thought Rubião on his way out; naturally that was the easiest way to get rid of him. Marry him off and make him her cousin. Rubião tramped over many a street before he reached another hypothesis—perhaps Sophia had not forgotten, after all, but was deliberately lying to her husband in order not to advance his plan. In that case, her feeling would be quite different. Rubião thought this explanation logical, and his soul recovered its former equanimity.

But there is no spiritual equanimity that can cut off even so much as an inch from the edge of time, if one does not have the means of shortening it. Indeed, Rubião's eagerness to go to Flamengo Beach in the evening made the hours drag more than ever. It was too early for everything, too early to go to Ouvidor Street, too early to return to Botafogo. Doctor Camacho was in Vassouras defending a criminal before the jury. There was no public entertainment, no fete or lecture. Nothing at all. Profoundly bored, Rubião pedalled his legs at random, reading the signboards, and tarrying to watch if there were any excitement due to an entanglement of carriages. One was not so bored in Minas. Why? He could find no answer to the enigma, since Rio de Janeiro had more amusements, amusements which really did divert him. Yet there were hours of deadly boredom.

Happily, there is a god that looks after the bored. Rubião remembered that Freitas—Freitas, who was always so cheerful—was seriously ill; he called a tilbury, and went to see him at Formosa Beach. He spent nearly two hours there, conversing with the sick man; finally the latter fell asleep, and Rubião said good-by to the mother—a frail old lady. At the door, before leaving, he said:

"You've probably had your money troubles." And seeing that she bit her lips and dropped her eyes: "Never mind. It's painful to be in need, but it's nothing to be ashamed of. I asked because I wanted you to accept something that I'm leaving to help defray expenses; you may pay it back some day, if you can—"

He had opened his pocket-book and now he took out six twenty-thousand reis bills, rolled them into a wad, and left it in her hand. Then he opened the door and went out. The old lady was so astonished that she was unable to thank him. Not until the tilbury rolled away did she run to the window; but her benefactor was already out of sight.

LXXXVI

All that had been so spontaneous an impulse with Rubião that only after the tilbury was in motion did he have time to reflect. It seems that he raised the curtain from the peephole in his mind; the old lady was coming in; he even saw the rest of her arm. Then he thought of all the advantages of not being an invalid. He leaned back, relieved his breast with a great sigh, and looked toward the beach; then he leaned forward. On the way out, he had not been able to see it very well.

"You're enjoying it," said the driver, pleased with the good customer he had.

"I think it's beautiful."

"Have you never come here before?"

"I believe that I came many years ago, when I was in Rio de Janeiro for the first time. I'm from Minas— Stop, fellow."

The driver stopped the horse; Rubião got out and told him to continue on slowly.

He was really curious. Those great bunches of thicket, springing from the mud and growing right there on a level with his face, made him want to go nearer to them. They were so close to the street! Rubião did not even feel the sun, and he had forgotten the sick man's mother. If the sea were like this everywhere, with land and verdure scattered over it, it would be worth while to go sailing. Not far beyond were Lazaros Beach and São Christovão. They were within walking distance.

"Formosa Beach," he murmured. "It is well named."

Meanwhile the shore was changing its appearance. Rubião was rounding the bend at Sacco do Alferes, and the seaside houses were coming into view. Here and there they were not houses, but overturned canoes, grounded in the mud or on land. Beside one of them he saw children playing around a man, who was lying face downward. They were all laughing; but one was laughing more than the others, because he was not able to stick the man's foot into the ground. He was a little fellow three years old; he would grab the leg and stretch it out until he had it on a level with the ground; but then the man would make a move and raise both his foot and the child into the air.

Rubião stopped to watch for a few moments. The child, seeing himself the object of attention, redoubled his effort, but ceased to be natural. The other children, who were older, stopped to look on in astonishment. Rubião, however, saw nothing clearly; for him it was all confused. He continued to walk for some time; he passed Sacco do Alferes, he passed Gamboa, paused in front of the English cemetery, with its old graves clambering up the hillside, and finally he reached *Saude*. He saw narrow streets, some mere lanes, and he saw streets that were cut into slopes. He saw houses clustering in the distance, and on the hilltops many old houses, some from the time of the king, worn and cracked and falling apart, their whitewash soiled— But there was life inside—and all that gave him a feeling of nostalgia—nostalgia for the tatters of poverty, humble but unashamed. It did not last long though. The magician inside of him made a quick transformation. It was so good not to be poor!

Rubião came to the end of *Saude's* main street. As he was going along aimlessly and inattentively, a woman passed close to him. She was not pretty, but she was fresh-looking, nor was she without a certain elegance, although evidently she did not have even moderate means. She was about twenty-five years old and she had a little boy by the hand. The child became entangled in Rubião's legs.

"What are you doing?" said the young woman, pushing the child along with her arm.

Rubião had leaned over the little fellow to protect him.

"Thank you very much, and excuse him," she said, smiling.

Rubião took off his hat, and he, too, smiled. Once again the idea of having a family seized him forcibly— "Marry and tell me whether I'm wrong!" —He stopped, turned around, and saw the young woman tripping along, clickity-clickity, and the child beside her taking many short steps in order to adjust himself to his mother's pace. Then Rubião proceeded slowly, thinking of the various women whom he might very well choose to execute the connubial sonata with him in duet, serious classical music composed in accordance with the rules. He thought of the Major's daughter, who knew only some old mazurkas. Suddenly he heard the guitar of sin as plucked by Sophia's fingers, which so delighted and troubled him at one and the same time, and there went all the chastity of his plan. He tried again; made an effort to change the compositions; thought of the young woman of *Saude* with her charming manner and her little child by the hand—.

The sight of the tilbury made him remember the sick man of Formosa Beach.

"Poor Freitas!" he sighed.

Immediately after, he thought, also, of the money that he had given to the invalid's mother and he considered that he had done well. The idea that he had given one or two bills too many may have fluttered in our friend's brain for a few moments. However, he quickly shook it off, though not without feeling annoyance with himself, and to forget it completely, he exclaimed in a loud voice:

"Good old lady! Poor old lady!"

LXXXIX

As the idea came back, Rubião hurried over to the tilbury, got in and sat down, speaking to the driver in order to escape from himself.

"I took a long walk. It's pretty around here, and rather unusual; those beaches and streets are quite different from the other districts. I like this. I'll come again."

The driver smiled to himself so oddly that our Rubião was suspicious. He did not understand the reason for the amusement; possibly he had let slip some word that might have a bad connotation in Rio de Janeiro; he said them over to himself, however, and discovered nothing; they were all most ordinary and of common usage. And yet, the driver was still smiling in that same rather sly fashion. Rubião was on the point of questioning him, but he refrained from it just in time. It was the driver who renewed the conversation.

"So you like this district?" he said. "Well, you mustn't mind if I don't believe you; I mean no offense. I'm not one to offend a good customer; but I don't believe you like the district."

"Why?" ventured Rubião.

The driver shook his head from side to side and insisted that he did not believe—not because the district was not worthy of appreciation, but because his customer was already very familiar with it. Rubião ratified the first statement, but, as to his being familiar with the place, he had gone there when he had been in Rio de Janeiro many years before, and he remembered nothing of it. The driver laughed, and all the while his customer was proving his point, he was becoming more and more familiar, making negative gestures with his nose, his lips, and his hand.

"I know all that," he concluded. "I'm not blind. You think I didn't see the way you looked at that young woman who went by just now. That alone is enough to show that you have a flair and good taste—"

Rubião, flattered, smiled a little, but he amended it immediately.

"What young woman?"

"What did I tell you?" the man retorted. "You're smart; but I can keep a secret, and that carriage over there has been used for many such trips. Not many days ago, I brought out a handsome young man, an elegant fellow, very well dressed—it was some skirt-chasing business, of course."

"But, I—" interrupted Rubião.

He could scarcely contain himself; he was pleased by the driver's supposition that he was hiding some guilty secret.

"Look," the driver went on. "I'll tell you just as I told the young man from Invalidos Street that you can rest easy; I'll not say anything. But do you expect me to believe that a person who has a carriage at his disposal will walk from Formosa Beach way out here just for pleasure? You came to the appointed place, the person didn't come—"

"What person? I went to see a sick man, a friend who is dying."

"Just like the young man from Invalidos Street. That one came to see his wife's seamstress, as if he were married—"

"From Invalidos Street?" asked Rubião, who for the first time noted the name of the street.

"That's all I'm going to say," said the driver. "He was from Invalidos Street, a good-looking young man with whiskers and large, very large eyes. Oh! if I were a woman, I could fall in love with him— I don't know where she was from, and I wouldn't say if I did know; I only know that she was an eyeful."

And, seeing that his customer was listening with wide open eyes:

"Oh! You've no idea! Tall, a good figure, her face half-covered by a veil of fine quality. Just because a person's poor, doesn't mean he can't appreciate what's good."

"But—what happened?" murmured Rubião.

"What happened? He came in my tilbury just like you, he got out and went into a house with latticework; he said he was going to see his wife's seamstress. As I didn't ask any questions, and he hadn't said a word on the whole trip, very much absorbed in himself, I understood the trick right away. Now it could be true, because it is a seamstress who lives in the house on Harmonia Street."

"Harmonia?" repeated Rubião.

"This is bad! You're drawing my secret out of me. Let's change the subject; I'll not say another word."

Rubião was looking dazedly at the man, who did, in fact, keep still for two or three minutes, but then continued:

"There isn't much more. The young man went in, and I waited; half an hour later I saw a woman's figure in the distance, and I suspected that she was going there. And so she was; she came along slowly, looking all around, furtively, when she came to the house, she didn't even have to knock; as if by magic the lattice opened and she went inside. Oh, I've seen that before. How do you suppose a person earns a few more coppers? Our regular charge barely gives us enough to eat; we have to do these odd jobs."

X C

"No, it couldn't be she," reflected Rubião. He was putting on his black suit.

From the moment he had arrived home, he had no thought for anything but the affair the driver of the tilbury had told him about. He tried to forget it by putting some papers in order or reading, or snapping his fingers to make Quincas Borba jump; but the vision pursued him. His reason told him that there are many women with good figures and that there was no proof that the one who had been seen on Harmonia Street was she; but, this consolation was fleeting. A moment after, a person, who was none other than Sophia would appear in the distance, and, walking slowly and with head down, would suddenly enter the door of a house, which would close immediately after her— Once the apparition was so clear that our friend stared at the wall as if the lattice on Harmonia Street were right there. He imagined himself going through a series of acts; —he knocked, and went in, seized the poor seamstress by the throat, and demanded the truth or her life. The poor seamstress, threatened with death, made a full confession, and let him see the woman, who turned out to be someone other than Sophia. When Rubião came to, he felt ashamed.

"No, it couldn't be she."

He put on his vest, and went to button it in front of one of the windows that looked out toward the back. Just at that moment, a procession of ants was marching along the sill. He had seen so many marching like that before, but this time, he never knew how it happened, he grabbed a towel, struck with it twice, and crushed the unhappy ants, killing a number of them. Perhaps one of them looked like "a fine figure of a woman." Immediately he repented his act; after all, what did the ants have to do with his suspicions? Fortunately, a cicada began to sing, so appropriately and so meaningfully, that our friend paused at the fourth vest button. Soooo—fia, fia, fia, fia, fia, fia,— Soooo—fia, fia, fia, fia, fia—

Oh! Sublime and compassionate precaution of Nature, that in compensation, places a live cicada by the side of twenty dead ants. That, of course, is the reader's reflection. It could not be Rubião's. He was not in a state to put things together and draw a conclusion from them—nor could he, even now that he is coming to the last vest button, all ears, all cicada— Poor ants! Go now to your Gallic Homer, that fame may reward you. The cicada is laughing, emending the text

> Vos marchiez? J'en suis fort aise.
> Eh bien! mourez maintenant.*

* You were marching? I'm very glad.
Ah well, go to your death anon.

The dinner bell rang; Rubião composed his face, so that his guests (he always had four or five) would notice nothing. He found them in the living room, conversing while they waited. They all rose and went to shake hands with him cordially, whereupon he had an inexplicable impulse to give them his hand to kiss. He refrained just in time, aghast at himself.

In the evening, he hurried over to Flamengo Beach. He was not able to speak to Maria Benedicta, because she was in her room upstairs with two neighboring girls, friends of hers. Sophia received him at the door and took him to the study where two seamstresses were working on her mourning dresses. Her husband had just returned home and had not yet come downstairs.

"Sit down here," she said.

He examined her; she was divine. Her words were grave and affectionate, interspersed with friendly, open smiles. She spoke of her aunt, her cousin, the weather, the servants, the theater, the water shortage, a number of things that, commonplace or not, seemed quite different when they came from her lips. Rubião listened, enraptured. Not to be idle, she was sewing on some embroidered edges, and whenever there was a pause in the conversation Rubião all but devoured her agile hands, which appeared to be playing with the needle.

"You know that I have formed a women's committee?" she asked.

"I didn't know. What for?"

"Didn't you read about that epidemic in one of the cities of Alagoas?"

Then she told him that she had been so moved by it that she decided immediately to organize a committee of women to seek contributions. Her aunt's death had interrupted the first steps, but she was going to go on with it after the seventh day's Mass. She asked him what he thought about it.

"I think it's fine. Aren't there any men on the committee?"

"Just women. The men merely give the money," she concluded, laughing.

Rubião mentally subscribed to a large sum, in order to compel those who followed to do likewise. It was all true. It was true too, that the committee was going to bring Sophia to the fore and give her a push upward. The women selected were not of our lady's circle; only one was a speaking acquaintance; but through the intervention of a certain widow, who had shone between 1840 and 1850 and who still preserved the nostalgia and refinement of her day, she had succeeded in getting them all to go into that charitable undertaking. For some days she had thought of nothing else. Sometimes in the evening before tea she would appear to be asleep in the rocking chair, but she was not asleep; she had her eyes closed so that she might see herself in the midst of her companions, who were all persons of quality. It's quite understandable, then, that this was the chief topic of conversation. From time to time, however, Sophia would turn to our friend. Why did he stay away so long, eight, ten, fifteen days and more? Rubião replied that it was for no reason at all, but he replied with such disconcertion that one of the seamstresses stepped on the other's foot. From then on, even when there was a prolonged silence, interrupted only by the sound of scissors and of the tearing of cloth and by the sound of the needle being pulled through the merino, neither one took her eyes off our friend, who, in turn, was gazing at the lady of the house.

A man, a bank director, came to make a call of condolence. They went to summon Palha, who came down to receive him. Sophia asked Rubião to excuse her for a few moments; she was going to see Maria Benedicta.

Rubião, remaining alone with the women, began to walk back and forth, muffling his steps so as not to disturb anyone. From the drawing room came an occasional word from Palha: "In any case, you may be assured—" "The administration of a bank is not a child's play—" "Positively—" The director was saying little, in a low, dry tone.

One of the seamstresses folded up her work and hastily gathered together scraps, scissors and spools of linen thread and silk twist. It was late and she was leaving.

"Dondon, wait a bit; I'm leaving too."

"No, I can't. Will you please tell me what time it is, sir?"

"It's half-past eight," replied Rubião.

"Heavens! It's very late."

Just to say something, Rubião asked her why she would not wait, as the other one had asked her to.

"I don't wait for anyone but Dona Sophia," said Dondon, respectfully. "But do you know where this woman lives? She lives on Passeio Street. I rest my bones on Harmonia Street, and from here to Harmonia Street it's a long stretch."

Sophia came down soon after. When she saw that Rubião was upset about something and was avoiding her eyes, she asked him what was the matter. He answered that it was nothing, just a headache. Dondon left, the bank director took his leave; Palha thanked him for coming, he appreciated his courtesy. Where was his hat? He found it, and gave him his overcoat also, and, seeing that he appeared to be looking for something else, asked if it was his cane he was looking for.

"No, it's my umbrella. I believe this is it; it is. Good-by."

"Once again, thank you, thank you very much," said Palha. "Put on your hat, it's damp; don't stand on ceremony. Thank you, thank you very much," he concluded, bent double and clasping the banker's hand in his.

Returning to the study, he found his partner determined to leave. Palha was just as insistent that he stay; he said he should take a cup of tea and his headache would soon pass. Rubião refused.

"Your hand is cold," remarked Sophia. "Why don't you wait? Extract of balm is very good. I'll get some."

Rubião stopped her. It wasn't necessary; he knew those attacks; they got better with sleep. Palha wanted to send for a tilbury, but Rubião said hastily that the night air would do him good, and that he would find a conveyance in Cattete.

XCV

"I'll catch her before she reaches Cattete," said Rubião to himself, going up Principe Street.

He calculated that the seamstress would probably have gone that way. He saw several figures in the distance, on either side of the street; one of them appeared to be a woman's. It must be she, he thought; and he went faster. You understand, of course, that his head was all confused; Harmonia Street, seamstress, a lady, and all the lattices open. Let it not surprise you that, distracted as he was and walking so rapidly, he collided with a man who was going along slowly, head down. He did not even ask his pardon; he quickened his pace, seeing that the woman, too, was walking fast.

XCVI

The man who was bumped into scarcely felt the bump. He was going along contentedly, absorbed in his own thoughts, expanding his soul, relieved of all care. It was the bank director, who had just made his call of condolence on Palha. He did feel the bump, but he did not become angry; he adjusted his overcoat and his soul, and went tranquilly on his way.

To explain the man's indifference, I should tell you that during the course of an hour he had experienced contrary emotions. He had gone first to the house of a minister of state regarding the petition of a brother of his. The minister, who had just dined, was quietly and peacefully smoking. Incoherently, the director stated his business, backtracking, jumping ahead, putting his phrases together only to take them apart again. Seated on the edge of his chair so as not to lose the proper posture of respect, a smile of veneration continually upon his lips, he kept bowing and asking pardon. The minister asked some question; the director replied enthusiastically and at great length, and finally handed him a written petition. Then he rose, thanked the minister, and shook his hand, and the latter accompanied him to the veranda. The director made two bows— one full one before going down the step, and the other at the bottom, in the garden, an empty one, so to speak, since, instead of the minister, he saw only the opaque glass door, and on the veranda the gas lamp hanging from the ceiling. He rammed down his hat and departed, departed in shame and humiliation. It was not the mission on which he had been bent that distressed him, but, rather, all the compliments that he had dispensed, the indulgence he had craved, the air of inferiority he had assumed, all the profitless acts one after the other. It was in this state that he arrived at Palha's house.

In ten minutes his spirit was all dusted off and restored, such were his host's courtesies, nods of approval, and perpetual smiles, to say nothing of the offer of tea and cigars. He became cold, severe, superior; he even turned up his left nostril disdainfully apropos of an idea expressed by Palha. Palha quickly withdrew his idea, agreeing that it was absurd. The director copied the minister's slow movements, and when he left, it was his host, not he, who dispensed the compliments.

By the time he reached the street, he was quite another person; hence his quiet and complacent procedure, the expansion of his spirit, which had once again become its former self, and the indifference with which he received the collision with Rubião. The remembrance of his bowings and scrapings was fading away; now it was Christiano Palha's bowings and scrapings that provided a savory morsel to chew upon.

XCVII

When Rubião reached the corner of Cattete, the seamstress was talking with a man who had been waiting for her. The man gave her his arm and Rubião saw them go off together connubially in the direction of Gloria. Husband and wife? Friends? They became lost to view at the first turning; and Rubião remained standing, recalling the driver's words, the lattice work, the young man with whiskers, the lady with a fine figure, Harmonia Street— Harmonia Street; she had said Harmonia Street.

He went to bed late. Part of the time he was at the window with lighted cigar, pondering over the matter, but finding no explanation for it. Dondon must be the third party in the love affair; she must be, for she had deceitful eyes, thought Rubião.

"I'll go there tomorrow; I'll leave earlier, and go wait for her at the corner. I'll give her one hundred thousand reis, two hundred, five hundred: she'll confess everything to me."

When he grew tired he looked up at the sky; there was the Southern Cross. Oh! if only she had consented to gaze upon the Southern Cross! Their lives would have been different. The constellation seemed to confirm this feeling by shining with extraordinary brilliance. Rubião stood looking at it, imagining a thousand charming and amorous scenes—the life of the man he might have been. When he had had more than enough of this amorousness that was forever unfulfilled, our friend recalled that the Southern Cross was not only a constellation, but an honorary order as well. He thought it a clever idea to make a national and privileged distinction out of the Southern Cross. He had seen the decoration on the chest of several public servants. It was handsome, and, above all, rare.

It was nearly two o'clock when he left the window; he closed it and got into bed. Soon he was asleep. He awoke at the sound of the voice of the Spanish servant, who was bringing him a note.

XCVIII

Rubião sat up in bed. Only half awake, he did not notice the writing on the envelope. He opened the note and read:

> We were very anxious yesterday after you left. Christiano can't come to see you now because he has an appointment with the customs inspector, and he overslept. Let us know if you're better. Regards from Maria Benedicta and from
>
> Your sincere friend,
> Sophia.

"Tell the bearer to wait."

Within twenty minutes the reply was in the hands of the Negro boy who had brought the note. It was Rubião himself who handed it to him. After inquiring about the ladies and learning that they were well, he gave the boy ten *tostões*, and told him that whenever he needed money he should come to him. The boy opened his eyes wide with astonishment, and promised that he would.

"Good-by," said Rubião benevolently.

He remained standing there while the note bearer went down the few steps. When the latter had reached the middle of the garden, he heard a shout:

"Wait!"

He turned back in answer to the call; Rubião had already descended the steps; they approached each other, and stopped, neither one saying anything. Two minutes went by without Rubião opening his mouth. Finally he inquired if the ladies had been well; the same inquiry he had made a little while before. The boy confirmed his reply. Then Rubião let his eyes rove over the garden. The roses and the daisies were pretty and fresh, some carnations were opening and other flowers and leaves, begonias and vines and that whole little world seemed to be turning its invisible eyes toward Rubião and clamoring:

"Timorous soul, go ahead and do what you'd really like to; gather us, send us—"

"Well," Rubião said at last, "regards to the ladies. Don't forget what I told you; come here if you need me. You still have the letter?"

"Yes, it's here, sir."

"You'd better put it in your pocket, but be careful not to crumple it."

"No, I'll not crumple it, sir," the boy answered, carefully putting the letter away.

XCIX

After the Negro boy left, Rubião walked about the garden, with his hands in the pockets of his dressing gown, and his eyes on the flowers. What would have been wrong if he had sent some? It was a natural gift, even an obligatory one, to repay one courtesy with another. He had made a mistake; he ran to the gate but the Negro boy was already far away. Then Rubião realized that cheerful remembrances of that sort were not to be sent in time of mourning, and he was reassured.

As he resumed his walking, he noticed a letter beside a flower bed. He stooped down, picked it up, and read the envelope— The writing was hers, no one's but hers; he compared it with that of the note he had received; it was the same. But the name was the very Devil's own: Carlos Maria.

Yes, that was it, he thought, after a few moments; the bearer of my letter had this one too, and dropped it.

And scrutinizing both sides of the letter, he questioned its contents. What could be inside? What would be written there, nside of that murderous envelope? Perversity, corruption, the whole language of evil and madness, resumed in two or three lines. He raised the letter to his eyes to see if he could read a word. But the paper was heavy, and he could read nothing. Realizing that when the bearer missed the letter, he would come back for it, Rubião dazedly put it into his pocket and hurried inside.

In the house he took it out and looked at it again. His hands altered, reflecting his state of mind. If he opened the letter, he would know everything. If it were read and burned, no one would know the contents, whereas he would be done once and for all with that terrible fascination that was making him suffer close to the abyss of shame— It is not I who am saying that; it was he; he who was putting that and other ugly words together, he who paused in the middle of the room, with his eyes on the carpet, in whose woof was the figure of an indolent Turk, pipe in mouth, gazing at the Bosporus.

"Infernal letter!" he mumbled, repeating a phrase he had heard at the theater several weeks before, a phrase that had been forgotten, but that came back now to express the spiritual analogy between the play and the playgoer.

He had the impulse to open it; but he merely made the gesture, the move; no one saw him, the pictures on the walls were quiet and indifferent, the Turk in the carpet went on smoking and gazing at the Bosporus. And yet, he had scruples; the letter, although found in the garden, did not belong to him, but to someone else. It was like a packet of money; would one not return the money to its owner? Vexed, he put the letter into his pocket again. Between the alternatives of sending it to the one for whom it was destined, and giving it to Sophia, he finally chose the latter, since it had the advantage of enabling him to read the truth in the writer's features.

"I'll tell her that I found a letter, just like that," thought Rubião, "and before giving it to her, I'll plainly see by her face whether she's upset or not. She may turn pale; then I'll threaten her, speak of Harmonia Street; I'll swear that I'm ready to spend three hundred, eight hundred, a thousand contos, two thousand, thirty thousand, if need be, to choke the wretch—"

None of the habitués of the house showed up for lunch. Rubião waited about ten minutes, and then sent a servant out to the gate to see if anyone were coming. No one. He had to lunch alone.

He could never bear solitary meals; so accustomed was he to the talk of his friends, to their observations and witty remarks no less than to their manifestations of respect and consideration, that eating alone was the same as not eating at all. Now, however, he was like a Saul in need of a David to drive out the malignant spirit that had entered into him. He felt resentful toward the bearer of the letter for having dropped it; ignorance was an advantage. And then his conscience wavered between relinquishing the letter or refusing to relinquish it and keeping it indefinitely. Rubião was afraid to find out; one minute he wanted to read Sophia's face, the next moment he did not. In short, his desire to learn everything was merely the hope that there was nothing to learn.

Finally, David appeared between the cheese and coffee in the person of Doctor Camacho, who had returned from Vassouras the evening before. Like the scriptural David, he was bringing an ass laden with loaves, a jug of wine and a kid. While he was taking his first swallows of coffee, Camacho explained that since a Mineiran deputy, who was in Vassouras, was gravely ill, he, Camacho, had written to persons of influence in Minas and prepared the way for Rubião's candidacy.

"I, a candidate?"

"Who else?"

Camacho pointed out that there could be none better. He had rendered services in Minas, had he not?

"Some."

"Here you have rendered very important ones. Helping me to maintain the organ of our principles, you have accepted the blows directed toward me, in addition to the pecuniary sacrifices that we all make. Don't deny it. I tell you, I'm going to do what I can. Besides, you're the best solution for the split."

"The split?"

"Yes. Doctor Hermenegildo of Cattas-Altas and Colonel Romualdo; they say that in case of a vacancy both will present themselves, and that would divide the vote—"

"Of course. But will they go through with it?"

"I believe they won't when I send in the leader's confirmation from here, because that's one of the things they threw up to me, that I had no power. I admitted that I didn't for the moment, but I said that I had the confidence of the leaders, who would support me. Rest assured that they will. So then what do you think? Do you think that it'll be to no avail that I'm working here, sacrificing time and money and some talent for a friend who has given so much proof of his loyalty to the principles? Oh no! They'll listen to me and adopt my proposal."

Rubião, very much excited, asked some other questions about the struggle and the victory, whether expenditures were necessary, or a request or a letter of recommendation, and how he would be able to get frequent news of the sick man, etc. Camacho replied to everything, but advised caution. "In politics," he said, "a trifle may divert the course of the campaign and give the victory to the adversary." And yet, even though he might not come out winner, Rubião would have the advantage of having had his name approved, and that counted as a service.

"Be patient and firm," Camacho concluded.

And then!

"Am I, myself, not an example of patience and firmness? My province is given over to a group of bandits; there's no other name for the Pinheiros gang; and besides that (I'm telling you this privately and quite frankly) I have some friends who are conspiring against me; profiteers, who want to see if the party will reject me and if they can take my place—the scoundrels! Ah! my dear Rubião, this business of politics may be compared to the passion of our Lord Jesus Christ: it's all there, the disciple who denies, and the disciple who betrays. The crown of thorns, the insults, the wood, and finally one is hung upon the cross of one's ideas, fastened by the nails of envy, calumny, and ingratitude—"

The phrase, dropped in the heat of conversation, seemed t him to be worthy of an article, so he kept it in mind, and befor going to sleep, wrote it down on a strip of paper. But in th course of the conversation, while he was fixing it in his mind Rubião was saying that were he, Camacho, to be aroused, h would be a man to undertake grand campaigns. And he mus not run away from threats.

"From threats? Certainly not. Nor from any genuine bogies either, if there are any. I'm waiting for them. Let them bewar the day we rise to power! They'll have to pay for everything Listen to this advice; nothing is ever forgiven nor forgotten One always pays; believe me, vengeance is a pleasure; there" a great deal of satisfaction— Finally, when one takes into ac count the good and the bad in politics, the good is on top There are ingrates, but they resign, or are caught and per secuted."

Rubião was listening in complete subjugation to the domina tion of Camacho. Camacho's eyes were sparkling, anathema were springing from his lips as from the lips of Isaiah; the triumphal palms were turning green in his hands. Every gestur seemed a principle. When he opened his arms, striking the air it was as though an entire program were unfolding. He wa becoming intoxicated with hope, and his spirits were soaring Once he paused in front of Rubião:

"Come, deputy, try a speech requesting that the discussion be closed: 'Mr. President—' Come, say it with me: 'Mr. Pres ident, I beg Your Excellency—'"

Rubião interrupted him, by rising. He felt a sort of vertigo He saw himself in the Chamber, entering to take oath, all the deputies standing, and he shuddered. Progress was difficult; bu he crossed the room, went up to the president's table, and too the usual oath— Perhaps his voice became faint on the oc casion—

It was in this state that the news of Freitas' death found him. He shed a hidden tear, took it upon himself to pay the funeral expenses, and the next day accompanied the deceased to the cemetery. When his late friend's old mother saw him entering the room, she tried to kneel at his feet, but he embraced her in time to prevent the gesture. That act on the part of our friend made a great impression on the guests. One of them went to shake hands with him, and later, in a corner he whispered the injustice of the dismissal he had had several days before; a dismissal prompted by intrigue and with the deliberate intent to offend him—

"You see, begging your pardon for the word, it's a den of rascals—"

Came the hour to leave for the interment; the mother's parting was sad: kisses, sobs, outcries, all heartbreakingly mingled. The women could not tear her away; two men had to use force; she screamed and insisted on going back to the corpse: "My son, my poor son!"

"It's a scandal," persisted the man who had been dismissed. "They say that the minister, himself, didn't like it, but you know, in order not to demoralize the director—"

Bang—bang—bang—the hammers sounded dully, nailing down the coffin.

Rubião acceded to the request that he take hold of one of the rings; so he left the dismissed man. Some people were standing outside; the neighbors at their windows were leaning over one another, their eyes full of that curiosity that death inspires in the living. Furthermore, there was Rubião's *coupé*, which stood out from the old calashes. There had already been considerable talk about that friend of the deceased, and now his presence confirmed the report. The dead man was now appreciated with true esteem.

At the cemetery, Rubião was not content with laying a shovelful of earth, which he, at everyone's request, was the first to do; with moist eyes he waited until the grave diggers, with the large shovels of their office, had completely filled the grave. Then, with others crowding on either side, he left, and, at the gate, with a single flourish of his hat to right and left, he greeted all the bowed, uncovered heads. As he got into his *coupé*, he heard these words spoken in a low voice:

"He looks like a senator or a judge of the Court of Appeals or something of the sort—"

CII

Night had fallen. Rubião was coming down into the city, thinking of the poor devil whom he had buried, when in São Christovao Street he passed another *coupé* with two orderlies behind It was a minister who was going to a meeting of state. Rubião stuck his head out, drew it in again, and continued to listen to the orderlies' horses, so alike in sound, so distinct, despite the noise of the other animals. Such was the tension of our friend's mind that he continued to hear them when distance would no longer permit it— Cloppety-clop—cloppety-clop—cloppety clop—

CIII

On the seventh day after Dona Maria Augusta's death, the usual Mass was said in São Francisco de Paula. Rubião went and there he saw Carlos Maria. That sufficed to precipitate restitution of the letter. Three days later, he put it into his pocket and hastened to Flamengo. It was two o'clock in the afternoon Maria Benedicta had gone to visit neighboring friends who had consoled her during the first days of her sorrow. Sophia was alone, dressed to go out.

"But it doesn't matter," she said, inviting him to sit down "I'll stay in, or I'll go out later."

Rubião replied that she wouldn't be long delayed; he had just come to give her a paper.

"Sit down anyway. One can give a paper sitting down, too."

She looked so pretty that he hesitated to say the harsh words that he had learned by heart. Mourning was very becoming to her, and her dress fitted her like a glove. When she was seated, half of her foot showed, and her flat-heeled shoe, and her silk stocking, all of which were pleading for compassion and forgiveness. As for the sword within the sheath—that is what an ancient writer calls the soul—it seemed to be blunt and ineffectual. Rubião was on the point of weakening; but the first word drew the rest.

"What paper?" Sophia asked.

"A paper that I suppose is important," he answered, restraining his emotion. "Don't you remember, or don't you know that you lost a letter?"

"No."

"Are you in the habit of writing letters?"

"I have written some; but I don't recall any important ones. Let me see."

There was a dazed look in Rubião's eyes. He neither said nor did anything. He got up to leave, but he did not leave. After several moments of perturbed silence, he continued, without anger:

"It's not a secret from you that I'm very fond of you. You know this, and yet you neither send me away nor accept me, but encourage me with your charming ways. I've not yet forgotten Santa Thereza nor our trip on the train when we came here, we two, with your husband sitting between us. Do you remember? That trip was an unfortunate one for me; from that day on you have held me captive. You are evil, you are like a snake. What harm have I ever done you? It's quite understandable that you may not care for me, but you might disillusion me then—"

"Hush, someone's coming," interrupted Sophia, rising too, and looking toward the door.

No one was coming; yet had there been anyone, Rubião could have been heard, because his voice was growing louder and

becoming more impassioned. It grew still louder. No longer wa
he contesting hope; now he was opening up his soul and freeing
it of its burden.

"I don't care if they do hear me," he shouted; "they can hea
me; I'm going to have my say now, and then you can throw me
out and it'll be over. No, a man can't be made to suffer so—"

"Hush, for Heaven's sake!"

"What Heaven are you talking about? Hear me out, because
I have no mind to hold anything back—"

Frantic with fear lest some servant might really hear, Sophia
clapped her hand over Rubião's mouth. At the touch of that
beloved epidermis, Rubião lost his voice. Sophia withdrew her
hand and prepared to leave the room; but when she reached the
door, she paused. Rubião had gone over to the window to re
cover from the outburst.

C I V

After listening for a few moments Sophia returned to the draw
ing room, and, with a great rustle of skirts, sat down on the blue
satin ottoman, which had been purchased just several days be
fore. Rubião turned around, and found her shaking her head
reproachfully. Before she spoke, Sophia put her finger on her
mouth, requesting silence; then she summoned him with her
hand. Rubião obeyed.

"Sit down in that chair," she said. And after she saw him
seated, she continued, "I have reason to be angry with you; I'm
not, because I know that you're good and I'm sure that you're
sincere. Say you're sorry for what you said to me, and all will be
forgiven."

Sophia tapped her fan on the right side of her dress to smooth
it down and arrange it; then she raised her arms, shaking the
black glass bracelets; finally she rested her arms on her knees
and opening and closing the ribs of her fan, she waited for his
answer. Contrary to what she was expecting, he shook his head

"I have nothing to be sorry for," he said; "and I'd rather you'd not forgive me. Whether you like it or not, you'll always be in my heart. I could die, but what's the good of dying? You've not been sincere with me, because you've deceived me—"

Sophia stiffened.

"Don't get angry. I don't wish to offend you; but let me say that you have deceived me grossly and pitilessly. It was all right for you to love your husband; I forgave you for that; but—"

"But—" she repeated in surprise.

Rubião put his hand into his pocket, pulled out the letter and handed it to her. When Sophia read the name Carlos Maria, Rubião noted her pallor. She seemed to be drained of every drop of blood. Controlling herself, she asked what it was, what was the meaning of the letter.

"The writing is yours."

"It's mine. But what would I be saying inside? Who gave this to you?"

Rubião wanted to tell how he had found it, but he thought that he had gone far enough and asked permission to take his leave.

"Pardon," she said, "open the letter yourself."

"I have nothing more to do here."

"Stay, open the letter; here it is; read it all—" said the young woman, seizing his sleeve. But Rubião jerked his arm away violently, went to get his hat and left. Sophia, afraid of the servants, remained in the drawing room.

C V

She was so nervous for the first few moments that she did not think of the letter. Finally, she turned it from side to side, without being able to guess its contents. Gradually, regaining her self-possession, however, she thought that it must be the circular of the Alagoas committee. She tore open the envelope; it

was the circular. How had such a paper gotten into his hands
And whence had come his suspicion? From within himself c
from outside? Could it be that some rumor was circulating
She went to find the servant who was to have delivered th
circular to Carlos Maria, and she asked him if he had given
to him. She learned that he had not. When he had reache
Invalidos Street, he had not found the letter in his pocket, an
being afraid, he had said nothing to his mistress.

Sophia went back to the drawing room, without any inclina
tion now to go out. She gathered together the letter and th
envelope to show them to Rubião so that he might see tha
it was nothing; but probably he would suspect a substitution
"Confounded man!" she murmured, and she began to pace aim
lessly.

A flock of memories made its way into Sophia's heart. Th
image of Carlos Maria set itself up before her, with his larg
eyes of a beloved and hated specter. Sophia tried to drive
away, but she could not; it followed from side to side withou
losing its slender masculinity or its air of sublime laughter. A
times she saw it bow, uttering the very words that had bee
uttered at a ball one night, words that had cost her many slee
less nights and hopeful days until they had become lost in u
reality. Sophia had never understood why that adventure ha
failed. The man seemed to be truly fond of her, and no one ha
compelled him to declare himself so boldly, or pass by her wi
dows late at night, as she heard him say that he did. She eve
recalled other meetings, stolen words, ardent glances, and sh
could not understand how all that passion could come to not
ing. Probably there was none; probably it was pure gallantry,
most a means of perfecting his powers of attraction— His w
a cynical, conceited nature.

What did she care about the mystery? He was a conceite
fellow, for whom she was more and more beginning to feel d
gust and contempt. She even laughed at him, and could fa
him now without remorse. Indeed, she was concerning herse
far too much with the matter, and she began to curse Rubiã
for having evoked such a man from oblivion with that unhap
circular—. Then, she went back to the first memories, to Carl

Maria's words. If everyone thought her beautiful, why did not he, who told her that he did? Perhaps she would have had him at her feet, had she not appeared so grateful, so humble—

Suddenly the maidservant, who was in the other room, hearing the sound of something breaking, ran to the drawing room, where she found her mistress standing alone.

"It's nothing," said the latter.

"I thought I heard—"

"It was that figurine of mine that fell; pick up the pieces."

"Oh! The Chinese one!" exclaimed the maid.

In fact it was a porcelain mandarin, that always stayed very quietly, poor thing, on top of a bookcase. Somehow, without knowing how it got there or how long it had been there, Sophia found it between her fingers, and when she thought of its deliberate humility, she had an impulse—anger against herself, it seems—and flung the figurine to the floor. Poor mandarin; it did not do any good that he was of porcelain, nor even that he had been given by Palha.

"But madame, how did the Chinese—"

"Go away."

Sophia recalled her behavior with Carlos Maria, the easy acquiescences, the anticipated forgiveness, the eyes with which she sought him out, the ardent handclasps— That was it; she had thrown herself at his feet. Then, however, she began to feel differently about it. Despite everything, he surely must care for her, and the spiritual harmony of both would not bring about the act of desertion by one. Perhaps the fault lay elsewhere. She dug out possible reasons, some cold, severe gesture, some lack of attention. She remembered that once, because she was afraid to receive him when she was alone in the house, she had the servant tell him that she was not at home. Yes, it might be that. Carlos Maria was proud; he was hurt by the least offense. Perhaps he learned that it was not true— Yes, that's where the fault lay.

—or more properly, the chapter in which the reader, disoriented, is unable to reconcile Sophia's distress with the tilbury driver's story, and asks in bewilderment: "Then the Harmonia Street tryst, Sophia, Carlos Maria, that whole clangor of noisy, delinquent rhymes was all calumny?" Calumny on the part of the reader and on Rubião's part, not on the part of the poor driver, who did not give any names or even tell a real story. You would have seen that, had you read carefully. Yes, unhappy reader, note that it was unlikely that a man bent upon an adventure of that sort would stop the tilbury right in front of the house of assignation. That would provide a witness to the crime. There are many more streets in heaven and earth than are dreamed of by your philosophy, side streets where the tilbury could wait.

Well, the driver did not know how to make up a story. But what interest did he have in inventing it?

He had driven Rubião to a house, where our friend stayed nearly two hours without dismissing him; then he saw him come out, get into the tilbury, and soon get out again and walk, ordering him to follow along. He thought that he was an excellent customer, but, even so, it did not occur to him to make up anything. However, a young woman went by with a child —she of Saude Street—and Rubião stood looking after her sadly and affectionately, whence the driver inferred that he was sensual as well as prodigal, and brought out his gifts for him. If he spoke of Harmonia Street, it was because it was suggested by the district from which they were coming; and if he said that he brought a young man from Invalidos Street, it was because he had, to be sure, transported someone from there the evening before—perhaps Carlos Maria himself—or because he may have lived there or may have had his coach-house there or because of some other circumstance that helped the improvisation, just as daytime memories serve as material for one's dreams at night. Not all coach drivers are imaginative and it's quite an accomplishment, after all, just to put together the tatters of reality.

There remains only the coincidence of one of the mourning seamstresses living in Harmonia Street. This certainly appears to be an intentional act of fate, but it was the seamstress's fault; she could have found a house nearer the center of the city, had she been willing to abandon her needle and her husband. They, however, were dearer to her than all else in this world; and yet that was no reason for me to interrupt the episode, or break the continuity of the book.

CVII

Sophia's reflections need not be explained. They were all based on reality. It was only too true that Carlos Maria had not corresponded to her first hope—nor, indeed, to her second and third; for there were successive ones, you see, each less green and less flourishing than the last. As for the reason for this lack of response, we have seen that Sophia, for want of one, attributed three in turn. It did not occur to her that he might have had a love affair that would make any other insipid. That would be a fourth reason, and, perhaps, the real one.

CVIII

For several months Rubião stopped going to Flamengo. It was not an easy resolution to carry out; often he repented it and hesitated as to whether he should persist. More than once he left the house with the intention of going to see Sophia and beg her forgiveness. For what? He did not know, but he did wish to be forgiven. However, whenever he started out, the remembrance of Carlos Maria made him turn back. Then, from a certain point on, the very lapse of time prevented his going; it would be queer if, like an unhappy prodigal son, he were to make his appearance one day merely to beseech the warmth of the lady's beautiful eyes. He continued to go to the warehouse to visit with Palha; at the end of five weeks the latter rebuked him for not having gone to see them, and when two months had gone by, he asked him if it were intentional.

"I have had a great deal to do," Rubião replied quickly. "These political matters take a great deal of one's time. I'll come on Sunday."

Sophia planned how she would receive him. She would watch for an opportunity to tell him about the letter, swearing by all that was holy so that he might see that the facts were not in her disfavor. Wasted schemes! Rubião did not appear. Came another Sunday, came other Sundays— Nevertheless, one day Sophia sent him a subscription to the Alagoas fund, and he subscribed five contos.

"That's a great deal," his partner said at the warehouse when Rubião took him the paper.

"I'd not give less."

"But see here, you could give generously without giving so much. Do you think that this subscription is made up among half a dozen people? It's in the hands of a number of women and some men; it's on the counters in the shops in Commercio Square. Sign up for less."

"How, if it's already written?"

"You can very well make a three out of this five. Three contos is a good subscription. There are larger ones, of course, but they are from persons who are obliged to give more because of their official position or their millions; Bomfin, for example, subscribed ten contos."

Rubião could not repress an ironical smile; he shook his head and insisted upon the five contos. He would amend it only by writing the figure one ahead of it—fifteen contos, more than Bomfin.

"Of course you can give five, ten or fifteen," Palha retorted "but your capital requires caution; you're going into it pretty deeply— Remember, it's bringing you less now."

Palha was the depositary of Rubião's titles (shares, policies and deeds) which were locked in the warehouse safe. He was collecting for him the interest, the dividends and the rental for three houses that he had had him buy some time before at a low price and that were bringing in a good sum. Also, he was keeping a number of gold coins for him, because Rubião had a mania for collecting them just to look at. Palha knew the total amount of the property better than the owner, and he was witness to the fact that though there was no storm, and though the sea was like milk, holes were being made in the caravel. Three contos were enough, he insisted, and he attested his sincerity by calling attention to the fact that he was the husband of the originator of the committee.

But Rubião did not desist from the five contos and he took advantage of the occasion to ask for ten contos more. He needed ten contos. Palha scratched his head.

"Pardon," he said, after a few moments, "but what do you want them for? Aren't you sure to lose them, or run the risk of losing them, at least?"

Rubião laughed at his objection.

"If I were sure that I was going to lose them, I'd not have come for them. It may be that I'm running a risk, but, nothing ventured, nothing gained. I need them for a business deal— three deals, I mean. Two are loans, perfectly safe and only one and a half contos. The eight and a half are for a certain enterprise. Why do you shake your head? You don't know what it's about."

"That's just it. If you were to consult me and tell me what the enterprise is and who the persons concerned are, I'd soon see if it could be risked; but I very much fear that nothing's any good but the money that'll be lost. You remember the shares in that Honest Capitans' Union Company? I told you right away that that was a pompous name, designed to fool people and give employment to some individuals who needed money. You wouldn't believe me and you were taken in. The shares are down now and there haven't been any dividends for the past six months."

"Well, then sell those shares; I'll be satisfied with the principal. Or give it to me from the firm's strongbox. I'll come by for it, if you wish—or you can send it to Botafogo. Or, if you think it would be better, use some insurance policies for security—"

"No, I'll not do a thing; I'll not give you the ten contos," Palha intercepted vehemently. "I've given in to everything long enough; it is my duty to be firm. Safe loans? What loans are they? Don't you see that they're just taking your money away from you and not paying what they owe? Fellows who carry it to the point of having dinner every day at their creditor's house, like a certain Carneiro whom I have seen there. I don't know whether the others owe you too. Quite possibly they do. It's too much. I'm speaking to you because I'm a friend; you'll not be able to say some day that you were not warned in time. What will you live on if you go through what you have? Our firm can fail."

"It won't fail," said Rubião.

"It can; anything can fail. I saw the banker Souto fail in 1864."

Rubião gave thought to his partner's advice, not because it was good or probably right, but because back of its crude exterior he discovered kindly intention. At heart he was grateful for it; but he rejected it. He wanted the ten contos. He could be more careful thereafter; besides, he had more than enough; he had money to give and to sell—

"Only to sell," Palha amended.

And, after a moment:

"Well, it's late now. Tomorrow I'll bring you the ten contos. And why not come and get them at our house in Flamengo? What have we done to offend you? Or what have the women done? Since I see you here, your quarrel appears to be with them. Tell me what it is, so that I may punish them," he concluded, laughing.

Rubião turned his eyes away from his partner, whose words impressed him as being sharp with irony—like someone who knew well what it was all about and was laughing at him. When he turned back, he saw the same questioning look, and he responded:

"They didn't do anything; I'll come tomorrow evening."

"Come for dinner."

"No, I can't come for dinner; I'm having some friends at the house. I'll come in the evening." And, making an effort to laugh:

"Don't punish them; they didn't do anything to me."

"He's under the influence of someone," reflected Palha, as Rubião left; "someone who's envious of our association— It may be, too, that Sophia did something to keep him away."

Before he had had time to reach the corner, Rubião appeared at the door again. He was returning to say that, since he needed the money early, he would come and get it at the warehouse; he would go to see them in the evening. He needed the money at two o'clock in the afternoon.

CIX

That night Rubião dreamed of Sophia and Maria Benedicta. He saw them on a great terrace, dressed only in their skirts, their backs entirely bare; Sophia's husband, armed with a leather whip with five iron-tipped prongs was lashing them pitilessly. The women were shrieking and begging for mercy; they were writhing, bathed in blood, their flesh falling away in pieces. Now why Sophia was the Empress Eugenia and Maria Benedicta one of her ladies-in-waiting I can't say precisely. "They are dreams, dreams, Penseroso," exclaimed one of our Alvares de Azevedo's characters. I prefer, however, the reflection of the old Polonius who had just heard a very mad speech of Hamlet: "There's method in his madness." There is method, too, in that merging of Sophia and Eugenia; and there is even method in what followed, which was still more extravagant.

Yes, Rubião, in indignation, commanded that the whipping cease, that Palha be hanged, and the victims withdrawn. One of them, Sophia, accepted a seat in the open carriage that was waiting for Rubião, and off they went at a gallop, she, elegant and with sound body, he, magnificent and imposing.

The horses, of which at first there were two, soon became eight, four beautiful pairs. Streets and windows filled with people, flowers showering upon them, acclamations—Rubião felt that he was the Emperor Louis Napoleon; the dog was in the carriage at Sophia's feet—

It all came to an end without any conclusion or fracas. Rubião opened his eyes; perhaps a flea bit him; something. "Dreams, dreams, Penseroso!" I still prefer Polonius' saying: "There's method in your madness."

C X

Rubião made the two loans and the deal. The deal was a project for improving embarkation and disembarkation in the port of Rio de Janeiro. One of the loans was to pay a delinquent bill for the *Atalaia*. The debt was pressing, since the publication was threatened with the possibility of having to discontinue.

"Fine," said Camacho, when Rubião took the money to his house. "Thank you very much. You see how our organ could be silenced by a wretched thing like this. Of course, those are the thorns to be expected in our path. The people are not educated; they do not recognize, they do not support those who work for them, those who descend each day to the arena in defense of constitutional liberties. Just think that if now we didn't have this money at our disposal, each one would go off to his own business and the principles would be left without their loyal expositor."

"Never!" Rubião protested.

"You're right; we'll redouble our efforts. The *Atalaia* will be like the character of the fable, who each time that he fell rose with greater vigor."

Saying this, Camacho looked at the wad of bills. "One conto two hundred milreis, is it not?" he asked, and put it into his pocket. He went on to say that they were secure now, and that the paper would prosper. He had certain material reforms in view. He went even further:

"We must develop the program, give a push to our fellow-believers, attack them if necessary—"

"How?"

"How? By attacking. That's just a manner of speaking, of course. I mean correct them. It's obvious that the party organ is growing lax. I call it the party organ because our paper is the organ for the party's ideas. Do you understand the difference?"

"I understand."

"It's growing lax," Camacho continued, holding a cigar between his fingers before lighting it. "We must emphasize the principles, but openly and honestly and by telling the truth. Believe me, the leaders need to hear it from their own friends and adherents. I never rejected the conciliation of the parties; I fought for it; but conciliation is not a game of intrigue. To give you an example, in my province the followers of Pinheiros have the government's support for the sole purpose of getting rid of me. And when my fellow-believers in the capital see that the government is strengthening the Pinheiros group, what do you think they do? They give them their support too."

"Does the Pinheiros group have any power?"

"None," Camacho answered, violently closing the match-box he was about to open. "There's a former convict among them, and someone who was once a barber's apprentice. To be sure, he matriculated in the Faculty of Recife in 1855, I believe, through the death of his godfather, who left him something. The man's career was so scandalous, however, that immediately after receiving his Bachelor's diploma, he entered the provincial assembly. He's stupid; he's as much of a bachelor as I am the Pope."

Camacho and Rubião came to an agreement concerning the political modification of the paper. Camacho reminded Rubião that the latter's candidacy had gone on the rocks because of opposition from the leaders. "Or, some of them," he amended. Rubião concurred. His friend had told him that at the time, and now the recollection of it aggravated his resentment of the failure. He could, he should be in the Chamber. They, the leaders, were the ones who didn't want him; but they would see, thought Rubião, they would suffer for their mistake. With eyes crossed from stupefaction, they would see him deputy, senator, minister. Our friend's head, enkindled by his companion, was burning by itself, not with hatred nor envy, but with naive ambition, heartfelt certainty and a dazzling anticipatory vision of grandeur. Camacho deemed that Rubião was now in accord.

"Our people are of the same opinion," he said. "I believe a little threat to our friends will not be amiss."

That very evening Camacho read him the article in which he advised the party of the propriety of not yielding to the perfidy of power by supporting certain corrupt and worthless people in some of the provinces. Here is the conclusion:

"The parties must be disciplined and united. There are those who pretend (*mirabile dictu!*) that discipline and union cannot be carried to the point of rejecting the benefits that fall from the hands of the adversary. *Risum teneatis!* Who can utter such a blasphemy without a quiver? But let us suppose that it is true, that the opposition can occasionally close its eyes to the government's transgressions, to its contempt of the law, to its abuse of power, to its perversity of errors. *Quid inde?* Such cases—and they are rare—could be admitted only if they favored the good elements, not the bad. Every party has its dissenters and sycophants. It is to the interest of our adversaries to see us become lax, while the party's corruption is encouraged. This is, indeed, the truth; to deny it is to provoke intestine conflict, that is, the laceration of the national soul— But, no, ideas do not die; they are the banner of justice. The vendors will be driven from the temple; the faithful and the pure of heart will remain, those who subordinate paltry local and momentary interests to the imperishable victory of the principles. All that is contrary to this will find us opposed. *Alea jacta est.*"

Rubião praised the article; he thought it excellent. Not forceful enough, perhaps. Vendors, for instance, was well put, but
vile vendors would be better:

"Vile vendors? There's only one thing wrong," said Camacho. "It's the repetition of the v's. Vile ven—vile vendors.
Don't you hear that the sound is disagreeable?"

"But before that there's vés vis—"

"Vae victis. But that's a Latin phrase. We can put something else: vile merchants."

"Vile merchants is good."

"Though merchants isn't as forceful as vendors."

"Then why don't you leave vendors? Vile vendors is strong;
no one notices the sound. I never pay any attention to that.
I like forcefulness. Vile vendors."

"Vile vendors, vile vendors," Camacho repeated in an undertone. "It's beginning to sound better to me already. Vile
vendors. I'll accept it," he concluded. And reread, emending:
"The vile vendors will be driven from the temple; the faithful and the pure of heart will remain, those who subordinate
paltry, local and momentary interests to the imperishable victory of the principles. All that is contrary to this will find
us opposed. Alea jacta est."

"Very good!" said Rubião, feeling that he, himself, had a
small part in the authorship of the article.

"Do you like it?" asked Camacho, smiling. "Some people
still find in my style the freshness of my student days. I don't
know; I can't say. I can say that the tenor is the same. I must
chastise them; we must chastise them."

Here is where I should like to have given this book the method
of so many others—old, all of them in which the contents of

the chapter was summarized; such as, "Concerning how this or that happened." That's the way Bernardim Ribeiro is and other glorious books. As for those in foreign languages, without going back to Cervantes or Rabelais, Fielding and Smollet suffice, many of whose chapters are read only because of the summary. Pick up *Tom Jones*, Book IV, Chapter I, and read this title: *Containing five pages of paper*. It is clear, simple, it deceives no one; there are five pages, no more; he who does not wish to read, does not; he who wishes to read, does, and it is for the latter that the author concludes obsequiously, "And now, without further preface, let us go on to the following chapter."

CXIII

If such were the method of this book, here is a title that would explain everything: *"How Rubião, Pleased with the Emendation Made in the Article, Composed and Pondered over so Many Phrases that in the End He Wrote All the Books that He Had Ever Read."*

There will probably be some reader for whom this will not be enough. Doubtless he will want a complete analysis of our friend's mental operation, without realizing that not even Fielding's five pages of paper would suffice for that. There is an abyss between the first phrase of which Rubião was co-author and authorship of all the works he had read. The hardest part, to be sure, was to progress from the phrase to the first book—from then on it went rapidly. No matter; even so, an analysis would be long and tiresome. It's better, then, to leave it like this: for a few minutes Rubião looked upon himself as the author of many another's work.

CXIV

On the contrary, I know not whether the chapter that follows could be summarized in a title.

CXV

Rubião was persisting in his resolution, not to go to see Sophia again; at least he did not go to Flamengo. One day he saw her pass in a carriage with one of the women of the Alagoas committee. She bowed smilingly, and waved good-by. He returned the courtesy, removing his hat with some agitation; but he did not stand still as he would have before; he merely glanced at the carriage, which was going on its way. He, too, was going on his way, thinking of the affair of the letter, and puzzled by that wave of the hand which seemed to be completely free from resentment or humiliation, as if there were nothing between them. Her preoccupation with the committee work, and the presence of a companion, might have explained Sophia's graciousness, but Rubião did not think of that possibility.

"Can she be so indifferent?" he wondered. "Doesn't she remember the letter I found, the one she sent to that fop of Invalidos Street? This is really carrying it pretty far, too far. She seems to be flaunting it in my face, as much as to say she doesn't give a hang, she'll write all the letters she pleases. Well, she can write them, but she'd better spend some money and register them at the Post Office; it's cheap—"

He thought himself rather clever and he laughed. This laughter, together with the greeting he was obliged to give to a man who passed at that moment, dispelled the bitterness of his melancholy thoughts; he forgot the matter, to think of another that was taking him to the Bank of Brazil.

As he entered the bank, he happened upon his partner, who was on his way out.

"I think I saw Dona Sophia just now," Rubião said.

"Where?"

"In Ourives Street; she was in a carriage with another lady, whom I don't know. How have you been?"

"You saw her, and yet you didn't remember something," observed Palha, without answering the question. "You didn't remember that Wednesday, day after tomorrow, is her birthday. I'll not invite you to dinner; I don't dare; that would be asking you to spend a boring evening. But one can drink a cup of tea quickly. Will you grant me that favor?"

Rubião did not reply immediately.

"I'll even come for dinner," he said finally. "Wednesday? Count on me. I had forgotten, I confess, but I have so many things on my mind. I'll be at the warehouse half an hour from now. Will you wait for me?"

Before the half hour was up he was there, asking for two contos. Palha no longer resisted the crumbling away of Rubião's capital, and, if occasionally, he did utter some mild protest, he handed him the money this time with indifference. Rubião did not return home without first buying a magnificent diamond, which he sent to Sophia on Wednesday, accompanied by a calling card and a few words of congratulation.

Sophia was alone in her dressing room, putting on her shoes when the maid brought the package. It was the third gift she had received that day; the maid waited for her to open it, so that she, too, might see what it was. Sophia was dazzled when she opened the box and saw the costly jewel, a beautiful stone, in the center of a necklace. She was expecting something nice, but after what had happened recently, she could scarcely believe that he would be so generous. Her heart was all aflutter.

"Is the bearer of the gift still here?"

"No, he left. How pretty, madame!"

Sophia closed the box and finished putting on her shoes. She remained sitting alone for awhile, reminiscing, and as she rose, she thought:

"That man adores me."

She started to dress, but as she passed in front of the mirror, she lingered for a few moments. She took pleasure in contemplating herself, her opulent figure, her arms, bare from shoulder to wrist, her dreamy eyes. She was twenty-nine years old, and she thought she looked the same as she had at twenty-five. She was not mistaken, either. As she pulled in and fastened her corset, she lovingly adjusted her bosom, leaving a large expanse of her beautiful neck uncovered. This prompted her to see how the diamond would look when worn; she took the necklace out and put it around her neck. She turned from left to right and vice-versa, approached the mirror, assumed an elegant pose, increased the light in the dressing room. It was perfect. She shut the jewel into the box and put it away.

"That man adores me," she repeated.

"He'll probably be there," thought Rubião, on his way to Flamengo for dinner. "I doubt that he has given a better present than I."

Carlos Maria was there, indeed, conversing with one of the Alagoas committee women and Maria Benedicta. There were not many guests; they had been purposely selected and limited. Neither Major Siqueira nor his daughter were there, nor the ladies and gentlemen whom Rubião had met at that dinner in Santa Thereza. Several of the Alagoas committee women were in evidence, the bank director even more so—the one who called on the minister. He was with his wife and daughters. There was someone else from the bank, an English business man, a deputy, a judge, a counselor, and not many more.

Although she was manifestly in her glory, Sophia forgot the others for a moment when she saw Rubião enter the drawing room and come toward her. Whether it was that he had changed, or whether she had become unaccustomed to him, she found him different, with firm step and head held high, quite the reverse, in short, of his former timid and shrinking manner. Sophia clasped his hand warmly, and whispered her thanks. She had him sit beside her at the table. The president of the committee sat on the other side of her. Rubião regarded everything with an air of superiority. He was not impressed by the guests' social standing, nor by the atmosphere of formality, nor by the luxurious table. None of it dazzled him. He found Sophia's special attentions agreeable, but they did not disconcert him, as before. As for her, she was more solicitous than usual, and her eyes were exceptionally kind and tender. Rubião looked for Carlos Maria; there he was between the same young women with whom he had been conversing in the drawing room— Maria Benedicta and the Alagoas committee woman. Rubião saw that Carlos Maria was paying attention only to them, that he was not looking at Sophia, nor she at him.

Rubião did think that they exchanged a glance as they rose from the table; but since the general movement of the gathering might have deceived him, Rubião made no further capital of the observation. Sophia had hastened to take his arm. On the way out she said to him:

"I've been waiting for you since that day, but you never came here after that. I had the right to demand it, so that I might explain myself. We'll talk presently."

After a little while, Rubião went to the smoking room, where he listened to the conversation in silence, his eyes wandering here and there. When the others went out, Rubião remained alone, half-reclining on a leather sofa. He was not thinking of anything; but his imagination was at work, though somewhat slowly, to be sure, perhaps because he had eaten a great deal. Outside, the guests for the evening were arriving; the house was becoming filled, the murmur of conversation was increasing. Yet our friend did not come down from his fine dreams. Even the sound of the piano, which silenced all the noises, did not bring him down to earth. A swish of silks coming into the room, however, made him sit up abruptly, wide awake.

"Here you are," said Sophia. "This is where you've taken shelter to escape boredom. You don't even want to hear good music. I thought you'd left. I came to find you."

And without further delay, because she could not waste a minute, she told him what we know about the letter that was found in the garden at Botafogo; she reminded him that before opening it, she had asked him to open it himself and read it. What better proof of innocence? The words came from her lips rapidly and excitedly, yet with proper gravity. Once her eyes grew moist; she wiped them, and they became red. Rubião took her hand, and saw one more tear—a little tear, sliding to the corner of her mouth. Then he swore that there was, indeed, no better proof of innocence, that he believed everything she had told him. What was her idea of crying? Sophia wiped her eyes again, and held out her hand in gratitude.

"Good-night," she said.

Rubião called her attention to the fact that the piano was still playing. While they listened, no one came to look for them.

"But I can't be away so long," said Sophia. "Besides, I have some orders to give. Good-night."

"One moment," Rubião insisted.

Sophia paused.

"Let me say this, and for all I know, it may be the last time—"

"The last time?"

"Who knows? It may be the last. I don't care whether that man lives or not, but I don't feel inclined to quarrel if I should run into him here."

"You'll meet him here every day. Hasn't Christiano told you yet? Carlos Maria's going to marry Maria Benedicta."

Rubião took a step backward.

"Yes, they're getting married," she continued. "The fact is surprising, because it came up when we were least expecting it; —either they dissimulated very well, or it happened suddenly. Anyway, they're getting married. Maria Benedicta told me a story, which was confirmed by someone else; but after all, it's always the same story. They fell in love, and that was that. They're getting married shortly. When she spoke to Christiano, Christiano answered that it depended on me— As if I were her mother! I consented immediately, and I hope they'll be happy. He seems like a good young man and she's a fine girl; so they can't help but be happy. It's a good match, you know. He has all his father's and mother's property. Maria Benedicta has no money, but she has the training I gave her.

You must remember that when she came to me, she was a rustic creature; she knew almost nothing; it was I who trained her. My aunt was very deserving, and Maria Benedicta, too. Well, it's really true; they're getting married shortly. Haven't you noticed today how they're together all the time? There's been no official announcement yet; but there's no reason why the family's intimate friends shouldn't know."

For one who was in such a hurry this was too long a speech. Sophia realized it a little too late; she repeated, "Good-night," and told Rubião that he should go to the drawing room. The piano had stopped playing; one heard a discreet murmur of applause and conversation.

CXVI

They were going to get married? But how was it then that— Maria Benedicta—it was Maria Benedicta who was marrying Carlos Maria; but then Carlos Maria— Now he understood; it was all a mistake, all confusion; what appeared to be true for one person was for another; and that is how one can be led to slander and to crime.

Rubião was musing thus as he left the dining room where the butlers were clearing the supper table. And he continued, walking the length of the room: "Remember, Palha wanted to marry me to his cousin, not knowing that destiny was holding another suitor in store for her. He's not a bad looking young man; he's much more attractive than she. Beside Sophia, Maria Benedicta is not very pretty, or not pretty at all; but when it's rather a matter of congeniality, it's often that way— And so they're going to get married soon— I wonder if it will be a big wedding. Probably. Palha's a little better off now —" and Rubião glanced at the furniture, the porcelains and glassware, the hangings. "It'll be big, no doubt. And the fiancé is rich." Rubião thought about the carriage and the horses that he would take. At Engenho Velho a few days before, he had seen a superb pair worthy of being painted. He was going to order another like it, whatever the price; he'd have to present one to the bride, too. As he was thinking of Maria Benedicta, he saw her entering the room.

"Where's Cousin Sophia?" she asked Rubião.

"I don't know. She was here a little while ago."

And when he saw that she was about to leave the room, he asked if he might have a word with her, and begged her not to be angry with him. Then, without any hesitancy, he told her he knew she was going to be married, and offered her his congratulations. Maria Benedicta flushed deeply and murmured that he should not tell anyone. As there was no servant present, Rubião took her hand and held it in his.

"I'm one of the household," he said. "You deserve to be happy, and I hope that you will be."

A little startled, Maria Benedicta withdrew her hand; but in order not to displease him, she smiled. She really would not have had to, because he was delighted anyway. Though the young woman was not pretty, as we know, her happiness had made her attractive. Indeed, she gave the impression of being one of nature's supreme achievements.

Rubião smiled too, and continued:

"It was your cousin who told me; she asked that I keep it secret. I'll not say anything before the proper time. But what is there to say to you? You're good and deserve the best of everything. You don't have to hide your eyes; marriage is nothing to be ashamed of. Come now. Lift your head and laugh."

Maria Benedicta looked at him with radiant eyes.

"That's the way!" approved Rubião. "What harm is there in confessing to a friend? Let me tell you; I believe that you'll be happy, but I admit that your husband will be even more so. You don't think so? You'll see if it isn't so. He, himself, will tell you how he feels, and if you're sincere, you'll acknowledge that I'm merely prophesying. Of course, I know there's no scale for measuring feelings; but what I mean is that you're a fine and lovely person— You'd better go now, or I'll be speaking out, and already your face is turning very red—"

Maria Benedicta was, in fact, blushing with pleasure as she heard Rubião's words. From the others in the house she had had only silent assent. Even Carlos Maria, who loved her with circumspection, was not so tender. He spoke to her of conjugal felicity as of a rate of interest that he was to receive from fate —a debt that was surely to be paid, and paid in full. And though she treated him with the same circumspection, she adored him above all else in the world. Rubião repeated his parting words, and stood looking after her as he might have had she been his daughter. He watched her cross the room; she was vivacious and happy now, so different from the way she had been formerly, when he had seen her disappearing through one of those doors. He could not refrain from saying:

"A fine and lovely person!"

CXVII

The story of Maria Benedicta's marriage is short; and though Sophia finds it ordinary, it's worth telling. Let it be admitted from the start that had it not been for the Alagoas epidemic, there would, perhaps, have been no marriage; whence it may be concluded that catastrophes are useful and even necessary. There are more than enough examples; but a little tale that I heard as a child and that I shall tell you here in two lines will suffice. Once upon a time there was a cabin on fire by the side of the road; the owner—an unhappy woman, all ragged and dirty, was sitting on the ground near by and bemoaning her misfortune. An intoxicated man who happened to pass, saw the fire and the woman, and asked her if the house were hers.

"Yes, it is mine, sir. It's all that I possess in this world."

"Then may I light my cigar there?"

The priest who told me this surely emended the original text; it's not necessary to be intoxicated to light one's cigar on the sufferings of others. Good Father Chagas!—His name was Chagas—Father, you were more than good, you who for many years implanted in my mind that consoling thought that no one in his right mind exploits another's misfortune; to say nothing of the inebriate's respect for the principle of ownership—to the extent that he did not light his cigar without first asking permission from the owner of the ruins. Consoling thoughts, these. Good Father Chagas!

CXVIII

Farewell, Father Chagas! I am going on to the story of the marriage. That Maria Benedicta liked Carlos Maria was obvious or foreseen from the time of that ball on Arcos Street at which he and Sophia waltzed so much. We saw her next morning quite ready to go back to the country, whereupon, her cousin pacified her with the promise of finding her a suitor. Thinking it was the waltzer of the previous evening, Maria Benedicta stayed on and waited. She did not confess her thoughts to her cousin— at first because she was ashamed—and afterwards not to spoil the effect of novelty when Sophia would disclose the person's name. Then, too, if she confessed right away, her cousin might become lax in her task, and the cause would be lost. Let us not give any heed to all this; they are merely a young woman's petty calculations.

The Alagoas epidemic came along and Sophia organized the committee, which brought new associations to the Palha family. Included among the women that formed a subcommittee, Maria Benedicta worked with them all; but in particular, she won the esteem of one, Dona Fernanda, a deputy's wife. Dona Fernanda was a little over thirty; she was florid and robust, and she was jolly and expansive. She had been born in Porto Alegre, and had married a bachelor of Alagoas, who was now deputy for another province and, according to rumor, about to become Minister of State. The fact that her husband had been born in Alagoas was her pretext for joining the committee; and it was well that she did, because her requests were commands; she was not backward, and would not accept a refusal. Carlos Maria, who was her cousin, went to see her as soon as she arrived in Rio de Janeiro. He thought that she was even more handsome than in 1865, the last year in which he had seen her, and perhaps it was true. He concluded that the southern air must be such as to invigorate people and redouble their charms, and he promised to end his own days there.

"Let's go there now, and I'll arrange a marriage for you," she said. "I know a young woman from Pelotas who's a *bijou*; and she'll only marry someone from the capital."

"Me, naturally?"

"Someone from the capital, and someone with large eyes. Look, I'm not just joking. She's a first-rate native daughter of Rio Grande do Sul. I have a picture of her here."

Dona Fernanda opened the album and showed the woman's picture.

"She's not bad-looking," he agreed.

"Is that all you can say?"

"Well, she's pretty."

"Where do you put your old slippers, Cousin?"

Carlos Maria smiled, but did not answer. He did not like the expression. He wanted to go on to some other subject, but Dona Fernanda returned to the marriage of her Pelotas friend. She was looking at the picture and she began to tint it verbally, telling the color of the eyes, the hair, the complexion. Then she gave a biographical sketch of Sonora. Such was the lady's name —a pretty name. The priest who had baptized her, however, had hesitated to give it to her despite the influential and respected position of the girl's father, a wealthy coal and timber merchant. But he had yielded, finally, considering that the father's virtues might place the name on the roster of the saints.

"Do you believe she'll attain the roster of the saints?" asked Carlos Maria.

"If she marries you I believe she will."

"That isn't an answer. She will if she marries the Devil, too; and even more surely, because of the martyrdom she'll suffer. Saint Sonora, it's not a bad name, it harmonizes well with its meaning. Saint Sonora— In any case, Cousin—"

"You've a Jewish streak in you; hush," she interrupted. "Then you refuse my friend from Rio Grande do Sul?" she continued, going to put the album away.

"I don't refuse her; but just let me keep my bachelorhood, which is the halfway point to Heaven."

Dona Fernanda burst out laughing.

"Lord of mercy! You really believe you're going to Heaven?"

"I'm already there, and have been for the past twenty minutes. For what else is this cool, quiet room, so far removed from the people outside there? Here we are, the two of us, talking together and not having to listen to blasphemies nor endure the unendurable outpourings of sick minds, and those that are scrofulous and distorted—Hell, in short. This is Heaven, right here, or a bit of Heaven. So long as there's room for us in it, it will do as well as the infinite one. We can talk about Saint Sonora, Saint Carlos Maria and Saint Fernanda, who, in contrast with Saint Gonçalo, has become a match-maker for young women. Where is there another such Heaven as this?"

"In Pelotas."

"Pelotas is so far away!" he sighed, stretching his legs and looking at the chandelier.

"Well, this is only the first assault. I'll make others until finally you'll come around."

Carlos Maria smiled and looked at the tassels that fell from the silk cord tied loosely around Dona Fernanda's waist. Perhaps he wanted to see the tassels; perhaps he wanted to observe the lovely body. At any rate, he saw clearly, once again, that his cousin was a beautiful woman. Her figure attracted his eyes—respect diverted them. It was not only friendship that had brought him to this house again and made him linger yet awhile. Carlos Maria liked the conversation of women as much as he ordinarily detested that of men. He thought men pedantic, coarse, tiresome, dull, frivolous, vulgar and trivial. Women, on the other hand, were neither coarse, nor pedantic, nor dull. Vanity was becoming to them, and some other defects were not unbecoming. There was always something to be obtained from even the most insignificant, he thought, and if ever he did find any that were stupid or vapid, he was convinced that they had, at first, been intended as men.

Meanwhile, the association between Dona Fernanda and Maria Benedicta was becoming closer. The latter, besides being naturally shy, was unhappy at that time, and it was precisely this disparity of temperament and circumstances that brought the two together. Dona Fernanda possessed the quality of sympathy to a generous degree; she loved the weak and the sad and felt that she must make them brave and happy. It was said that she had performed many acts of pity and devotion.

"What's the matter?" she asked her little friend one day. "You almost never laugh; you're always so pensive, and your eyes look so frightened."

Maria Benedicta answered that nothing was the matter, that that was just her way; and, as she said it, she smiled out of pure condescension. She did allude to the loss of her mother as one of the causes of her sadness. Dona Fernanda began to take her with her everywhere; she took her to dinner and gave her a seat in her box if she went to the theater. Thanks to this and to her jolly nature, she dispelled the hateful crows of melancholy that were fluttering about in the girl's heart. Habit and affection soon made the two women intimate; yet Maria Benedicta still withheld her secret.

"Whatever it is," thought Dona Fernanda one day, "I think the best thing is to see that she marries Carlos Maria. Sonora can wait."

"You should get married, Maria Benedicta," she said to her one morning, two days later. They were at Dona Fernanda's country house in Matta-cavallos; Maria Benedicta had gone to the theater with her and had spent the night there. "Now don't start shaking all over; you should get married, and you're going to— I've been wanting to tell you this since day before yesterday, but it's useless to broach such subjects in the drawing room or on the street. Here in the country it's different. And best of all would be if you had the courage to go out walking with me —there's a little hill we could climb. Shall we go?"

"It's hot—"

"That makes it more poetic, child. Ah! bloodless carioca! You have only water in your veins. Well then, let's stay here on this bench. Sit down; I'll be right here beside you ready to take up the cudgels. Now then, get married or die. Don't answer me back. You're not happy," she continued, changing her tone. "However much you may try to conceal it, I see that you have no joy in life. Come, tell me frankly, are you in love with anyone? If you are, confess, and I'll send for him."

"I'm not."

"No? So much the better. And it won't be necessary to put a for sale or for rent sign on your heart, because I know a good tenant—" Maria Benedicta turned squarely toward her, her lips half open, her eyes wide. She appeared either to be afraid of the suggestion or eager for it. Since she was not certain which it was, Dona Fernanda first took her hand and begged her to tell her everything. She loved someone, that was evident; one could see it in her eyes. She must confess; she, Dona Fernanda insisted, implored—if need be, she would cite the law. Maria Benedicta's hand had become cold, her eyes were boring a hole in the ground, and for a few moments neither of the women said anything.

"Come, speak," said Dona Fernanda.

"I have nothing to say."

Dona Fernanda gave signs of incredulity; she kept squeezing Maria Benedicta's hand more tightly, and she put her arm around her waist, and drew her close, whispering into her ear that it was just as though she were her mother. She kissed her face, her ear, her neck; she put Maria Benedicta's head on her shoulder, caressing it with her other hand. Everything, everything, she wanted to know everything. If her lover were in the moon, she'd send to the moon for him—wherever he might be, unless he were in the cemetery, and if he were in the cemetery she would give her a much better one, who would make her forget the first in a few days. Benedicta was listening in agitation, her heart throbbing, not knowing how to escape—ready to speak, and then refraining just in time, as if she were defending her modesty. She made no denial, no confession; but as she did not smile either and was shaking with emotion, it was easy to guess at least half the truth.

"But then am I not your friend? Don't you have confidence in me? Pretend that I'm your mother."

Maria Benedicta did not hold out much longer; she had spent her strength, and she felt the need of telling her secret to someone. Dona Fernanda listened, affected with emotion. The sun was licking the ground around the bench; soon it climbed onto their shoes, and up to the hems of their dresses and to their knees, but neither one noticed. They were engrossed in love; the exposition of the one had a rare fascination for the other. Maria Benedicta's was an unknown, unguessed, unshared passion; a passion that was losing its own nature and becoming pure adoration. At first, when she saw the beloved one she experienced two very distinct reactions—one that she could not define, one of joy and bewilderment, of throbbing heart, and near-trance; the second, one of contemplation. Now it was almost solely the latter. She had wept much when by herself, and she had spent many sleepless nights in sorrowful longing; she had paid dearly, indeed, for the aspiration of her hopes. And yet she would never lose the certainty that he was superior to all other men, a divine being, who, though he took no notice of her, would always be worthy of her worship.

"Well," said Dona Fernanda, when her friend finally became silent, "let's get to the essential point, which is not to go on grieving to no purpose. No, my dear, this worship of a man who takes no notice of one is sheer poetry. Let's be done with poetry. You'll be the one to lose in the business, because he'll marry someone else; the years will go by, taking passion with them, and one day when you're least expecting it, you'll awaken with neither love nor a husband. And who is the boor?"

"That I'll not tell you," said Maria Benedicta, rising from the bench.

"Well, then, don't tell me," said Dona Fernanda, clasping Maria Benedicta's wrists and making her sit on her lap. "The main question is to get married—if you can't marry that one, it will be someone else—"

"No, I'll not marry."

"You'll marry no one but him, you mean?"

"I don't know even whether I'd marry him," replied Maria Benedicta, after a few moments. "I feel about him as I feel about God in Heaven."

"Holy Mother! What blasphemy! Two blasphemies, child: the first, no one should love anyone as he loves God—the second, a husband, even a bad one, is better than the best of dreams."

"A husband, even a bad one, is better than the best of dreams."

The maxim was not idealistic, and Maria Benedicta protested. Was it not better to dream than to weep? Dreams come to an end or change, whereas bad husbands can live a long time. "You could say that, because God gave you an angel— Look, there he comes."

"Never mind; you'll have your angel too. I know a wonderful one for you; all the angels look me up."

Theophilo, Dona Fernanda's husband, who had seen them from a distance, was coming toward them, a crumpled daily in his hand. He did not greet the guest, but went straight to his wife.

"Do you want to know what they've done to me, Nannan?" he asked, with gritted teeth, "My speech of the fifth came out today. Look at this phrase. I had said, *When in doubt, be moderate is a wise man's advice*, and they put, *When in debt, be moderate*— It's intolerable! You see, it was a question of an amount owed the Ministry of the Navy, and it was alleged in my speech that there had been much expenditure. So that it may well appear rudeness on my part, as if I were advising non-payment of debt. At any rate, it's a stupid mistake."

"But didn't you read the proofs?"

"I did, but the author is the one least apt to read them well. *When in debt, be moderate*—" he snorted, his eyes on the paper.

He was aghast. He was a serious man, talented and hard-working; but at that moment, all great undertakings, all the most fearful problems, the most decisive battles, the most profound revolutions, the sun and the moon, and all the constellations, and the beasts of creation, and all the generations of man were less significant than the substitution of an *e* for an *ou*. Maria Benedicta was looking at him uncomprehendingly. She thought she was suffering the greatest unhappiness, but here was another as great as hers, and much more distressing. So a young girl's gnawing anguish was no greater than that occasioned by a typographical error. Theophilo, who only then noticed her, held out his hand; it was cold. As no one can feign cold hands, he must really be suffering. A few moments later, he hurled the sheet to the floor with a violent gesture and turned away.

"But, Theophilo, it will be corrected tomorrow," said Dona Fernanda, rising.

Without looking back, Theophilo shrugged his shoulders despairingly. His wife ran to him; her friend followed in alarm. Only the bench remained, disencumbered from them now, receiving the full rays of the sun, which neither likes speeches nor makes them. Dona Fernanda took her husband to the study, and, by dint of kisses, consoled him for the blow. At lunch he was already smiling, albeit with a wan smile. To divert him from his preoccupation, his wife aired the plan to get Maria Benedicta married. She must marry a deputy, she said, if there were any bachelor in the Chamber, whatever his political opinion. He might be for the government, for the opposition, for both or for neither—so long as he might be a husband. Good woman that she was, she made some gay, witty remarks on this subject which passed time and were meant to destroy all memory of the substitution of letters. As Theophilo listened to his wife, he became cheerful, and he agreed that it would be well to see that Maria Benedicta got married.

"The unfortunate part of it," said his wife, looking at her friend, "is that she is in love with someone whose name she won't tell."

The following Sunday Dona Fernanda went to the church of Santo Antonio dos Pobres. After Mass was over, she saw appear from among the faithful, who were moving about greeting one another or bowing before the altar, no one other than her cousin. He was in sober attire. Erect and smiling, he held out his hand.

"You too came to Mass?" she asked in surprise.

"I did."

"Do you always come?"

"Not always, but often."

"Frankly, I wouldn't expect such piety in you. Men are unbelievers, ordinarily. Theophilo never sets foot in church, except to baptize his children. Then you're devout?"

"I can't say for certain, but I do despise a banal disparagement of religion. And that's all I need say; I came to Mass, not to confession. I'll escort you home now, and if you offer it to me, I'll have lunch with you. Unless you'd like to have lunch at my house; it's right in this street you know."

"I'll go if for no other reason than to tell you about something that will take quite a long time to tell."

"Then we'll go slowly," said Carlos Maria, offering her his arm at the church door. And after they had taken a few steps, "Is it important?"

"Important and delightful."

"It is generally hoped that God, ever merciful, will take our beloved Theophilo unto Himself, leaving the nicest of widows helpless— You needn't make that face, Cousin; don't take your arm away. Let's get to the news. I'll wager the young woman from Pelotas is here?"

"I'll not tell you anything, if you won't be serious."

"I'll be serious."

Dona Fernanda confessed that she hesitated to have him marry her fellow-countrywoman from Pelotas; he shouldn't be disappointed, because she had discovered someone here who had a great love for him. Carlos Maria smiled and started to joke, but the announcement intrigued him. "Great love?" "Great love, violent passion," confirmed his cousin, adding, however, that perhaps the definition no longer fitted the person's present feeling. Now it was rather silent adoration. She had cried for him night after night, as long as hope had lasted— And Dona Fernanda continued thus to repeat Maria Benedicta's confidence. Only the name was left to be told. Carlos Maria wanted to know what it was, but she refused to tell him. She said she could not disclose it. Why give him the satisfaction of knowing who it was who adored him if he did not respond to her heart? It would be better that she remain unknown. She did not cry any more now; modest, and without ambition, she had lost hope of being loved, and, in time, had become merely a devotee: and, indeed, a devotee without equal; for she did not even hope to be heard by the god whom she worshipped, nor thanked one day by a kindly glance from his eyes.

"Cousin, you—"

"I what?"

Carlos Maria concluded, saying as a lawyer she was worthy of her case. Truly, if that young woman so adored him, it was only natural and right that his cousin should take a keen interest in her. "But why not tell her name?"

"I'll not tell you now; perhaps, someday— But you understand that it would be very hard for me to marry you off to my countrywoman, knowing that someone else loves you dearly. And yet it's quite possible that the one here wouldn't suffer very much, if she saw that you were married. Yes, it seems absurd, but one has to know her— I swear, as long as you're happy, she'd be ready to bestow blessings upon her lovely rival."

"That's no longer romanticism, it's mysticism," argued Carlos Maria, after walking a little way, his eyes on the ground. "Have you any proof of such a state of mind?"

"I have— That's your house, isn't it?" asked Dona Fernanda, stopping.

"It is."

"An attractive and substantial structure."

"Very substantial."

"One, two, three, four—seven windows. Does the salon run from end to end? It would be fine for a ball."

And as she walked along, she continued:

"If I had a larger house than mine here, I'd give a big ball before going back to Rio Grande. I like parties. My two sons don't give me much trouble. By the way, I want to put Lopo into private school; where'll I find a good one?"

Carlos Maria was thinking of his unknown devotee; and was a long, long way from teaching and its institutions. How good it was to feel oneself an adored god, adored, too, in an evangelical manner, the devotee secretly locked in her room rather than being out in the synagogues, within view of everyone. "And thy father, who sees what is going on in secret will give thee thy pay!" Oh, he would give his pay if he knew who she was. Might she be married? No, she wouldn't be; or she would not confess her secret to anyone; she would be widow or spinster, spinster rather. The whole affair suggested a spinster. In what room did she lock herself to pray, call forth his image, weep for him and give him her blessing? He would no longer insist upon knowing the name, but he would want to know the room at least.

"Where shall I find a good school?" Dona Fernanda asked again.

"A school? I don't know. I'm thinking about the stranger. Someone who worships me silently and hopelessly is to be thought about somewhat, you know. Tall or short?"

"Maria Benedicta."

Carlos stood stock-still.

"That young woman? It can't be. I've talked to her many times, and I've never discovered anything. I've always thought her indifferent. It must be a mistake. Have you heard her speak my name?"

"No, despite all my insistence. She confessed the miracle, without naming the saint. But what a miracle! You can boast of unparalleled devotion— Whose house is that?"

"Unparalleled devotion? It may not be quite that. You usually exaggerate things, Cousin. And how did you learn that it was I?"

"Theophilo was the one who first found out. When she told

him she turned red as a *pitanga*.* Later she denied it, when talking with me, and from that day hasn't come back to the house."

That is how the affair began. Carlos Maria was pleased with that quiet adoration; and his prejudice became sympathy. He began to notice the girl, and he enjoyed her confusion and timidity, her modesty and cheerfulness, her manner that seemed almost an entreaty, all the acts and sentiments that comprised the apotheosis of the man she loved. That is how the affair began, and that is how it ended. And that is how we happened to see them on the evening of Dona Sophia's birthday. Once upon a time he had spoken very sweetly to Dona Sophia; but that's the way men are, no different from the passing shower or the howling wind.

C X X I

"Good, he's going to get married! So much the better!" thought Rubião. Between that evening and the wedding day Rubião plucked from the air some glances cast by Sophia—glances whose intention, he suspected, was to entice Carlos Maria. If Carlos Maria responded, it was more for the sake of politeness than anything else. Rubião concluded that they were fortuitous occurrences; he still remembered the tear Sophia had shed the evening of her birthday, when she explained to him about the letter. Oh kind, unanticipated tear! Thou that sufficed to persuade one man may not be explicable to others; so goes the world. What does it matter that the eyes were not accustomed to weeping, or that the evening would appear to arouse feelings very different from melancholy? Rubião saw it fall; even now he can see it in retrospect. Rubião's confidence, however, came not from the tear alone but from Sophia's present manner; never had she been so solicitous nor so devoted to him. She seemed to regret all the hurt she had caused, and to be ready to

* The fruit of the *pitangueira*. (*Translator's Note.*)

heal his wounds, either through belated affection or through the failure of her other adventure. Sometimes virtual crimes lie dormant, and operas are stored away in a maestro's head, only to await the creative influence of genius to inspire their opening bars.

CXXII

"It's well that he's getting married," Rubião repeated.

The wedding took place three weeks later. On the morning of the appointed day, Carlos Maria awoke with some perplexity. Was it really he who was going to get married? There was no doubt; it was himself whom he saw in the mirror. He thought over the past days, the rapid march of events, the genuineness of the affection he held for his fiancée and, finally, the pure felicity she would bring him. This last thought filled him with a great and rare contentment. He was still musing while taking his usual morning canter; this time he had chosen the district of Engheno Velho.

He was used to admiring glances, but now he had the impression that everyone who looked at him had heard of his coming marriage. Some *casuarina* trees that were in the garden of a suburban villa, quite still before he passed them, spoke to him in a very special way; the light-headed would ascribe it to the breeze that, too, was passing, but the wise would recognize it for what it was—the nuptial language of *casuarina* trees. Birds were hopping about, twittering a madrigal. A pair of butterflies —which the Japanese consider the symbol of fidelity, since they have observed that as they flit from flower to flower they almost always go in pairs—a pair of them accompanied the horse for some time. They would fly over to the enclosure of a villa that bordered the road, fluttering gaily here and there, their wings gleaming brightly yellow. And together with all this, there was the fresh air, the blue sky, the happy faces of men riding donkey-back, necks craning from carriage windows to have a look at him with his elegant appearance befitting a bridegroom. Truly, it was hard to believe that all those gestures and attitudes of people and animals and trees were expressing any sentiment other than Nature's homage to marriage.

The butterflies became lost in one of the thickest tangles of growth beside the enclosure. Another estate came into view, bare of trees, its gate standing open. In the back, facing the gate, was an old house whose five balconied windows looked like so many crinkled eyes. They, too, had seen weddings and festivities. At the beginning of the century they had been aglow with life and hope; now, after the loss of so many tenants, they were weary.

But do not think that this saddened the heart of the rider. No, he had the faculty of rejuvenating ruins and reliving the past. He even enjoyed seeing the faded old house in such contrast to the bright butterflies he had seen a little while before. He checked his horse, and evoked the women of another day, who had entered there, their faces, their manners, their festive attire. Perhaps the ghosts of these happy people would come now to greet him and express their esteem with unseen lips. He even fancied he could hear them and he smiled. But a shrill voice broke into the harmony of sound—a parrot was in a cage hanging from the outside wall of the house: "A royal parrot, a parrot for Portugal; who's going by? Currupá, pepá—Grr—Grr—" The ghosts took flight, and the horse continued on its way. Carlos Maria hated parrots, just as he hated monkeys. He said that they were both fraudulent imitators of man.

"Will the happiness that I give her be interrupted thus?" he reflected, as he rode along.

Cambaxirras were flying back and forth across the road, and when they alighted they compensated for the parrot's shrieking by singing in the language that is peculiar to them. That wordless language was unintelligible; yet it expressed much that was clear and beautiful. Carlos Maria even saw in it a symbol of himself. When his wife, troubled by the parrots in this world, was drooping with weariness and aversion, he would make her spirits rise at the trilling of that divine flock that within itself harbored golden thoughts uttered by a golden voice. Oh how happy he would make her! Already he could see her kneeling, her arms resting on his knees, her head in her hands, her eyes upon him, eyes that were grateful, devoted, loving. And she, all beseeching and wholly submissive.

CXXIII

Now, at the same hour that this vision was appearing before the eyes of the bridegroom, it was being reproduced in the mind of the bride. At the window, as she watched the waves break in the distance and on the shore, Maria Benedicta was visualizing herself kneeling at her husband's feet, quiet, contrite, as if at the Communion table to receive the Host of felicity. And she said to herself: "Oh, how happy he will make me!" The words and the thought were different, but the position and the hour were the same.

CXXIV

They were married; and three months later they went to Europe. When Dona Fernanda said good-by to them she was as happy as if she were welcoming them back. She did not cry. The pleasure of seeing them happy was greater than the sorrow of parting.

"Are you happy?" she asked Maria Benedicta for the last time as she stood near the gunwale of the ship.

"Oh, very!"

Dona Fernanda's heart, fresh and ingenious, leaned out and looked down from her eyes, singing a fragment in Italian—because the proud lady from Rio Grande do Sul preferred Italian music—perhaps this aria from Lucia: O bell' alma innamorata. Or this excerpt from the Barber:

> Ecco ridente in cielo
> Spunta la bella aurora.

Sophia did not go on board; she fell ill and sent her husband. No one will believe that it was due to displeasure or grief, because for the wedding she conducted herself very discreetly; she attended to the bride's trousseau, and took leave of the bride with many tearful kisses. But she thought that it would be humiliating to go on board. So she fell ill, and not to belie her pretext, she remained in her room. She picked up a recent novel that Rubião had given her. There were other things there, too, to remind her of him, a number of watch charms, to say nothing of jewelry that was put away; and finally, a strange remark that she had heard him make the night of her cousin's wedding was added to the inventory of her recollections of our friend.

"Of them all you are already the Queen; wait, I shall still make you Empress."

Sophia was not able to understand those enigmatic words. She was tempted to suppose that it was a lure of grandeur to persuade her to become his mistress, but she excluded such an intention as too conceited. Though Rubião was no longer the shy, timid man he had been, he did not appear so vain that she could charge him with such presumption. Yet what did it mean? Sophia believed anything possible. She had received not a few gallantries; she had heard that declaration from Carlos Maria which was no more than an expression of vanity; she would hear others, probably. But they were all ephemeral. Only Rubião persisted. Occasionally he would desist, becoming suspicious, but his suspicions went as they came.

He deserves to be loved, read Sophia on the open page of the novel as she started to continue her reading; she closed the book, closed her eyes, and became lost in thought. The slave who came in with some broth a little later, supposed that her mistress was asleep, and went out on tip-toe.

Meanwhile Rubião and Palha were leaving the ship for the launch and were returning to the Pharoux wharf. They were thoughtful and quiet. Palha was the first to speak:

"For some time I have been going to tell you something important, Rubião."

Rubião was aroused from his thoughts. It was the first time he had been on a ship. He was coming away full of the sounds he heard on deck, the hustle and bustle of people going in and out, natives and foreigners of various nationalities, French, English, Germans, Argentinians, Italians, a confusion of tongues, a medley of hats, cordage, sofas, binoculars to be carried over the shoulder, men going up or down the inner stairways, women, tearful, curious, or laughing, many of them with flowers or fruit that they had brought from shore—all new sights for Rubião. In the distance, the bar through which the ship had to pass, and beyond the bar, the vast sea, the closed-in sky, and solitude. Rubião renewed his dreams of the ancient world; and, though he knew nothing of the tradition, he created an Atlantis of his own. Having no notion of geography, he formed a confused idea of the other countries, and his fancy encircled them with a mysterious nimbus. As it was easy for him to travel by imagination, he traveled thus for some time, in that high and extensive vapor, where there are neither seasickness nor waves, winds nor clouds.

"You have been going to tell *me* something?" Rubião asked, after a few moments.

"Yes, you," confirmed Palha. "I should have told you sooner, but what with the wedding and the Alagoas committee, I was prevented from doing so; I didn't have the opportunity. Now, however, before lunch— You'll have lunch with me?"

"Yes, but what is it?"

"Something important."

Saying this, he pulled out a cigarette, opened it and spread the tobacco with his fingers, rolled the paper again, and struck a match, but the wind blew the match out. Then he asked Rubião to be good enough to hold onto his hat so he could light another. Rubião complied impatiently. It may well be that by prolonging the wait, his partner was deliberately trying to make him believe that the matter in question was of no less gravity than an earthquake, so that the reality would seem trivial. After two puffs, he said:

"I'm planning to liquidate the business. I have been asked to become director of a banking house here, and I think I'll accept."

Rubião breathed a sigh of relief.

"Why, yes. Shall you liquidate immediately?"

"No, at the end of next year."

"And is it necessary to liquidate?"

"Yes, for me it is. Of course, if the bank offer weren't safe, I'd not have the courage to risk a sure thing for something doubtful, but it's perfectly safe."

"Then at the end of next year, we'll sever our ties—"

Palha coughed.

"No, before that, at the end of this year."

Rubião did not understand; but his partner explained that it would be well to dissolve the partnership so that he might liquidate the firm alone. The bank might be organized sooner or later than planned; why should Rubião be subjected to the exigencies of the occasion? Besides, Doctor Camacho declared that Rubião would be in the Chamber before long, and that the Ministry was sure to fall.

"Be that as it may," he concluded, "it is always well to dissolve a partnership in time. You're not living on the business, anyway. You came in with the capital it needed—but you could have given it to some other business or kept it."

"Why, yes, no doubt," agreed Rubião.

And after a few moments:

"But tell me one thing. Is there some hidden motive behind this proposal? Is it a personal break, a break in our friendship—? Be frank, tell me—"

"What false notion is this?" Palha retorted. "Severance of friendship—why, you're mad. It must be from the motion of the sea. Would I, who have worked so hard for you, who have introduced you to my friends, treated you as a kinsman, as a brother, quarrel for no reason? You know that had it not been for your refusal you would have been the one to marry Maria Benedicta, instead of Carlos Maria. One can break one tie without breaking them all. The contrary would be absurd. Then all those who are social or family friends are business partners, and all those who are not are business men without a partner?"

Rubião thought the reasoning excellent, and embraced Palha. The latter grasped his hand, highly satisfied. He would be free of a partner whose growing extravagance could be somewhat dangerous. The house was sound; it would be easy to give Rubião the part that belonged to him except for his personal debts of long standing. There were still some of those that Palha confessed to his wife that evening at Santa Thereza, Chapter L. One day, wanting to force some money upon Rubião, Palha repeated the old proverb, "Pay what you owe and see what you have left." But Rubião joked:

"Well, don't pay, and see if you don't have more left."

"That's a good one," Palha replied, laughing and putting the money away in his pocket.

There was no bank, nor directorship, nor liquidation; but how could Palha justify dissolution of the partnership merely by telling the truth? Hence the invention, all the more ready, since Palha loved banks and was dying for one. The man's career was becoming more and more prosperous and striking. His business was expanding; indeed, one of his reasons for severing relations with Rubião was to avoid having to divide future profits with him. Furthermore, Palha owned shares from all over and stock in the Itaborahy loan, and, together with a person of influence, he had furnished some of the war supplies, which were highly profitable. He had already engaged an architect to build him a mansion, and he was thinking vaguely of baronage.

"Whoever would have thought the Palhas would treat us like this? We're no longer any good. You needn't defend them—"

"I'm not defending them; I'm explaining; there must have been some mistake."

"A birthday, the cousin's wedding, and not even one little invitation to the Major, the great Major, the priceless Major, his old friend the Major. That's what he used to call me; I was great, priceless, his old friend, and that isn't all he called me. Now, nothing, not even one little invitation, not even delivered by a Negro boy by word of mouth: 'It's my mistress's birthday,' or 'her cousin's getting married, she says you're to come to the house and it's to be formal.' We wouldn't have gone; formality is not for us. But it would have been something, it would have been a message, a Negro boy, for the priceless Major—"

"Papa!"

Seeing that Dona Tonica interrupted, Rubião summoned courage to defend the Palha family at some length. This was at the Major's house; the Major was no longer living on Dous de Dezembro Street but in a modest little two-story house on Barbonos Street. Rubião had been passing by, the Major was in the window and called him in. Dona Tonica did not have time to leave the drawing room for so much as a glance at the mirror; she was barely able to smooth her hair, rearrange the ribbon bow at her neck and pull down her dress to cover her shoes, which were not new.

"I tell you that there could have been a mistake," insisted Rubião; "everything is very much in confusion there with that Alagoas committee."

"See here," Major Siqueira interrupted; "why didn't they put my daughter on the committee? I've been wondering about that for a long time. They never used to do anything without us; we were always the life of the party. The change began some time ago; they started to receive us coolly, and whenever he can avoid me, the husband doesn't even greet me. It began some time ago, but before that they never did anything without us. What do you mean by confusion? The day before her birthday, suspecting that they wouldn't invite us, I went to see him at the warehouse. He didn't say much, and dissembled. Finally I said to him, 'Yesterday, at home, Dona Tonica and I were discussing the date of Dona Sophia's birthday; she said it had passed and I said it hadn't; that it was today or tomorrow.' He didn't answer, pretended to be absorbed in an account, called the bookkeeper and asked for an explanation. I understood the beastly fellow well enough; so I repeated my story, and he repeated his procedure. Then I left. And that was Palha—a poor, common fellow. He's ashamed of me now. I used to drink many a toast to him, I had a certain knack for it. We used to play *voltarete* together. But now he has a swelled head and hobnobs with fine folk. Ah! worldly vanity! Why, the other day didn't I see his wife in a *coupé* with another woman? Sophia in a *coupé*! She pretended not to see me, but she looked out of the corner of her eye to see if I saw her and was admiring her. Worldly vanity! He who eats olive oil for the first time, spills it all over himself."

"Excuse me, but the committee work demands a certain amount of display."

"Yes," said Siqueira, "that's why my daughter didn't go into the committee; she doesn't want to spoil the carriages."

"Besides, the *coupé* might belong to the woman who was with her."

The Major took a few steps, his hands behind his back, and stopped in front of Rubião.

"To her—or to Father Mendes. How is the Father? Living well, of course."

"But Papa, there may be nothing in all this," interrupted Dona Tonica. "She's always nice to me, and when I was sick last month she sent the Negro boy over twice to inquire how I was."

"The Negro boy," her father shouted. "The Negro boy! A great favor indeed! 'Boy, go over to the house of that retired army man, and ask him if his daughter is better; I'll not go myself because I'm polishing my nails!' A great favor indeed! You don't polish your nails! You work! You are my worthy daughter, poor but honest!"

Here the Major wept, though he quickly checked his tears. His daughter felt ashamed, as well as touched. To be sure, the house bespoke the family's poverty; just a few chairs, an old round table, a worn settee; on the walls two lithographs framed in pine wood painted black, one a portrait of the Major in 1857, the other a copy of *Veronese in Venice*, bought in Senhor dos Passos Street. However, the daughter's diligence was everywhere in evidence. The furniture shone, on the table was an embroidered runner that she had made, and on the settee was a pillow. And it was not true that she did not polish her nails; she probably had neither powder nor chamois skin, but she went at them every morning with a bit of cloth.

C X X X I

Rubião assumed a sympathetic attitude and, in order not to irritate the Major, he stopped defending the Palhas. A little later he took his departure, and, though he was not invited, he promised that he would have dinner with them "one of these days."

"It will be a poor man's dinner," said the Major; "if you can, let us know when you're coming."

"I don't want a banquet. I'll come when I feel like it."

He took his leave. After accompanying him to the landing (she did not go to the door because of her shoes), Dona Tonica went to the window to watch him go out.

CXXXII

As soon as Rubião turned the corner of Mangueiras Street, Dona Tonica went back to her father, who had stretched out on the settee to reread the old *Saint-Clair das ilhas ou os desterrados da ilha da Barra*. It was the first novel he had known. The copy was over twenty years old, and it constituted the entire library of father and daughter. Siqueira opened the first volume and cast his eyes on the beginning of Chapter II, which he already knew by heart. Now he found therein a particular savor because of his recent indignation: *"Fill your glasses," cried Saint-Clair, "and let us drink in unison; here is the toast that I propose. To the health of the good and courageous, to the oppressed and to the chastisement of their oppressors." All gathered around Saint-Clair and joined in the toast.*

"Do you know something, Papa? You buy some canned goods, tomorrow, peas, fish, etc.; and we'll put them aside. Then the day he comes for dinner, we'll put it on the fire, and it'll only have to be warmed up. We'll have a better dinner that way."

"But I have just enough money for your dress."

"My dress? That can be bought next month or the month after. I'll wait."

"But wasn't it ordered?"

"It can be countermanded. I'll wait."

"And what if there's no other of the same price?"

"There will be. I'll wait, Papa."

CXXXIII

I have not yet told you—because the chapters come tumbling over one another under one's pen—but here is one to tell you that by that time Rubião's acquaintanceship had increased. Camacho had put him in contact with a number of politicians and too, there were the women of the Alagoas committee, the personnel of the banks, the business houses, and the Exchange, the theater-goers, and all the people of Ouvidor Street. His name was now often repeated. He was well known. Whenever his beard and long whiskers appeared, his broad chest, his tight-fitting topcoat, his cane with the head of a unicorn, and his firm and masterful step, everyone would say that it was Rubião—a rich man from Minas.

They had built up a legend around him. They said he was the disciple of a great philosopher who had bequeathed him immense wealth—one, three, five million contos. Some were surprised that he never talked about philosophy, but the legend explained that silence by the master's philosophical system, which consisted of teaching only men of good will. Where were those disciples? They went to his house every day—some twice a day, in the morning and in the afternoon. This, then, was the definition given to those who shared Rubião's table. They may not have been disciples, but they were men of good will. They would suffer the pangs of hunger as they waited, and they would listen quietly and smilingly to their host's discourse. There was some rivalry among the old and the new, which the former emphasized by manifesting greater intimacy, giving orders to the servants, asking for cigars, assuming the freedom of the house, whistling, etc. Habit, however, enabled them to tolerate one another, and, in the end, they would all pleasantly agree as to the admirable qualities of their host. After some time the new ones also would owe him money, either in currency or in a promissory note to the tailor or an indorsement of bills of exchange, which he paid secretly so as not to abash the debtors.

Quincas Borba would spring into their laps and they would snap their fingers to see him jump. Some even gave him a kiss on the forehead; one of them, more clever than the rest, found a way of holding the dog on his knees at lunch or dinner to give him bread crumbs.

"Ah! Don't do that!" protested Rubião the first time.

"What's wrong?" retorted his guest. "There are no strangers here."

Rubião pondered a moment.

"It's true, of course, that there's a great man inside of him," he said.

"The philosopher, the other Quincas Borba," added the guest, looking around at the novices to display the intimacy of his relations with Rubião. However, he was not able to enjoy exclusive advantage, because the other friends of the same era repeated in chorus:

"That's right, the philosopher."

And Rubião explained to the novices the allusion to the philosopher, and the reason for the dog's name, which they all thought he had given. Quincas Borba (the deceased) was described as one of the greatest men of all time—superior to his countrymen. A good philosopher, a great soul, a great friend. And, finally, after a silence, Rubião shouted, tapping his fingers on the edge of the table:

"I'd make him Minister of State!"

Unconvinced, but simply out of a sense of duty, one of the guests exclaimed:

"Oh, of course!"

None of those men really knew the sacrifice that Rubião was making for them. He would refuse dinners and drives, he would interrupt agreeable conversations just to hurry home and eat with them. One day he conceived a way to arrange everything. If he were not at home at six o'clock sharp, the servants were to serve dinner for his friends. There were protests: no, they would wait until seven or eight. A dinner without him would have no charm.

"But it may be that I can't come," Rubião explained.

And so the guests complied. They set their watches by the clocks in the house at Botafogo, and at the stroke of six, all were at table. There was some reluctance the first two days; but the servants had strict orders. Occasionally Rubião would arrive a little later, and then there would be laughter and witty talk and merry intrigue. Once one of them had wanted to wait, but the others had gainsaid him; in the end it was he who dragged out the dinner because he was so hungry—so hungry that nothing but the dishes were left. And Rubião laughed with them all.

CXXXIV

To compose a chapter just to tell that at first, when Rubião was away, the guests smoked their own cigars after dinner—may seem frivolous to the frivolous; but those of considered judgment will say that it may have some interest in this apparently trivial instance.

In fact, one evening one of the guests of longest standing took it into his head to go to Rubião's study: he had been there several times. That was where the cigar boxes were kept; not four or five, but twenty or thirty. They were of different brands and they were all wide open. A servant (the Spaniard) lighted the gas. The other guests followed the first, selected some cigars, and those who were not yet familiar with the study admired the well-made and well-arranged furniture. The secretary won general admiration; it was of ebony, with beautiful marquetry, substantial and with severe lines. But there was something new waiting for them; two marble busts on top of it, the two Napoleons, the first and the third.

"When did this come?"

"Today at noon," answered the servant.

They were two magnificent busts. Beside the uncle's penetrating gaze, the nephew's meditative one seemed to be staring into space. The servant told that as soon as his master had received and placed the busts, he had stood admiring them for a long time, so oblivious to everything that he, too, had been able to contemplate them, but without any admiration. *"No me dicen nada estos dos pícaros,"* the servant concluded, making a lofty and sweeping gesture.

C X X X V

Rubião patronized literature generously. Books that were dedicated to him went to press with the guarantee of two or three hundred copies. He had innumerable diplomas from literary, choreographic and religious societies and he was a member of a Catholic Congregation and a Protestant Association, having forgotten the one when he was approached for the other; what he did was to pay his monthly dues regularly for both. He subscribed to papers that he never read. One day he was paying his six months' subscription to one that had been sent to him, and when he learned from the collector that it was a paper of the Government party, he consigned the collector to the Devil.

C X X X V I

The collector, however, did not go to the Devil; he received the six months' payment and with a collector's natural perspicacity, he muttered in the street:

"Now there's a man who despises the sheet, yet pays. How many there are who love it, yet do not pay!"

Oh, coincidence of fortune! Oh, equity of Nature! If our friend's prodigality was without remedy, it was not without compensation. No longer did time pass for him as for an empty-pated idler. If Rubião was lacking in judgment, he now had imagination. Formerly he had depended upon others rather than upon himself; he had found no inner equilibrium, and idleness had stretched the hours so that they seemed unending.

Now everything was changing. Imagination was beginning to take up its perch in his head. Seated in Bernardo's shop, he would while away a whole morning, without time hanging heavy or the narrowness of Ouvidor Street hemming him in. Delightful visions, like those of the wedding (Chapter LXXXI) were repeated, and in such form that their grandiose nature did not deprive them of their charm. More than once he was seen to jump up from his chair and go over to the door to see the back of someone who was passing. Did he know the person? Or was it, perhaps, someone who happened to have the features of the imaginary person at whom he had been looking? There are too many questions for one chapter alone; suffice it to say that one of those times, no one passed, and he, himself, aware of the illusion, went back inside and bought a bronze watch charm for Camacho's daughter who was having a birthday and getting married soon. Then he left.

And Sophia? the feminine reader asks impatiently, like Orgon: *Et Tartufe?* Here, my friend, the answer is the same, naturally; she, also, was eating well and sleeping well, all of which does not keep one from being in love, if one wishes to be in love. If this last reflection is the secret reason for your query, let me tell you that you are very indiscreet, and I wish to have nothing to do with those who cannot dissemble.

I repeat that she was eating and sleeping well. The work of the Alagoas committee had been completed and she had been much praised by the press; the *Atalaia* called her "the angel of mercy." And though this name flattered her, don't think that she was pleased with it. Since it restricted the whole charitable undertaking to Sophia, it might offend her new friends and make her lose in a day the work of many long months. This explains the article that the same paper carried in the next issue, naming individually and glorifying the other committee women—"stars of the first magnitude."

Not all the friendships continued; most of them, however, were firmly established, and our friend did not lack the talent to make them lasting. Her husband was too noisily effusive, too obsequious, showing quite plainly that he was overwhelmed by courtesies which he did not expect and which he scarcely thought he deserved. To correct him, Sophia shamed him with advice and criticism. She would say, laughingly:

"You were intolerable today; anyone would have thought you were a servant."

"Christiano, be more composed; when we have guests, don't let your eyes pop out and shift from side to side like a child who's being given candy—"

He would deny it, explain or justify himself; finally he would conclude that she was right, one should not humble oneself; politeness, affability, but no more—

"Precisely, but don't fall into the opposite extreme," said Sophia, quickly. "Don't be sullen."

After that Palha was both ways; sullen, at first, indifferent, almost contemptuous; but either reflection or unconscious impulse restored our man's habitual animation, and, with it, depending upon the occasion, excess and noise. In truth, it was Sophia who made amends for everything. She observed and imitated. Through necessity and inclination, she had gradually acquired what neither birth nor fortune had given her. Furthermore, she was at that age between youth and maturity when women inspire equal confidence in girls of twenty and women of forty. Some would have laid down their lives for her; others praised her to the skies.

And so it was that little by little our friend cleared the atmosphere. She severed old, familiar relations, some so intimate that they could be dissolved only with difficulty. However, the art of receiving coolly, of listening without interest, and saying good-by without regret, was not the least of her accomplishments. One by one they were disappearing—those poor, modest, unpretentious women who did not have fashionable wardrobes; unimportant friends with simple diversions, and unassuming ways. Toward the men whom she passed in a carriage—which was her own, incidentally—she acted exactly as the Major had said. Only she no longer looked to see if they saw her. The honeymoon of ostentation had ended; now she would coldly turn her eyes aside, exorcising with a peremptory gesture the danger of any hesitancy on their part. It was in this way that she compelled her old friends not to raise their hats.

CXXXIX

Rubião still tried to help the Major, but the air of annoyance with which Sophia interrupted him was such that he preferred to ask her whether if it were not raining the next morning they would be going to Tijuca.

"I spoke to Christiano, and he told me that it'll be next Sunday because he has some business to attend to."

After a moment, Rubião said,

"Let's go, the two of us. We'll leave early, we'll ride, and have lunch there; by three or four o'clock we'll be back."

Sophia looked at him with such evident desire to accept the invitation that Rubião did not wait for a verbal answer.

"It's agreed; we'll go," he said.

"No."

"What do you mean, no?"

And he repeated the question because Sophia would not explain the reason for her refusal, which, after all, was obvious. Compelled to do so, she said that her husband would be envious and might postpone his business just to go along. She did not wish to interfere with his business, and, anyway, they could wait a week. But the look that accompanied the explanation was like a bugle accompanying an Our Father. She wanted, oh, she did so want to go up the road with Rubião next morning, firmly seated on her horse, not dreamy and poetical, but bold, with flaming cheeks, completely of this world, galloping, trotting, and occasionally stopping. Up at the top, she would dismount for awhile; all alone, the city far away, the sky above. Leaning against her horse, combing his mane with her fingers, she would hear Rubião praise her daring and her elegance— She even felt a kiss on the nape of her neck—

CXL

Since we're speaking of horses, it will not be amiss to say that Sophia's imagination was now a fiery and capricious steed, capable of leaping over hills and laying waste to woodlands. There would be some other comparison if the occasion were different, but a steed is the best. It conveys the idea of running away and of spirit and impetuosity as well as that of the quietness with which it returns to the straight road and, finally, to the stable.

CXLI

"It's decided, we'll go tomorrow," Rubião repeated, watching closely Sophia's flushed face. But the steed was weary from its run, and stood drowsily in its stable. Sophia had already changed; the giddy adventure, the imagined ardor, the joy of going up the Tijuca road with him were past. When Rubião said that he would ask her husband to let her go, she answered indifferently:

"You're mad! It'll be next Sunday."

And she fixed her eyes on the lace that she was making—
frioleira it is called—while Rubião turned his toward a modest
little patch of garden beside the workroom where they were.
While Sophia, seated in an angle of the window, was moving
her fingers back and forth, Rubião envisaged an imperial fete
out in the garden where there was nothing but two common
roses and he forgot the room, the woman there, and himself.
It cannot be said for certain how long they remained thus, not
speaking and each a stranger to and far away from the other.
It was a maid who aroused them, bringing coffee. After he had
drunk his coffee, Rubião adjusted his beard, drew out his watch,
and took his leave. Sophia, who had been eagerly waiting for his
departure, was very glad; however, she covered her pleasure with
surprise.

"So soon!"

"I have to see someone before four o'clock," explained
Rubião. "No ride then, in the morning. I'll countermand the
horses. But it will surely be next Sunday?"

"I can't say that it will surely be; but if Christiano decides in
time, I believe it will be. My husband, you know, is the one
who sometimes makes it difficult."

Sophia accompanied him to the door, listlessly held out her
hand, smilingly made a flat remark and went back to the little
room in which she had been—to the very same angle of the
very same window. She did not go on with her work immediately. She crossed her legs, pulling her skirt down from force of
habit, and glanced at the garden in which were the two roses
that had inspired our friend with an imperial vision. Sophia saw
nothing but two mute flowers. Nevertheless, she looked at them
for some time; then she picked up her *frioleira*, worked a little,
and again stopped awhile, letting her hands lie idle in her lap.
Again she took up her work, only to put it down once more.
Suddenly, she stood up and tossed the shuttle and linen thread
into the little wicker basket in which she kept all her pretense
of work. The basket, too, was a memento from Rubião.

"What a tiresome man!"

She went to lean against the window that looked onto the

modest garden where the two common roses were withering. When roses are fresh, they are concerned little or not at all with man's anger; but if they are dying they will vex the human soul at the slightest provocation. I like to believe that this habit springs from the shortness of their lives. Someone has written: "In the eyes of a rose, its gardener is eternal." And what better way to strike at the eternal than to make fun of its anger? "I am ephemeral, you are enduring; but I blossomed and scattered my fragrance, I served matrons and maidens, I was the message of love, I adorned the buttonholes of men, I died upon my own bush and all hands and all eyes sought me and looked upon me with admiration and affection. Not so with you, O eternal one! You become angry, you weep, you suffer, and are distressed; your eternity is not worth a single moment of my life."

And so when Sophia went over to the window that looked on the garden, both the roses were laughing with their outspread petals. One of them said that it was "quite right, quite right, quite right!"

"You are right to be angry, my pretty one," it added, "but it should be with yourself, not with him. What is there in his favor? A sorry man without any charm, he may be a good friend, he may be generous, but he's repulsive, isn't he? And what the deuce makes you, who are sought by other men, listen to that one who has intruded upon your life? Humble yourself, O proud woman, because you are, yourself, the cause of your unhappiness. You swear to forget him, but you do not forget him. And do you have to forget him? Is it not enough to look at him and to listen to him, to despise him? That man says nothing, O strange woman, and yet, you—"

"It's really not like that," the other rose interrupted with a calm and ironical voice. "He does say something, and he has been saying it for a long time. He never forgets nor changes it; he is constant, he forgets sorrow, and believes in being hopeful. His entire love life is like the ride to Tijuca that you were talking about not long ago: 'It'll be next Sunday.' Have pity, at least. Be compassionate, O kindly Sophia! If you are to love someone out of wedlock, love him who loves you and is discreet. Come, repent of that impulse you had just now. What harm has he done you, what fault is it of his if you're pretty? And if there is any fault, it's not the basket's, just because he bought it, nor the linen thread's; not the shuttle's, that you, yourself, sent the maid to buy. You're wicked, Sophia, you're unfair—"

CXLII

Sophia lingered on, listening, listening— She questioned other plants, and they did not say anything different. There can be just such a wonderful concurrence. He who knows the soil and subsoil of life knows well that a fragment of a wall, a bench, a carpet, an umbrella are rich in thoughts or feelings when we, ourselves, are, and the association of inanimate objects with men and their reflection of them is one of the most interesting of terrestrial phenomena. Though the expression, "to converse with one's buttons," appears mere metaphor, it has true and direct meaning. Our buttons operate in synchronization with ourselves; they form a sort of cheap and comfortable senate, which always votes in favor of our motions.

CXLIII

They took the ride to Tijuca without any incident other than a fall from the horse as they were going down. It was not Rubião who fell, or Palha, but the latter's wife, who was thinking of I know not what, and angrily struck her animal with the whip. It took fright and threw her to the ground. Sophia fell gracefully; attired in her riding habit, the vest of which was alluringly close-fitting; she was singularly slender. Othello would have exclaimed, had he seen her: "Oh, my beautiful warrior maiden!" At the beginning of the ride, Rubião had merely said: "You're an angel."

"I hurt my knee," she said, limping into the house.

"Let's see."

In the dressing room, Sophia lifted her foot to a little bench and showed her husband her bruised knee; it had swollen a little, very little, but it made her cry out when it was touched. Not wanting to hurt her, Palha only lightly brushed it with his lips.

"Were my clothes disarranged when I fell?"

"No. After all, with such a long skirt— One could barely see the tip of your foot. It was quite all right, I assure you."

"You swear?"

"How suspicious you are, Sophia! I swear by all that is most holy, by the light that is shining on me, by the good Lord. Now, are you satisfied?"

Sophia was covering her knee.

"Let me see it again. I don't think it will get any worse. Put a little something on it. Ask at the pharmacy."

"All right. Let me go and take my things off," she said, trying to pull down her skirt.

But Palha had dropped his eyes from the knee to the rest of the leg, where it touched the top of the boot. It was, indeed, a beautiful bit of nature; the silk stocking revealed its shape to perfection. With kindly concern, Palha kept asking his wife if she had hurt herself here, or here, or here, indicating the places with his hand, which was moving downward. "If a tiny bit of this masterpiece did show, the sky and the trees would have been stunned," he concluded, while his wife lowered her skirt and removed her foot from the bench.

"Maybe, but it was not only the sky and the trees that were there," she said. "There were Rubião's eyes, too."

"Oh, Rubião! That's right. There was never any recurrence of the Santa Thereza foolishness?"

"Never. But, still, I'd not like— Do you really swear, it, Christiano?"

"What you want me to do is to swear by something more

and more holy. I've sworn by God, but, no, that wasn't enough. So now I swear by you; are you satisfied?"

All this was nothing but playful sentimentality. He left his wife's room finally, and went to his own. Sophia's timid and doubting modesty pleased him. It showed that she was his, completely his; but for the very reason that she was his, he considered that it behooved a lord and master not to be distressed by a fortuitous momentary glimpse of a part of his queen that was usually hidden. He was sorry that fortuity had stopped at the boot top. That was only the frontier; the outlying towns of the city hurt by the fall would have given some idea of its sublime and perfect civilization. And as he soaped himself, scrubbing his face and neck and head in the enormous silver basin, and, afterwards, as he dried himself, and brushed his hair and perfumed himself, Palha imagined what would have been the amazement and the envy of the mishap's sole witness, had the mishap been less incomplete.

CXLV

It was at that time that Rubião astonished all his friends. On the Tuesday following the Sunday of the ride (it was then January, 1870), he asked a barber and hairdresser of Ouvidor Street to send some one to his house to shave him next day at nine o'clock in the morning. A Frenchman, called Lucien, went there, and, according to the orders given to the servant, he was sent to Rubião's study.

"Grr—" growled Quincas Borba, from Rubião's knees.

Lucien bowed to the master of the house; the latter, however, did not see the courtesy, just as he had not heard Quincas Borba's signal. He lay on an elongated couch, quite bereft of his mind, which had broken through the ceiling and had become lost away up in the air. How many leagues had it gone? Neither condor nor eagle could say. On its way to the moon—it saw only the perennial felicity that had showered on it from the cradle, where the fairies had rocked it to sleep, to the shore of Botafogo, where they had taken it, resting on a bed of roses and jasmine. No reverse, no failure, no poverty—a peaceful life, made up of joy, and with more than enough income. —It was on its way to the moon!

The barber glanced about the study, where the most prominent thing was the secretary with the busts of Napoleon and Louis Napoleon on top. Hanging on the wall over the latter were an engraving or lithograph of the Battle of Solferino and a portrait of the Empress Eugenia.

Rubião was wearing a pair of gold-embroidered damask slippers on his feet, a cap with a black silk tassel on his head, and bright blue laughter on his lips.

CXLVI

"Sir—"

"Grrr—" repeated Quincas Borba, standing on his master's knees.

Rubião recovered his senses and noticed the barber. He recognized him, since he had seen him recently in the shop. He rose from his chair and Quincas Borba barked as if to protect him against the intruder.

"Quiet! Hush!" said Rubião; and, crestfallen, the dog went to hide behind the wastepaper basket. In the meantime, Lucien was unwrapping his instruments.

"You're going to lose a fine beard," he said in French. "I know persons who have done the same thing, but to please a lady. I have been the confidant of honorable men—"

"Precisely," interrupted Rubião.

He had not understood a word; though he knew some French, he could only read it—as we know—and he did not understand the spoken language. But, curiously enough, his answer was not hypocritical, he heard the words as if they were a greeting or an acclamation, and, what is still more curious, he believed he was speaking French.

"Precisely," he repeated. "I wish to restore my face to its former appearance; there it is."

And, as he pointed to the bust of Napoleon III, the barber answered in Portuguese:

"Ah! The Emperor! A fine bust, indeed. An excellent piece of work. Did you buy this here or send to Paris for it? They're magnificent. And there's Napoleon I, the Great; there was a man of genius. Had it not been for the betrayal, you see, sir, traitors are worse than Orsini's bombs."

"Orsini! a poor fellow!"

"He paid dearly."

"Just what he should. But neither bombs nor an Orsini avail against the destiny of a great man," Rubião continued. "When a nation's fortune places an imperial crown upon a great man's head, no malice is of any use— Orsini! He was a fool!"

In a few minutes the barber began to shave Rubião's beard, so that only the goatee and mustache of Napoleon III would be left. He commended his own work, saying that it was difficult to make an exact copy of anything; and as he cut off the beard, he praised it. What a fine growth of hair! He was really making a great sacrifice—

"You're presumptuous, barber," interrupted Rubião. "I've told you what I want; make my face as it used to be. There's the bust to guide you."

"Yes, sir, I'll carry out your instructions; you'll see what a likeness there'll be."

And, clip, clip, he gave the final touch to Rubião's beard and began to scrape his cheeks and jaws. The operation lasted a long time, the barber serenely scraping and comparing, and dividing his eyes between the bust and his man. Sometimes, to compare them better, he would step back a little, look at them alternately, lean forward and ask his man to turn to one side or the other, and then go back to look at the corresponding side of the bust.

"Is it going all right?" Rubião would ask.

Lucien would gesture to him to be quiet, and then he would proceed. He trimmed the goatee, left the mustache, and then went over everything a second time, slowly, lovingly, tiresomely, sensing with his fingers some imperceptible little point of hair on the chin or cheek. Occasionally, weary of looking at the ceiling while the barber went over and over his jaws, Rubião would ask for a rest. While he was resting, he would touch his face and feel the change.

"The mustache isn't very long," he observed.

"The ends have to be fixed; I have my small irons here to curl it over the lip and then I'll do the ends. Oh! I'd rather do ten original styles than one copy."

Ten minutes more passed before the mustache and the goatee were touched up. At last it was ready. Rubião bounded up and ran to the floor mirror in his bedroom; it was the other man whom he saw there, it was both of them, in short, it was he, himself.

"Precisely," he exclaimed, returning to the study, where, having collected his instruments, the barber was patting Quincas Borba. Going over to the secretary, he opened a drawer, took out a twenty thousand reis bill, and gave it to the barber.

"I haven't any change," said the latter.

"You needn't give back any change," Rubião said quickly, with a haughty gesture; "take out what you must to pay the establishment and the rest is yours."

CXLVII

After he was alone, Rubião threw himself into an armchair and watched a parade that was passing in his mind. He was in Biarritz or Compiègne, we don't know exactly, he heard the ministers and ambassadors, he danced, he dined—and he did other things that had been reported in newspaper dispatches that he had read and that had stayed in his mind. Not even Quincas Borba's whining succeeded in arousing him. He was far away and high above. Compiègne was on the road to the moon, and he was on his way to the moon.

When he came down from the moon, he heard the dog's whining, and his jaws felt cold. He ran to the mirror and ascertained that there was, indeed, a great difference between the bearded face and the shaven one, but that the shaven one was not unbecoming. His dinner guests reached the same conclusion.

"It looks fine! You should have done it a long time ago! Not that the beard detracted from the dignity of your face; but as it is now, it has all it had before and a modern look in addition—"

"Modern," repeated the host.

Other people were equally surprised. All sincerely thought that this new appearance was more becoming to him than the old. Only one person, Doctor Camacho, though he thought the goatee and mustache suited his friend very well, declared that it was wise not to alter the face, which is the true mirror of the soul, whose strength and constancy it should reproduce.

"I shouldn't speak of myself," he concluded. "But you'll never see my face any different from what it is now. With me that is a moral necessity. My life, sacrificed to principles—because I never tried to conciliate principles, but, rather, men—my life, I say, is a faithful image of my face, and vice-versa."

Rubião listened seriously, and nodded that indeed it should be so. At the moment he was thinking of himself as Emperor of the French, traveling through, incognito; when he descended to the street, he returned to his former self. Dante, who saw so many remarkable things, asserts that he witnessed in the Inferno the punishment of a Florentine shade, whom a six-footed serpent so encircled in its coil that the two merged, and finally one could no longer distinguish if it were one creature or two. Rubião was still two. His own person and the Emperor of the French did not fuse within him. They took turns, and even forgot each other's existence. When Rubião was just himself, he was the same as ever. When he rose to the position of Emperor of the French, he was just the Emperor. Each offset the other, each was a complete individual.

"Why the change?" Sophia asked, when he showed up at the end of the week.

"I've come to find out about your knee. Is it well?"

"Thank you, yes."

It was two o'clock in the afternoon. Sophia had just dressed to go out when the maid came to tell her that Rubião was there—so changed that he looked like someone else.

"But why the change?" she repeated.

Not having any imperial feeling at the moment, Rubião replied that he thought the mustache and goatee was more becoming.

"Or am I uglier?" he concluded.

"It's better, much better."

And Sophia said to herself that she might be the cause of the change. She sat down on the sofa and began to pull on her gloves.

"You're going out?"

"Yes, but the carriage hasn't come yet."

She dropped one of her gloves; as Rubião started to pick it up, she did the same. Both touched the glove, and since each was determined to pick it up, their faces collided in midair, and her nose struck his. Their mouths, however, were left intact, so that they could laugh; and they did.

"Did I hurt you?"

"No! I should ask you—"

And again they laughed. Sophia put on her glove, and until the servant came to say that the carriage had come, Rubião watched one of her feet, which was furtively restless. Then they rose, and once more they laughed.

Stiffly, and with bared head, the lackey opened the *coupé* door when Sophia appeared at the door of the house. Rubião offered to assist her; she accepted the courtesy, and got in.

"For now, good—"

She could not finish; Rubião had gotten in after her, the lackey closed the door, climbed onto the cushion, and the carriage started off.

It all went so fast that Sophia could neither speak nor move; however, after a few moments, she said:

"What's this? —Mr. Rubião, stop the carriage."

"Stop it? But didn't you tell me that you were going out and waiting for it?"

"I wasn't going out with you— Don't you see that— Stop it."

Distracted, she, herself was about to order the driver to stop; but the fear of a possible scandal detained her half way. The *coupé* had entered Bella da Princeza Street. Sophia again implored Rubião to consider the unseemliness of their being together in the eyes of God and all the world. Rubião respected her scruple, and proposed that they pull down the curtains.

"I don't think that there's any harm in their seeing us; but if the curtains are down, nobody will see us. Shall I?"

And without waiting for an answer, he drew the curtains down on each side. The two were left alone, then, because if they could see an occasional passerby, no one could see them from outside. Alone, completely alone, as on that day in her home at the same hour—two o'clock in the afternoon—when Rubião had flung all his despair into her face. There, at least, the young woman had been free; here, inside of a closed carriage, she was unable to calculate the consequences.

Sophia had shrunk as far as possible into the corner. Perhaps it was because of the strangeness of the situation or because of fear, but mainly it was because of repugnance. Never had that man made her feel such aversion, such loathing, or something else less strong, if you wish, but which was really nothing more nor less than incompatibility of—how shall I put it so as not to offend the ear?—incompatibility of the epidermis. Where were the dreams of a few days before? At the mere invitation to a ride alone to Tijuca, she had galloped up the height with him, dismounted, listened to adoring words, and felt a kiss upon the nape of her neck. Where were those imaginings? Where were the large, gazing eyes, the long, affectionate handclasps, the gentle words, the compassionate ears? All forgotten, all vanished, now that they were really alone together, insulated by the carriage and by scandal.

The horses went on their way, thrusting their hooves forward, slowly dragging the carriage over the stones of Bella da Princeza Street. What would she do when she reached Cattete? Would she go to the city with him? She considered going on to the house of some friend; she would leave him inside and tell the driver to go on. She would tell her husband everything. In the midst of that agony, some banal or irrelevant thoughts went through her mind, such as the news of a jewel robbery that she had read about in the papers that morning, the strong wind of the day before, a hat. Finally she concentrated on a single concern. What was she going to say to Rubião? She saw that he was still looking straight ahead, saying nothing, the head of his cane resting against his chin. The pose, quiet, serious, all but indifferent was not unbecoming to him; but why had he gotten into the carriage? Sophia wanted to break the silence; twice she nervously moved her hands; she was almost annoyed by the quiet of the man, whose action could be explained solely by his old and violent passion. Then she supposed that later he, himself, would be sorry, and she told him so with kind words.

"I don't see that I can be sorry for anything," he said, turning around. "When you said that it was unseemly for us to be together thus in the eyes of the public, I lowered the curtains. I didn't agree, but I obeyed."

"We're coming to Cattete," she interrupted. "Do you wish me to take you home? We can't go to the city together."

"We can go at random."

"What do you mean?"

"At random; the horses going along and we conversing, without anyone's hearing us or even guessing—"

"For the love of Heaven! Don't talk to me that way. Leave me, get out of the carriage, or I'll get out myself, right here, mark my words. What do you wish to say? You'll not need more than a few minutes. Look, we're turning in the direction of the city; have him go to Botafogo; I'll leave you at your door—"

"But I just left my house; I'm going to the city.

"What harm is there in taking me there? If we aren't seen, I'll get out anywhere—at Santa Luzia Beach, for instance—on the ocean side."

"It would be best to get out right here."

"But why can't we go to the city?"

"No, it's impossible. I beseech you, by all that's most holy. Don't make a scandal. Come, tell me what I must do to obtain such a simple thing? Do you want me to kneel right here?"

Despite the narrow space she was already bending her knees; but Rubião quickly made her sit down again.

"You needn't kneel," he said softly.

"Thank you. Then I beg you, for the sake of God, for the sake of your mother, who is in Heaven—"

"She must be in Heaven," agreed Rubião. "She was a saintly woman. Mothers are always good; but no one who knew her will be able to say anything but that she was a saint. And there were not many as accomplished as she. What a hostess! It was all the same to her if there were five or fifty guests, she attended to everything in its turn and right on time. She became famous. The slaves called her *Sinhá Mãe* because she really was a mother to everyone. She must be in Heaven!"

"Well, well," interrupted Sophia, "then do this for the sake of your mother. Will you do it?"

"What?"

"Get out right here!"

"And walk to the city? I can't. It's just a whim of yours; no one's going to see us. And then these horses are magnificent. I've noticed how they throw out their hooves slowly, clop—clop—clop—clop—"

Weary of imploring, Sophia said no more, folded her arms, and, if such a thing were possible, moved even closer into the corner of the carriage.

"Now I know," she thought. "I'll have it stopped at the entrance to Christiano's warehouse; and I'll tell him the way this man got into the *coupé*, how I entreated him to get out, and how he answered me. That'll be better than having him get out mysteriously on some street."

Meanwhile, Rubião was quiet. Now and again he would turn the diamond ring on his finger—a splendid solitaire. He did not look at Sophia, nor say anything to her, nor ask her for anything. They were like a bored husband and wife. Sophia was beginning to be wholly baffled as to why he had gotten into the carriage. It couldn't have been mere need of transportation. Nor vanity, either, because he had drawn the curtains at her first complaint that they were exposed to public observation. Not one amorous word, not one allusion, however remote, timid, worshipful, and beseeching. Really, he was inexplicable, a freak.

CLIII

"Sophia—" Rubião said, suddenly, and continued hesitatingly: "Sophia, the days pass, but no man ever forgets the woman who truly loved him, or he does not deserve the name of man. Our love will never be forgotten—by me, that is certain, nor by you, I am sure. You have given me everything, Sophia; your very life was in danger. Of course it is true that I would avenge you, my beautiful one; if vengeance can please the dead, you will have the greatest pleasure possible. Happily, my destiny protected us, and we were able to love freely and without bloodshed—"

The young woman was looking at him aghast.

"Do not be afraid," he continued. "We shall not separate; no, I am not speaking of separation. Do not tell me that you would die. I know that you would shed copious tears. Not I— for I did not come into the world to weep—yet, for all of that, my sorrow would not be less; on the contrary, sorrows that are kept within the heart are more painful than the other kind. Tears are good because they mitigate one's suffering. Dear one, I am saying this because we must be careful; our insatiable passion may forget that need. We have grown very lax, Sophia; since we were born for each other, it seems to us that we are married and we have grown lax. Listen, my beloved! Listen, dearheart— Life is beautiful! Life is grand! Life is sublime! And yet, when it is shared with you, what adjective is there that can describe it? Do you remember our first meeting?"

As Rubião spoke this last word, he tried to take Sophia's hand, but she drew back in time. She was confused, bewildered, and afraid. His voice was growing louder, the driver would hear— And then a suspicion struck her—perhaps Rubião's intention was precisely to make himself heard in order to frighten her into submission—or in order that she be defamed. She had the impulse to throw herself at him, to cry for help, and save herself through scandal.

After a brief pause, he murmured:

"I remember as if it were yesterday. You arrived in a carriage; it was not this one; it was a silver carriage, a calash. You got out of it timidly, with a veil over your face; you were quivering like a leaf— But my arms supported you— The sun must have stopped that day, as when it obeyed Joshua— And yet, my blossom, those hours were deucedly long, I don't know why; by all rights they should have been short. Perhaps it was because our passion was never-ending; it has never ended, nor will it ever end. —We didn't see the sun again anyway, because it was dropping behind the mountains when my Sophia, timid still, went out into the street and took another calash. Another or the same one? I believe it was the same one. You can't imagine the state I was in; I was like a madman; I kissed everything you had touched; I even kissed the threshold of the door. I believe I have already told you that. The threshold of the door. And I almost, almost crawled to kiss the steps of the stairway—I didn't though—I went back and locked myself in, so as not to lose your fragrance—violet, if I remember correctly."

No, it could not be that Rubião's plan was to make the driver believe a fictitious adventure, because his voice was so faint that Sophia could scarcely hear it. But if she had difficulty hearing the words, she was completely unable to comprehend their meaning. What was the purpose of that false story? Whoever might have heard it would have accepted it as true, such was its note of sincerity, the gentleness of its tone, and the verisimilitude of its details. And on and on he went, sadly expressing his beautiful memories—

"But what jest is this?" Sophia interrupted, finally.

Our friend did not answer—he had the vision before his eyes; he did not hear the question and he continued. He referred to a concert of Gottschalk. The divine pianist was playing; and they were listening, but the confounded music made them look into each other's eyes, and everything else was forgotten. When the music stopped, there was a burst of applause, and they awakened from their trance. Alas, unhappily they awakened with Palha's eye upon them like the eye of a wild panther. That night he thought he would kill her.

"Mr. Rubião—"

"Napoleon. No, call me Louis. I am your Louis, your dear Louis. Yours, yours; call me yours, your Louis, your dear Louis. Oh, if you know how happy you make me when you say those two words: 'My Louis!' You are my Sophia—the sweet, dear Sophia of my heart's desire. Let us not waste these moments; let us speak tender words, but more softly, very softly, so that the tattlers up on the driver's cushion won't hear. Why must there be drivers in this world? If the carriage went by itself, one could speak as one pleased and go to the ends of the earth."

They were now driving alongside the Passeio Público. Sophia, however, did not notice; she was staring at Rubião. Calculated perversity it could not be, nor did she accuse him of mockery— Delirium, yes, that was it, for he was speaking with all the sincerity of one who actually sees or has seen the things of which he speaks.

"I must put him out here," thought that young woman. And, summoning her courage: "I wonder where we are?" she asked. "This is a chance to separate. Look out your side. Where are we? It looks like the convent; we're in Ajuda Square. Tell the driver to stop; or, if you wish, you may get out at Carioca Square. My husband—"

"I'll appoint him ambassador," said Rubião. "Or senator, if you wish, senator would be better, because both of you then could stay here. Even if he were ambassador, I'd not let you go with him and evil tongues— You know all the opposition and slander I have to put up with— Oh, people can be mean. The Ajuda Convent, did you say? Why are you interested in it? Do you wish to become a nun?"

"No, I said that we'd already passed the Ajuda Convent. I'll let you out at Carioca Square. Or shall we go on to my husband's warehouse?"

Sophia was again leaning toward the second alternative, because in that way the driver would not be so suspicious of her, and she could better prove her innocence to Palha by telling him everything from the moment of Rubião's unexpected entrance into the carriage to that of his raving. And what was the meaning of his raving? The thought came to Sophia that she, herself, might be the cause of it, and the conjecture made her smile with pity.

"Why?" said Rubião. "I'll get out right here; it's safer. Why should he distrust us and mistreat you? I can punish him, of course, but I should always feel remorseful for any harm he might do you. No, dear, lovely flower, be assured that I should drive from space as unworthy any wind that dared to touch you. You do not yet know my power, Sophia. Come, confess that you don't."

As Sophia made no confession, Rubião told her she was pretty and offered her the solitaire that he was wearing on his finger; but, although she loved jewelry and had an intuitive appreciation of solitaires, she was afraid to accept the offer.

"I understand your scruple," he said, "however, you'll not lose thereby, because you'll receive an even finer stone from your husband. I'll make you a duchess. Did you hear? The title is given to him, but it is you who are the reason for it. Duke— Duke of what? I'll see if I can find an attractive title; or, choose it yourself, because it's for you; it's not for him, it's for you, my pet. You don't have to choose now; go home and think it over. Don't hesitate; let me know by message what you consider the most attractive, and I'll have the decree prepared at once. Or you can choose, and tell me the first time we meet at our accustomed place. I wish to be the first to call you Duchess. 'Dear Duchess—' the decree will follow— Beloved Duchess!"

"Yes, yes," she said, distractedly, "but let's tell the driver to take us to Christiano's warehouse."

"No, I'll get out here— Stop! Stop!"

Rubião raised the curtains, and the lackey came to open the door. To dispel any suspicions of the latter, Sophia once more begged Rubião to go with her to her husband's warehouse; she said that Palha had to speak to him about an urgent matter. Rubião looked at her somewhat surprised; then he looked at the lackey and at the street, and said that he would not go now, he would go later.

CLIV

The moment they were separated, a contrasting mood came upon them.

Rubião looked all about in the street; reality was taking hold of him and his delirium was disappearing. He walked ahead, stopped in front of a shop and detained an acquaintance, whom he asked for news and his opinions regarding it, all of which was an unconscious effort on his part to shake off his borrowed personality.

As soon as her surprise and alarm were past, Sophia, on the other hand, plunged into revery; all Rubião's fiction made her long—long for what?—"Long for Heaven" is what Father Bernardes said of a good Christian's feelings. Various names gleamed like so many lightning flashes in the blue of that vision that might so well have been reality. What a wealth of interesting detail! Sophia reconstructed the old calash that she had quickly entered and from which she had tremulously alighted to glide through the corridor, and climb the stairs to meet the man, who had said the most delightful things, and had repeated them just now at her side in the carriage. But it was not Rubião, it could not be. Who might it be? Again various names gleamed like so many lightning flashes in the blue sky of that vision that might so well have been reality.

C L V

The news of Rubião's obsession spread. Some, who happened to meet him when his madness was upon him, experimented to see if the rumor were true; they would lead the conversation to the affairs of France; the Emperor Rubião would slip into the abyss, and they would be convinced.

C L V I

Several months passed, the Franco-Prussian war broke out, and Rubião's crises became more acute, and far less apart. When the European mail arrived early, he would leave Botafogo before lunch, and hurry to await the papers; he would buy the *Correspondencia de Portugal* and go to the Carceler * to read it.

* *Translator's Note:* The *Carceler* was an elegant restaurant in Rio de Janeiro used as a gathering place by the upper classes. It no longer exists.

Whatever the news, he always interpreted it as victory. He would count up the dead and wounded, and invariably found a large balance in his favor. For him Napoleon's fall was King Wilhelm's capture, and the revolution of the fourth of September a banquet for the Bonapartists.

His dinner guests at home did not try to dissuade him; nor, abashed by the other's presence, did they confirm what he had to say. They merely smiled and changed the subject. Meanwhile, all had acquired military titles, Marshal Torres, Marshal Pio, Marshal Ribeiro, and they answered to their title. To Rubião they appeared to be in uniform; he would order a reconnoitre or an attack, and they would not have to leave to obey; their host's brain did the whole thing. When Rubião returned from the battlefield to the table, the latter was no longer the same. Without silver now, almost without porcelain or crystal, it still appeared royally splendid in the eyes of Rubião.

Upon wretched, skinny hens was conferred the title of pheasants; mediocre stews, poorly cooked, had the savor of the daintiest tidbits. The guests would make some comment among themselves—or to the cook—but Lucullus always dined with Lucullus. And all the rest of the house, too worn from time and lack of care, faded carpets, soiled curtains, furniture that was broken and falling apart, had not its true appearance, but another, shining and magnificent. Language, too, was different; round and full so that ideas, some of them extraordinary, like those of his deceased friend, Quincas Borba—theories that he had not comprehended when he had heard them formerly in Barbacena—he now repeated clearly and with understanding, occasionally using the same expressions as the philosopher. How explain that repetition of the obscure, that knowledge of the inscrutable, when the ideas and the words that expressed them seemed to have gone with the wind of another day? And why did all those memories vanish with the return of reason?

Once Sophia had explained Rubião's malady by the love he had
for her—her compassion was midway between pure sympathy
and uncompromising egotism; it was neither, exclusively, one
nor the other, but it was partly both. Provided she could avoid
any incident like that of the *coupé*, all went well. During
Rubião's periods of lucidity, she listened and talked to him
with interest—because, though it made him bold during moments of crisis, his illness redoubled his timidity when he was
normal. She did not smile as Palha did, when Rubião ascended
the throne or commanded an army. Believing herself the cause
of his ailment, she forgave him for it; and the thought that the
man had loved her to the point of madness sanctified him in
her eyes.

"Why doesn't he have treatment?" Dona Fernanda asked one
evening. She had met him there the year before. "It's possible
that he can be cured."

"It doesn't appear to be serious," said Palha. "He has these
attacks of megalomania, but they're mild, and they soon pass;
and notice that outside of that he converses perfectly well. And
yet, it's possible— What do you think?"

Dona Fernanda's husband, Theophilo, replied that it was
quite possible.

"What did he do before, or what's he doing now?" the deputy
continued.

"Nothing either before or now. He was wealthy—but extravagant. We met him when he came from Minas, and we were his
guide, so to speak, in Rio de Janeiro. He had not been there
for many years. He's a good man. He always lived in luxury,
you know. But no amount of wealth is inexhaustible when
one goes into the capital, and that's what he did. I believe he
has little today—"

"You could save that little for him if you had yourself named his guardian while he's being treated. I'm not a doctor, but I think it quite possible that your friend can be cured."

"I don't deny it. Really, it's a pity— He gets along with everyone, and is always ready to help. You know he nearly became a relative of ours. He wanted to marry Maria Benedicta."

"Speaking of Maria Benedicta," interrupted Dona Fernanda, "I was forgetting that I have a letter from her to show your wife. I received it yesterday. Did you know that they'll soon be back? Here it is."

She handed the letter to Sophia, who opened it without enthusiasm, and read it with boredom. It was more than an ordinary transatlantic letter, it was a spiritual deposit, the full and intimate confession of a happy and grateful person. She recounted the trip's most recent events, but without any fixed order, since superimposed upon everything were the travelers themselves. More important than the finest works of man or Nature were the eyes that looked upon them.

Sometimes an incident pertaining to a particular hostelry or a particular street had been of greater interest than others and had consumed more paper in the telling, for the reason that it had more clearly revealed her husband's virtues. Maria Benedicta was as much or more in love than the first day. Finally, in a timid post-script, asking that Dona Fernanda say nothing to anyone, she confessed that she was to become a mother.

Sophia folded the paper, not with boredom this time, but with resentment for which there were two contradictory causes. But then, contradiction is characteristic of this world. If that letter were compared with the ones she had received from Maria Benedicta, one would say that she was merely an acquaintance with no bond of kinship or affection, and yet she really would not want to be the confidante of that happiness whispered across the ocean, filled with details, adjectives, exclamations, Carlos Maria's name, Carlos Maria's eyes, Carlos Maria's witty sayings, and, finally, Carlos Maria's child. It appeared premeditated and almost made one suspect complicity on the part of Dona Fernanda. Clever as she was, Sophia managed to recover her composure quickly; she concealed her resentment and handed back her cousin's letter. She wanted to say that, judging from the contents, Maria Benedicta's happiness must be as intact as the day she had carried it away with her, but her voice stuck in her throat. It was Dona Fernanda who took upon herself the responsibility to conclude:

"It's obvious that she's happy!"

"It appears so."

Had the following morning not been rainy, Sophia's mood would have been different. Not that the sun is always a guarantee of good humor; but it does, at least, allow one to go out, and a change of scene alters one's feeling. When Sophia awakened, it was raining hard and steadily, and so low were the clouds and so thick was the fog that sea and sky were one.

Gloom inside and out. Nothing to divert the eyes and repose the soul. Sophia laid her soul away in a cedar coffin which she enclosed in the leaden one of the day's mist and rain. Then she was sincerely convinced that she was dead. She did not know that the dead think, that a swarm of new thoughts takes the place of the old, and that just as spectators leave the theater criticizing the play and the actors, so do these new thoughts emerge criticizing the world. The deceased felt that some of her ideas and sensations were a continuation of life. They were all higgledy-piggledy, but they did have a common point of departure—the letter of the day before, and the memories that it brought of Carlos Maria.

Indeed, she had thought that she had put that despised figure away from her, and here it was again; that egotistical, infatuated idler, smiling, looking intently at her, whispering into her ears the same words that one day invited her to dance the waltz of adultery and then left her standing in the middle of the room. Other figures clustered around this one, that of Maria Benedicta, for example, whom she had taken from the country to give her some urban polish, and who forgot all the favors and remembered only her ambition. And Dona Fernanda, too, the patroness of her love affair, who, the day before, had deliberately brought Maria Benedicta's letter with its confidential postscript. She did not realize that her friend's pleasure might have sufficed to explain her having forgotten the secret part of the letter; even less did she ask herself if Dona Fernanda's ethical sense allowed of such a supposition. There came other thoughts and images, and they were all continually coalescing and separating. Among them appeared a recollection of the day before. Dona Fernanda's husband had enveloped Sophia in a deeply admiring gaze. It was, indeed, one of her best days; her frock attractively emphasized the contours of her bust, the slenderness of her waist, and the graceful outline of her hips;—it was of straw-colored foulard.

When Dona Fernanda admired it, shortly after her arrival, Sophia laughingly stressed the word straw *—"straw-colored as a memento of that gentleman."

It is not easy to hide the pleasure of flattery; the husband smiled proudly, searching the others' eyes for the effect of that meticulous proof of his wife's love. Theophilo, too, praised the dress; however, it was hard to look at it without looking also at the body of its wearer; hence the admiring glances that he cast upon it; but it seemed to Sophia that his admiration, that unsolicitated gesture, had been free from lust for, when she thought of it, the memory of the previous day's admiration which had, indeed, been without desire, intervened.

And, as was stated in Chapter CLIV, Carlos Maria, Theophilo—other names gleamed like so many lightning flashes in the sky of that vision that might so well have been real. They all came to her now because the rain, which was falling still, and sea and sky, were fused by the heavy mist. They all came, those names, with the individuals that corresponded to them, and there even came some nameless individuals—the casual strangers—who had passed by only once, sung their hymn of praise, and received their little good will offering. Why had she not retained one of so many, so that she might hear him sing

* The Portuguese word for straw is *palha*.

and make him rich? Not that alms make anyone rich, but there are gifts of greater value. Why had she not retained one of all those elegant and even illustrious names? That wordless question ran through her veins, her nerves and her brain, but perturbation and wonder were its only answer.

C L X

The rain stopped a little, a ray of sunlight succeeded in breaking through the fog—one of those misty rays that appear to come from eyes that have been crying. Sophia thought that she might still be able to go out; she was eager to look about, to walk, to shake off that torpor, and waited for the sun to sweep away the rain and take possession of the sky and earth. The great celestial body perceived, however, that she intended to make him a lantern of Diogenes, and so he said to the misty ray, "Come back, come back to my breast, chaste and virtuous ray; you must not lead her to the destination of her desire. Let her be in love, if she wishes; let her answer love notes—if she receives them and does not burn them—but, light of my bosom, child of my heart, ray, brother of all my other rays, do not serve as her torch."

And the ray obeyed, returning to its focal point, a little surprised by the trepidation of the sun, that has seen so many things, both ordinary and extraordinary. Then the veil of clouds became heavy once more, and darker, and again the rain beat down.

C L X I

Sophia resigned herself to staying in. Her mind was now as confused and diffuse as the scene outside. All the images and names became lost in the one desire to be in love. It is only fair to say that whenever she roused herself from these nebulous and obscure states of conscience, she would try to escape from them and direct her thoughts to other channels; but then she would have an experience like that of one who is sleepy, and whose eyes, though he is fighting against his drowsiness, keep opening and shutting. Finally she withdrew her gaze from the rain and fog; she was tired, and, to rest, she opened the pages of the most recent number of the *Revue des Deux Mondes*. One day, when the work of the Alagoas committee had been at its height, one of the fashionable ladies of the moment, the wife of a senator, had asked her:

"Are you reading Feuillet's novel in the *Revue des Deux Mondes?*"

"Yes, I am," said Sophia. "It's very interesting."

She was not reading it, nor did she know the *Revue*; but the next day she asked her husband to subscribe to it. She read the novel and every one that came out afterwards, and talked about them all. After she had opened the current number and finished a story, Sophia retired to her room and threw herself on the bed. As she had had a bad night, she fell easily into a long, deep sleep, which was dreamless except at the last, when she had a nightmare. She was in front of the same wall of fog that she had been looking at before she fell asleep, but at sea, in the prow of a launch, lying prone and writing a name on the water with her finger—Carlos Maria. The letters remained engraved upon the water, and were made all the more clear by furrows of foam. Up to this point there was nothing startling unless it were the mysteriousness of it, but it is a known fact that in dreams the mysterious seems natural. Then the wall of fog broke and none other than the owner of the name appeared before Sophia's eyes, went toward her, took her in his arms, and spoke many tender words like those she had heard from Rubião several months before. And they did not trouble her as the latter's had; on the contrary, she listened to them with pleasure, leaning partly backwards as though in a faint. She was no longer in a launch, but in a carriage with Carlos Maria, who was holding her hands and making love to her with a tongue of gold and sandalwood. Nor was there anything alarming about this. Alarm came when the carriage stopped and was surrounded by a number of masked figures who killed the driver, pulled off the doors, stabbed Carlos Maria and flung his corpse to the ground. Then, one, who appeared to be the leader, took the dead man's place, removed his mask, and told Sophia not to be afraid, that he loved her a hundred thousand times more than the other man had. Then he seized her wrists and gave her a kiss; but it was a kiss wet with blood and smelling of blood. Sophia uttered a cry of horror and awoke. Her husband was beside her bed.

"What is it?" he asked.

"Ah!" sighed Sophia. "I cried out. Did I not cry out?"

Palha made no reply; he was thinking about business matters which gave him an absent-minded air. Then a fear struck his wife; she wondered if she had, in fact, spoken, murmured some word, some name—the one she had written on the water. And then, stretching her arms up into the air, she let them fall on her husband's shoulders, interlocked her finger tips on the back of his neck, and murmured, half gaily, half sadly:

"I dreamed that you were being killed."

Palha was touched. To have made her suffer for his sake, even in dreams, filled him with pity; a pleasing pity, however, a very special feeling, deep and intimate—that in all likelihood made him want more nightmares so that he might again be killed before her eyes, and so that she would be convulsed with anguish and cry out in terror.

CLXII

The following day the sun appeared bright and warm, the sky was clear, the air fresh. To seek release from seclusion, Sophia got into her carriage and went visiting. The day itself put her into a happy mood. She had hummed while dressing. The conversation of the women who received her in their homes and of those whom she met on Ouvidor Street, the society gossip, the hustle and bustle of the city, the genial aspect of so many friendly people sufficed to dispel the previous day's troubles.

CLXIII

And so, what had appeared to be an imperious desire was no more than a caprice; after an interval of a few hours all the evil thoughts withdrew to their hideaways. If you should ask me for some remorse on the part of Sophia, I know not what to say. There is a scale of distress and reproach; and it is not in actions alone that the conscience passes gradually from novelty to habit and from fear to indifference. Sins committed in thought alone are subject to that same variation, and the habit of thinking about things so affects them that finally they cease to startle or repel the mind. In such cases, too, there is always a moral refuge in outward exemption, that is, in more explicit terms, in an immaculate body.

CLXIV

A single incident perturbed Sophia on that clear, bright day— a meeting with Rubião. She had gone into a bookstore on Ouvidor Street to buy a novel; while she was waiting for change, she saw her friend come in. She turned her face away quickly and looked at the books on the shelf—some books on anatomy and statistics. She received her money, put it away, and, with lowered head, swift as an arrow, went out and started up the street. Not until Ourives Street was left behind did her blood flow quietly.

Some days later, as she was entering Dona Fernanda's house, she met him in the vestibule. She thought that he was going to mount the stairs, and it was not without reluctance that she, too, started up. Rubião, however, was coming down. They shook hands familiarly and parted, saying they would see each other again in the afternoon.

"Does he come here often?" Sophia asked Dona Fernanda, after telling her about the meeting in the vestibule.

"This is the fourth time, fourth or fifth; but only the second time did he appear to be raving. The other times he was as you saw him now, calm and even in a conversational mood. There's always something about him, though, that's obviously not quite right. Haven't you noticed it in the rather vague look in his eyes? That's what it is; otherwise, he converses well. Rest assured, Sophia; that man can be cured. Why don't you make your husband do something about it?"

"Christiano does plan to have him examined and treated; but don't worry, I'll press the matter."

"Yes, do. He seems to be a very good friend of you both."

"In his madness can he have said something about me that he shouldn't?" thought Sophia. "Will it be well to tell her the truth?"

She concluded that it would not. Rubião's ailment itself would explain anything that he might say amiss. She promised that she would press her husband, and, indeed, she broached the subject to Palha that very afternoon. "It's a big nuisance," he retorted. He asked what interest Dona Fernanda had in concerning herself with it. Let her treat him herself! It was annoying to have to take care of someone else and look after him, and, as he would probably have to do, put aside and manage what little money he might have left, becoming his guardian as Doctor Theophilo had said. It was a confounded bother.

"I already have a big load on my shoulders, Sophia. And, then, what'll we do? Shall we bring him to the house? Hardly. Where'll we put him? In some sanitarium—yes, but what if they can't take him? I'll not send him to Vermelha Beach. And all the responsibilities? Did you promise that you'd speak to me?"

"I promised, and I said that you'd do it," said Sophia, smiling. "It may not be so bad as it seems."

Sophia continued to insist. Dona Fernanda's pity had greatly impressed her; she found that there was something distinguished and noble about it, and she thought that if the other woman, who was neither an old nor close friend of Rubião, showed such an interest, it would be good taste on her part to be no less generous.

C L X V

It was all done quietly. Palha rented a little house on Príncipe Street, near the sea, where he put our Rubião, with a few pieces of furniture and his devoted dog. Rubião accepted the change willingly, and, when his madness was upon him, enthusiastically. He was in his palace at Saint-Cloud.

Not so with the friends of the house, who received the news of the move as if it were a decree of exile. Everything in the former abode had become a part of them: the garden, the grating, the flower beds, the stone steps, the bay. They knew it all by heart. It was just a matter of going in, hanging up their hats, and entering the drawing room to wait. They had lost the notion that it was a courtesy that they were receiving. And then there was the neighborhood. Everyone of Rubião's friends was used to seeing the people of that district, the same faces every morning and every afternoon. Some of these would come in to greet them, as if they were their neighbors. But! have patience! Like the exiles from Zion, they would go now to Babylon. Wherever might be the Euphrates, they would find a willow tree upon which to hang their nostalgic harps—or, more properly, hooks, upon which to put their hats. The difference between them and the prophets is that, at the end of a week, they would again take up their instruments and pluck them with the same grace and force; they would sing the old hymns, as new as they had been on the first day, and Babel would become the same old Zion, lost and redeemed.

"Our friend needs rest for awhile," Palha said to them in

Botafogo the day before the moving. "You must have noticed that he is not well; he has moments of forgetfulness and aberration; he is going to undergo treatment, and so he needs rest. I have found a small house for him, but even so, he may have to go to a sanitarium."

They listened in astonishment. One of them, Pio, regaining his composure more quickly than the others, said that that should have been done long ago, but only someone to whom Rubião would listen could persuade him.

"I often told him politely that he must consult a doctor, as it appeared to me there was something wrong with his stomach— Of course that was just a euphemism, you understand— But he always answered that there was nothing wrong with him, that his digestion was good— 'But you're eating less,' I said. 'There are days when you're eating almost nothing; you're thinner and slightly sallow—' I couldn't tell him the truth, you know. I even consulted a doctor friend of mine, but Rubião wouldn't see him."

The other four were nodding corroboration of that fictitious tale; after all, following such a stunning blow, that's all that could be expected of them, and all they could do. Finally they asked the number of the new house so that they might go there to inquire about their poor friend. Poor, poor friend! When at last they tore themselves away, and took leave of one another, they had a strange experience that they were not counting on; they found that they could scarcely bear to part with one another. Not that they were bound by friendship or esteem; in fact, since each was looking out solely for himself, they each had an instinctive dislike for one another. However, the habit of seeing one another every day at the same table for lunch and dinner had, as it were, welded them together; necessity had made them mutually tolerable, and time, mutually necessary. In short, the eyes of each were going to miss the familiar gestures, faces, whiskers, mustaches, bald spots, and peculiar mannerisms of his companions; their ways of eating, and talking, and doing things. It was not just separation, it was dismemberment.

Rubião noticed that they had not accompanied him to the new house, and he sent for them. No one came, however, and their absence filled our friend with sadness. His family was abandoning him. He tried to remember whether he had in any way offended them by word or deed; but he could think of nothing.

"I talked with the man and found that he had some crazy ideas. However, though I'm not an alienist, I think that he can recover— But would you like to know an interesting discovery that I made?"

"You think he can recover?" said Dona Fernanda, disregarding Doctor Falcão's question.

Doctor Falcão, a family friend, was a deputy and a doctor, a learned man, skeptical and unfeeling. Dona Fernanda had asked him, as a favor, to examine Rubião, shortly after the latter had moved to the little house on Príncipe Street.

"Yes, I think he'll recover as soon as he has regular treatment. It may be that there's not been any such illness in the family before. Have him see a specialist. But don't you want to know my interesting discovery?"

"What is it?"

"Perhaps someone whom you know has had something to do with his ailment," he answered, smiling.

"Who?"

"Dona Sophia."

"How could she have?"

"He talked about her enthusiastically, told me that she was the finest woman on earth, and that he had made her a duchess since he could not make her Empress. But they should not play with him, he said, because, like his uncle, he could get a divorce and marry her. I concluded that he must have been passionately in love with the young woman, and then, no doubt, they became intimate— Forgive me, but I believe that they were lovers—"

"Oh, no!"

"Dona Fernanda, I am convinced that they were lovers. What's so strange about that? I hardly know her. Apparently you haven't known her for a long time, and have not been close. Perhaps they had an affair, and perhaps some violent emotion— She may have discarded him. —Of course, he has megalomania, but it all ties in together."

Dona Fernanda was not looking at him. She was vexed by his supposition, and since the subject was a delicate one, she did not care to discuss it. She thought his suspicion without foundation, absurd, unlikely. She could not believe in that spurious love affair, even if she heard it from Rubião himself. He was demented, of course. But even if he were not, she would probably still not believe him. No, she would not believe him. She could not believe that Sophia had had an affair with that man; not because he was what he was, but because she was so decorous, so pure. It was impossible. She wanted to defend Sophia, but despite the fact that Doctor Falcão was a close friend, she recoiled again from discussing the subject. She repeated the question she had just asked:

"You do think, then, that he may recover?"

"He may, but my examination is not enough. You know that a specialist is better in such cases."

Out on the street a little later, Doctor Falcão smiled at Dona Fernanda's reluctance to accept his hypothesis. "Surely, there was something," he said to himself. "He's good-looking; he's not a dandy, to be sure, but he's personable, and has passionate eyes. Surely—" He repeated a few of Rubião's expressions, recalled his gestures and soft tone of voice, and he became more and more convinced of his suspicion— "Surely—"

It was impossible that they had not had an affair; Dona Fernanda's refusal to believe it was naive—unless it were really a subterfuge to change the subject and not discuss the matter. It must have been that—

At this point the deputy stopped involuntarily. A new suspicion struck him. After a few brief moments, he deliberately shook his head as if to give himself the lie, as if he thought himself ridiculous; and he continued on his way. The suspicion was stubborn, however; after all, what is really inside a man pays no heed to the head nor its motions. "Who knows if Dona Fernanda, too, may not have sighed for him? Might not her devotion be a prolongation of love, etc.?" Thus, questions kept arising that found an affirmative answer in Doctor Falcão's mind. He hesitated to believe even now; he was a family friend, he respected Dona Fernanda, knew her to be honorable, and yet, he thought, it might have been a secret, hidden feeling— that might even have been inspired by the other woman's passion— Who knows? There can be temptations like that. Leprosy can pollute the purest blood; one little bacillus can destroy the sturdiest organism.

The whims of resistance were gradually yielding to the notion of possibility, probability and certainty. To be sure, he knew something about Dona Fernanda's works of charity, but this case was different. This special devotion to a man who was neither an habitué of the house nor an old friend, relative, follower, or colleague of her husband, and who, therefore, had no reason, whether through friendship, kinship or habit, to participate in their family life, was inexplicable without some secret motive. Love, surely; because it's curious but true that an honest woman can stray from the path of righteousness into wrongdoing and remorse. Dona Fernanda had probably drawn back in time; but a morbid sympathy had remained— "And hence, who knows?"

CLXVIII

"And hence, who knows?" Doctor Falcão repeated next morning. The night had not allayed his suspicion. "And hence, who knows?" Yes, it was probably not morbid sympathy alone.

Though he was not familiar with Shakespeare, he emended Hamlet: "There are more things in Heaven and earth, Horatio, than are dreamt of in your vain *philanthropy*." No, it bore the imprint of love. But Doctor Falcão had neither mockery nor pity for anything. As I have said, he was a skeptic. However, he was discreet at the same time; so he transmitted his suspicion to no one.

<h2 style="text-align:center">CLXIX</h2>

The return of Carlos Maria and his wife broke into Dona Fernanda's concern over Rubião. She went on shipboard to welcome them, and took them to Tijuca, where an old friend of Carlos Maria's family had rented and furnished a house, following his instructions. Sophia did not go out to the ship; she sent her *coupé* to await them at the Pharoux wharf; but Dona Fernanda already had her calash there, and they went in it, together with Palha and herself. In the afternoon, Sophia made her call.

Dona Fernanda was beside herself with joy. However, she was not immediately able to read in the couple's eyes and manner confirmation of the wild happiness about which Maria Benedicta had written. They did appear contented. Maria Benedicta did not restrain her tears when she embraced her friend, nor did the latter restrain hers, and both clung to each other as if they were blood sisters. Next day, Dona Fernanda asked Maria Benedicta if she and her husband were happy, and when she learned that they were, she seized her hands and gazed at her a long time without finding any words. She could only repeat over and over:

"Are you happy?"

"We are," answered Maria Benedicta.

"You don't know how your answer pleases me. It's not only because I would have had remorse had you not had the happiness that I thought I was giving you, but also because it is good to see others happy. Is he as much in love with you as on the first day?"

"More, I believe, because I adore him!"

Dona Fernanda did not understand that: *More I believe, because I adore him*. In truth, the conclusion did not appear to be in the premise; but it was another case of emending Hamlet: "There are more things in Heaven and earth, Horatio, than are dreamt of in your vain *dialectics*." Maria Benedicta began to tell her about the trip, and to recount her impressions and recollections in detail. When her husband came over to them a little later, she had recourse to his memory to fill in the gaps.

"How was it, Carlos Maria?"

Carlos Maria recalled, explained or rectified, but without interest, almost impatiently. He had guessed that Maria Benedicta had just confided their adventures to the other woman, and he could ill conceal the disagreeable effect it had upon him. Why had she had to tell that she was happy with him, if that were inevitable? Why had she had to divulge his every word, every affectionate gesture, and his god-like compassion?

The return to Rio de Janeiro was a condescension on his part. Maria Benedicta wanted to have her child there, and her husband had yielded; it was not without reluctance—but he had yielded. Why with reluctance? It is hard to explain no less than to understand. Concerning motherhood, Carlos Maria had some peculiar ideas of his own, which he confided to no one. He considered Nature shameless to make of human gestation a public spectacle of deformity and suggestiveness conducive to disrespect. Hence his desire for solitude, secrecy and isolation. He would gladly have spent the last days in a house on a hilltop, forbidden to the world, whence his wife would descend one day with a child in her arms and a divine light in her eyes.

He did not propose this to his wife, however. He would have to argue, and he did not like to argue; he preferred to yield.

Naturally, Maria Benedicta felt quite differently about it; she considered herself a divine and secret temple, wherein dwelt a god, son of one who was also a god. The pregnancy was tiresome and painful, and entailed many discomforts that she concealed from her husband as best she could; all that, however, only made the expected child the more precious. She accepted her suffering with resignation if not joy, since it was inevitable; gladly she accepted the duty of her species and wordlessly she repeated Mary of Nazareth's reply: "Behold, I am the handmaiden of the Lord; let it be to me according to your word."

C L X X

"What's wrong with you?" Maria Benedicta asked her husband as soon as they were alone.

"With me? Nothing. Why?"

"You looked displeased."

"No, I wasn't displeased."

"Yes you were," she insisted.

Carlos Maria smiled but did not answer. Maria already knew that particular inexpressive smile of his, without tenderness or reproof, superficial and pallid. She desisted from her questioning, bit her lips, and withdrew. For some time in her room she thought of nothing but that colorless, mute smile that was a sign of some displeasure for which she alone could be to blame. She reviewed everything she had said and done, but found nothing to explain Carlos Maria's coolness, or whatever his attitude was. Perhaps she had talked too much; it was her way, if she were happy, to put her heart in her hands and distribute it to friends and strangers alike. Carlos Maria reprimanded that generosity, because it made the state of his moral and domestic affairs appear to be a grand lottery, and because he considered it vulgar and common. Maria Benedicta recalled that more than once in the Brazilian colony in Paris, she had felt the effects of her unbridled tongue and had curbed it. But would she have to do so with Dona Fernanda? Was she not the cause of their happiness? Maria rejected that supposition and tried to find another. Not being able to, she went back to the first, and, as happened invariably, she justified her husband. After all, however close a friend Dona Fernanda might be and however sweet, Maria ought not to tell her all the trifling details of her life. That was indiscretion on her part—

Nausea interrupted her at this stage of her reflections. Nature reminded her of a reason of state—the reason for the existence of the species—more urgent and more important than her husband's displeasure. She yielded to necessity, but a few minutes later she was beside Carlos Maria, encircling his neck with her right arm. He was sitting and reading an English review; he took her hand, which lay on his breast, and finished the page.

"Will you forgive me?" his wife asked, when she saw that he had closed the pamphlet.

Carlos Maria took both her hands smilingly, and nodded. Her heart filled with joy; for it was as though he had cast a wave of light over her. It was almost as though the unborn child were responding to the feeling and giving his father his blessing.

CLXXI

"Fine! That's the way I want to see you!" shouted a voice from the side of the veranda.

Maria Benedicta quickly moved away from her husband. One of the doors by which the veranda communicated with the drawing room was open. It was from it that the voice had come, and it was through it that Rubião's laughing face was peering. It was the first time they had seen him. Without getting up, Carlos Maria looked toward him seriously and expectantly. And the face with its full, needle-point-tipped mustache, continued to laugh, looking at them both and repeating:

"Fine! That's the way I want to see you!"

Rubião came in and held out his hand, which they took without any affection. Then he heaped words of admiration and praise upon Maria Benedicta, telling how gracious she was and how elegant Carlos Maria was, and finally he announced the fall of the ministry.

"Has the ministry fallen?" Carlos Maria asked, involuntarily.

"That's all that's being talked about in the city. I'll sit down, if I may, since you haven't offered me a chair," he continued, sitting down and pulling his cane out from under his arm and clasping his hands on it. "Yes, it's true; the ministry asked to resign. I'll organize another. Palha, our Palha, your cousin Palha, and you, too, if you wish, will be a minister. I need a good Cabinet, all strong people, in sympathy with me and capable of laying down their lives for me. I will call Morny, Pio, Camacho, Rouher, and Major Siqueira. Do you remember the Major? I think that he'll be Minister of War, because I don't know anyone more suitable for military matters."

Bored and impatient, Maria Benedicta was walking about the room, waiting for her husband to send her on some errand. The moment that Carlos Maria gave her a look that signified she was to leave, she excused herself and withdrew. After she left, Rubião praised her again—"a flower," he said, and laughingly corrected himself: "two flowers; for I believe there are two flowers. God bless them." Carlos Maria held out his hand as if to say good-by.

"My dear sir—"

"May I include you in the ministry?" asked Rubião.

Hearing no reply, he interpreted it as an affirmative one and promised him a good post. The Major would be for war, and Camacho for justice. Did he not know them, by chance? Two great men, Camacho even greater than the other. And as he was following Carlos Maria, who was going toward the door, he was himself withdrawing, though he was unaware of the fact. He did not leave immediately, however. On the veranda, before going down the steps, he reported on several matters of the war. For example, he had returned Germany to the Germans, which was a fine and politic gesture. He had now given Venice to the Italians, because he did not need more territory; the Rhine provinces, to be sure, but there was time to get them.

"My dear sir—" Carlos Maria insisted, holding out his hand.

He took leave of Rubião and closed the door; Rubião profferred a few more words, and went down the steps. Maria Benedicta, who had been spying on them from an inner room, came to her husband, took hold of his hand, and watched Rubião crossing the garden. He was not walking straight ahead, quickly and quietly; he kept stopping, gesticulating and clutching at a dry twig, all the while seeing in the air around him a thousand things more gracious than the lady of the house and more elegant than the master. They watched our friend from the window, and once, when Rubião did something particularly grotesque, Maria Benedicta could not repress her laughter. Carlos Maria, however, looked on placidly.

CLXXII

"But if the ministry really has fallen," she said, "do you know who is minister?"

Carlos Maria looked at her with eyes that asked, "Who?"

"Your cousin, Theophilo. Nanan told me that he was hoping for it, and that that's why he stayed in the capital this year. He suspected that the ministry would fall or there was already some talk of it. I don't quite remember what she told me. Anyway, it seems he's coming in."

"Maybe."

"Look, there goes Rubião; he's stopped, he's looking up; perhaps he's waiting for the coach or carriage. He used to have a carriage. There he goes—"

CLXXIII

"So, Theophilo is minister!" exclaimed Carlos Maria.

And, after a moment:

"I believe that he'll make a good one. Would you like to see me minister, too?"

"If you want to be, how could I help it?"

"Which means that I'd not be if it depended on your vote alone?" asked Carlos Maria.

"What shall I answer?" she thought, scrutinizing her husband's face.

And he, laughingly:

"Admit that you'd adore me if I were only a minister's orderly."

"Quite," the young woman exclaimed, throwing her arms around his shoulders.

Carlos Maria stroked her hair and murmured seriously: "Bernadotte was King, and Bonaparte Emperor. Would you like to be the Queen Mother of Sweden?"

Maria Benedicta did not understand the question, nor did he explain it. To explain, it would have been necessary to say that she might be carrying a Bernadotte under her heart; that supposition, however, would signify a desire, and the desire a confession of inferiority. Carlos Maria again spread his hands over his wife's head with a gesture that seemed to say, "Maria you chose the better part—" And she seemed to understand the meaning of that gesture.

"Yes, yes!"

Her husband smiled and went back to the English review. Leaning against the armchair, she ran her fingers through his hair very lightly and softly, so as not to disturb him. He went on reading, reading, reading. Maria Benedicta kept lightening her caress and gradually withdrawing her fingers until finally she slipped away from the room. Carlos Maria continued to read a study by Charles Little, M.P. on the famous statue of Narcissus in the Museum of Naples.

CLXXIV

When Rubião went to Dona Fernanda's house, the servant told him that he could not go up. The lady was indisposed; the gentleman was with her; apparently they were waiting for the doctor. Our friend did not persist, and left.

The truth was just the opposite; it was the gentleman who was ill and the lady who was with him; but the servant could not change the message that they gave him. Another servant suspected, indeed, that it was he rather than she who was ill, because he had seen him come in utterly crushed. Upstairs in their room, there was a sound of voices, now loud, now low, with intervals of silence. A little maid, who had gone up on tiptoe, came down saying that she had heard the master lamenting; probably the mistress had been dishonored. Downstairs there was a muffled palaver, pricked up ears, conjectures; they noticed that there were no requests for water, nor for any remedy, nor even for broth, coming from upstairs. The table set, the servant with his tie on, the cook proud and anxious— One of the best dinners!

What was the trouble? Theophilo still looked as crushed as when he had come in; he was sitting on a sofa; he was without a vest, and his eyes were staring. Seated beside him, holding his hands, Dona Fernanda was begging him to calm himself, assuring him that it was not worth it. She bent forward to look into his face, she drew him toward her, wanted him to put his head on her shoulder—

"Leave me alone, leave me alone," murmured her husband.

"It's not worth it, Theophilo! Is a position then—? Can a position that lasts only a short time and involves much unpleasantness and much work and a great many insults be worth so much? Is not a quiet life better? Of course, there's injustice; indeed there is, because you've served well. But can the loss be so great? Come, my dear, calm yourself; and let's have dinner."

Theophilo was biting his lips and pulling his whiskers. He had heard nothing of what his wife had said, either as exhortation or consolation. He had, indeed, heard the conversation of the previous evening and of that morning, the political combinations, the various names suggested, those rejected and those accepted. No combination had included him, although he had expounded to many people the country's actual state of affairs. He had been heard with attention by some, with impatience by others. Once, the organizer's spectacles appeared to question him; but the gesture was rapid and illusory. Theophilo was reliving now all the excitement of those many hours and places —he was recalling those who had looked at him askance, those who had smiled, and those who were wearing the same expression as he. Finally he had not spoken any more; his last hopes were dimly flickering before his eyes like a lamp at dawn. He had heard the names of the ministers, and had been obliged to approve them. But what an effort it had required to articulate a single word! He feared that his frustration and anger might be discovered; yet all his efforts to conceal them only accentuated them the more. He was pale, and his fingers were shaking.

CLXXV

"Come, let's have dinner," Dona Fernanda repeated.

Theophilo slapped his knee with his open hand, and got up uttering disconnected, irate words, pacing back and forth, stamping and threatening. As Dona Fernanda was unable to subdue the violence of this new attack, she hoped that it would be short, and it was. Theophilo shook his head, and fell into an arm chair, once again prostrated. Dona Fernanda pulled a chair over and sat beside him.

"You're right, Theophilo, but you must be a man. You're young and strong; you still have a future, perhaps a great future. Who knows but had you entered the ministry now, you would have lost later? You'll enter another one. Sometimes what appears to be misfortune is really good fortune."

Theophilo squeezed her hand in gratitude.

"It's perfidy, it's a plot," he muttered, looking at her. "I know all that rabble. If I were to tell you everything, every-thing— But what for? I'd rather forget— It's not because of a wretched position that I'm upset," he continued, after a few moments. "Positions are worth nothing. If a person is a good worker, and has talent, he can snap his fingers at positions and prove that he is superior to them. Most of those men, Nanan, don't come up to my bootstraps. Of that I am sure, and they are, too. Dirty traitors. Where'll they find greater sincerity, greater loyalty, greater enthusiasm for the fight? Who worked harder through the press at the time when the party was out of power? They excuse themselves by saying that the cabinets are formed in São Christovão—* Ah! I'd like to speak to the Emperor!"

"Theophilo!"

"I'd say to the Emperor: 'Sir, Your Majesty doesn't know that your government is being run by court favorites all jockeying for position. Your Majesty wants the best men working in your councils, but it is the mediocre who manage to get in— Merit is pushed aside!' That's what I'll tell him some day; maybe even tomorrow—"

He stopped talking, and after a long pause, he got up and went to his study, which was next to the bedroom; his wife went with him. As it was already dark, he lighted a gas jet and looked around the room, his eyes veiled with melancholy. There were four broad cases filled with books, and Treasury reports, budgets, and balances. The secretary was in order. Three high, open cabinets contained manuscripts, notes, memoranda, and calculations all methodically stacked and labeled—outside credit—supplementary credit—war credit—navy credit—1868 loan—railways—internal debt—fiscal year 61-62, 62-63, 63-64, etc. It was there that he worked from morning till night, adding, calculating, collecting the data for his speeches and statements of policy, and usually he did his own work and that of his six colleagues as well: they just listened and signed, and if the statements were long, one of them just signed.

"Man, you're a past master," he would say, "hand over the pen."

Everything there indicated careful, assiduous work, meticulous and useful. From hooks on the wall hung the newspapers of the week, that were afterwards taken down, put away, and finally bound every six months for reference. The deputy's

* *Translator's Note:* São Christovão is the name of the district in Rio de Janeiro where Emperor Don Pedro II lived.

243

speeches, printed in the form of brochures, stood in a row in one case. There was no picture or bust, no ornament of any kind to repose the eye and give it something to admire; everything was orderly and neat and businesslike!

"What's the good of all this?" Theophilo asked his wife, after a few moments of sorrowful contemplation. "Weary hours, long hours, from night until morning, occasionally— It can't be said that this is the study of an idle man; you're witness to the fact that I work. And what's it all for?"

"Seek consolation in your work," she murmured.

"Poor consolation! No, this will be the end; I just don't know what it's all about. Look, they all consult me in the Chamber, even the ministers, because they know that I apply myself earnestly to administrative matters. What's the reward? The opportunity to applaud the new gentlemen in May?"

"Don't applaud at all," his wife said, gently. "Will you do something for me? Let's go to Europe in March or April, and let's not come back until a year from now. Ask permission from the Chamber, wherever we happen to be—Warsaw, for instance; I very much want to go to Warsaw," she continued, smiling, and taking his face between her hands with a charming gesture. "Say yes; answer so that I may write to Rio Grande; the boat leaves tomorrow. Agreed; we're going to Warsaw?"

"Don't joke, Nanan; this isn't a joking matter!"

"I'm speaking seriously. For a long time, I've been on the point of proposing a trip to see if you could get some rest from this confounded lot of papers. It's too much, Theophilo! You can barely manage to make a call; a ride is a rarity, you scarcely converse. Our children barely see their father, because one can't come in here while you're working. You must rest; I beg of you to take a year's respite. You see, it's serious. Let's go to Europe in March."

"It's not possible," he stammered.

"Why not?"

It was not possible; it was like asking him to get out of his skin. Politics was all that mattered. Of course there was politics outside of the country also, but what was his concern with it? Theophilo was completely ignorant of external affairs except for our debt in London, and he did know of a half dozen econo-mists. However, he was grateful to his wife for her well-meant suggestion.

"You're good."

A vague feeling of hope restored to the deputy's voice the gentleness that it had lost during the great moral crisis. All his papers heartened him. That mass of work had for his eyes the aspect that earth, that has been fertilized and sown, has for the eyes of the farmer. It would soon germinate, and his work would be rewarded; the shoots would sprout and the tree would bear fruit. That's precisely what his wife had said in more straightforward and appropriate words; but only now was he beginning to see the possibility of harvest. He remembered his outburst of indignation, and despair, and his recent com-plaints; and he was ashamed. He tried to laugh, but did not succeed very well. At dinner and breakfast he played with the children, who retired later than usual that evening. Nuno, who was already going to secondary school, where he had heard of the change in Cabinet, told his father that he wanted to be a minister. Theophilo became serious.

"My son," he said, "choose to be something other than a minister."

"They say that it's nice, Papa; they say that one rides in a carriage with a soldier behind."

"I'll give you a carriage."

"Has Papa been a minister?"

Theophilo made an effort to smile, and looked at his wife, who seized the opportunity to send the children to bed.

"Yes, I've been a minister," the father answered, kissing Nuno's forehead. "But I don't want to be one any more; it's not at all nice; and it's a lot of work. You shall be a chaplain."

"What's a chaplain?"

"That means you'll go to bed," replied Dona Fernanda. "Go to bed now, Nuno."

At lunch the following day, Theophilo received a letter through an orderly.

"An orderly?"

"Yes, he says that he was sent by the President of the Council."

Theophilo opened the letter with trembling hand. What could it be? He had read in the papers the report about the new ministers; the Cabinet was full. There was no departure from the original names. What could it be? Dona Fernanda, opposite her husband, was trying to read the contents of the letter from his face. She saw that his face was brightening, and that he was suppressing a smile of satisfaction—or hope, at least.

"Tell him to wait," Theophilo ordered the servant.

He went to his study, and came back a few minutes later with his reply. He sat down at the table, saying nothing, waiting for the servant to hand the letter to the orderly. This time, his ears alerted, he heard the stamping of the horses hooves and then, in a moment, he heard it gallop away. He felt a glow of satisfaction.

"Read," he said.

Dona Fernanda read the letter from the President of the Council; it was a request for an interview at two o'clock that afternoon.

"But then, the ministry—"

"It's complete," the deputy said quickly; "the ministers are appointed."

However, he did not in the least believe what he was saying. He was imagining some eleventh-hour vacancy, and the urgent need to fill it.

"It must be some political conference, or perhaps he wishes to talk with me about the budget—or entrust me with some piece of work."

While he was saying this to deceive his wife, he realized how very probable the suppositions were, and again he felt depressed. Three minutes later, however, the butterflies of hope were fluttering inside him, not two nor four, but a swarm that obscured the sky.

CLXXVII

Dona Fernanda waited, filled with anxiety, as if the ministry were for her and as if it were a source of pleasure rather than bitter vexation. So long as her husband were satisfied, however, all would be for the best. Theophilo returned at half-past five. From his appearance she saw that he was pleased. She ran and seized his hands.

"What is it?"

"Poor Nanan. We shall have a burden to shoulder. The marquis asked me at once to accept a presidency of the first order. Since he couldn't put me in the Cabinet, where he had a place designated for me, he asked, with much insistence, that I share the political and administrative responsibility of the government by assuming a presidency. By no means could he dispense with my prestige (those are his words) and he hopes that I'll assume the post of majority leader in the Chamber. What do you say?"

"That we'll have to adjust the burden," replied Dona Fernanda.

"Do you think I could refuse?"

"No."

"I couldn't. You know, one can't deny such services to a friendly government. If one does, one's out of politics. The marquis was very cordial; of course, I already knew that he's a superior man; but you can't imagine how smiling and affable he was! He also wants me to attend a gathering of the ministers and a few of his friends, not many, a half dozen. Already he's confided to me the program of the Cabinet—"

"When do we leave for Europe?"

"I don't know. I am to be with him tomorrow evening. The gathering is tomorrow at eight o'clock— But don't you think I did well to accept?"

"Of course."

"Yes; had I refused, I should have been criticized, and quite rightly. The first thing that one loses in politics is one's freedom. If you like, you could stay home; the Chambers will open in four or five months; I'll barely have time to get over there and look around."

CLXXVIII

Dona Fernanda acceded to the suggestion; in that way her son's education would not be interrupted; it would have been a four months' break. Theophilo left in a few days. Early on the morning of sailing, he went to say good-by to his study. He took a last look at the books, reports, budgets, and manuscripts, all that part of the family that was the only part that meant anything to him. He had tied the papers and pamphlets together so that they would not be lost, and he gave his wife important instructions. Standing in the center of the room, he looked at each case in turn, and dispersed his heart among them. Then it was that he took leave of his friends and saints with genuine sorrow. For Dona Fernanda, who was beside him, the leave-taking lasted only ten minutes; for Theophilo, it seemed to last many years.

"Don't worry, I'll take care of them; I'll dust them myself, every day."

Theophilo gave her a kiss— Another woman would have received it sadly, seeing that he loved his books so much that he seemed to love them more than he loved her. Dona Fernanda, however, felt lucky.

After the day of the ministerial crisis, Rubião did not return to Dona Fernanda's house; he knew nothing of the presidency, nor of Theophilo's sailing. He was living with the dog and a servant, his ailment marked neither by great crises nor by prolonged respite. The servant did his work irregularly, squandered his tips, and often received the title of marquis. Furthermore, he was amused. When his master took it into his head to talk with the walls, the servant would run and spy upon him; it would be a dialogue, because Rubião would speak for them, answering as though he had asked some question. Then, at night, the servant would go and chat with his friends in the neighborhood.

"How's the crazy man?"

"The crazy man's all right. Today he asked his dog to sing; the dog barked loudly and he was tickled pink; but he put on airs over it. Whenever he's off his nut, you'd think that he ruled the world. Only yesterday, while he was having lunch he said to me: 'Marquis Raymundo—I want you to—' and he stammered the rest, so that I couldn't hear. In the end, he gave me ten *tostões.*"

"Of course you put them right away—"

"Oh, come now."

When Rubião came out of his garrulous delirium, he would become momentarily quiet and sad. His consciousness was trying to throw off the remnants it still bore of that previous state. He was like a man painfully coming up from an abyss, climbing up the walls, scraping his skin and wearing down his fingernails, to reach the top lest he fall down again and become lost. Then he would go to see some friends, some new ones, and some old ones like the Major's family and Camacho's.

The latter had been less talkative for some time. Even politics did not furnish material for discussion as in the old days. When he saw Rubião appear at the door of his study, he would make a gesture of impatience, which, however, he would immediately suppress. Rubião noticed the change, and wondered whether through some inadvertence, he had offended him, or if it were just that he was beginning to dislike him. And, in an effort to undo the dislike or resentment, or whatever it was, he would laugh and speak with sauvity, and with long, respectful pauses, waiting for Camacho to say something. In vain did he resort to the Marquis of Paraná, whose portrait was still hanging on the wall; he repeated the names that he had heard—the great marquis, the consummate statesman! Camacho would just nod, and go right on writing, consulting documents and rules of court procedure, Lobão and Coelho da Rocha, quoting, scratching and begging his pardon. He had a libel suit to present that day. Then he interrupted his work and went to the book case.

"Excuse me."

Rubião drew in his legs to let him get by; Camacho pulled out a volume of *Ordenácões do Remo* and thumbed through its pages, looking ahead and turning back without really looking for anything, but just to get rid of the nuisance. The nuisance, however, stayed on, for that very reason, and they kept eyeing each other furtively. Camacho returned to his libel and in order to read, sitting as he was, he leaned away over to the left from where the light was coming, and turned his back on Rubião.

"It's dark in here," Rubião ventured to say, one day.

He heard no reply, so intent did the lawyer seem upon the reading of the documents. "It may really be that I'm bothering him." He looked closely at the grim, serious face, at the gesture with which Camacho picked up his pen to continue the interminable libel. There were twenty minutes more of absolute silence. At the end of this time, Rubião saw him lay aside his pen, straighten up, stretch his arms and rub his eyes. He said, with a show of interest:

"You're tired, aren't you?"

Camacho nodded and prepared to go on; then our man got up and took advantage of the pause to make his departure.

"I'll come back when you're not so busy."

He held out his hand. Camacho took it limply, and went back to his paper. Rubião descended the stairs, perturbed and hurt by his illustrious friend's coolness. What could he have done to him?

CLXXX

As he left he had the good fortune to meet Major Siqueira.

"I was just going to your house," he said. "Are you on your way there?"

"I am; but we're no longer in the same house. We've moved to Princeza Street in the Cajueiros district."

"Wherever it is, let's go there."

At that moment Rubião needed a piece of rope to fasten him to reality, because once again his mind felt itself seized with giddiness. However, so sanely was he speaking that the Major thought he was in full possession of his faculties, and said:

"You know I have some great news for you?"

"Let's hear it."

"When we get to the house."

They got there. It was a two-story house; Dona Tonica came to open the latticed door. She was wearing a new dress and earrings.

"Take a good look at her," said the Major, tweaking his daughter's chin.

Dona Tonica drew back, abashed.

"I'm looking," answered Rubião.

"Can't you see right off that she's a person who's going to get married?"

"Ah, congratulations!"

"That's right, she's going to get married. She had a hard time, but she made it. She found a fiancé here who adores her, in the way that all fiancés do. When I was betrothed, I adored my late wife, who was the prettiest thing I'd ever laid eyes on— Yes, she's going to get married. He's a steady man, middle-aged; he spends his evenings here. When he passes by in the morning on his way to the office, I think he taps on the window, or, at any rate, she waits for him there. I pretend not to notice."

Dona Tonica was shaking her head, but she was smiling in a manner that seemed to say that it was true that he did tap on the window. She was so bubbling over with excitement she did not even remember any more that she had once set her cap for

251

Rubião, that he had, in fact, been one of her last hopes. They had entered the drawing room; Dona Tonica went over to the window and back aimlessly, her head erect, reconciled with life.

"She's a fine person," said the Major, "a fine girl— Tonica, go and get the picture— Go on, go and get the picture of your fiancé—"

Dona Tonica went to get the picture. It was a photograph; it showed a middle-aged man with sparse, close-cropped hair, startled eyes, a peaked face, scrawny neck, and a buttoned-up topcoat.

"What do you think of him?"

"He's good-looking."

Dona Tonica took the picture and looked at it a few moments. Then she withdrew her eyes and as she sat there, her imagination went out to wait for Rodrigues. His name was Rodrigues. He was shorter than she—which did not show in the picture—and he was employed in an office of the War Ministry. He was a widower, with two sons, one of whom was in the youth battalion, the other, a boy of twelve, a hopeless tubercular case. What matter? He was her fiancé. Every night, upon retiring, Dona Tonica knelt before the image of Our Lady, her patron saint, to express her gratitude, and to pray that she make her happy. Already she was dreaming of a son; she would call him Alvaro.

CLXXXI

Rubião listened in silence to a speech from the Major. The wedding would take place in a month and a half; the fiancé had to make the house ready; as he was not a capitalist, he had had to borrow. The house in which they would live would be the same one in which he was living now, and it did not require expensive new furniture, but there are always some necessities— In short, in a month and a half, or five weeks, at least, they would be united in the holy bonds of matrimony.

"And I'll be free of my encumbrance," concluded the Major.

"Oh!" protested Rubião.

The daughter laughed; she was used to her father's jokes, and so happy that nothing would annoy her. Even had her father referred to her forty-odd years, it would not have shocked her greatly. All brides are fifteen.

"He's going to miss you and come after you, you just see," said Rubião to Dona Tonica.

"What! Maybe I'll get married too!"

Suddenly Rubião stood up and took a few steps. The Major did not see the expression on his face, nor did he realize that Rubião's mind was quite possibly on the point of going off the track and that Rubião himself was aware of it. He asked him to sit down again, and began to tell him about the days when he had been married and had been campaigning. When he came to tell about the Battle of Monte-Caseros, with all the marches and counter marches, that formed a part of the telling, it was Napoleon III who was in front of him. Silent at first, Rubião proffered a few words of approbation, cited Solferino and Magenta, promised Siqueira a decoration. Father and daughter looked at each other; the Major said that a heavy shower was on the way. (It had, in fact, darkened a little). Rubião had better leave before it started to rain; he had not brought an umbrella and his own was an old one and the only one he had.

"My coach is coming for me," replied Rubião serenely.

"It's not coming here; it's gone to wait for you in the Campo. Can't you see the coach from here, Tonica?"

Dona Tonica made a vague, reluctant gesture. She did not want to lie, but she was afraid, and she did want Rubião to go. It was not possible to see the Campo da Acclamação from the house. Her father already had Rubião by the arm, and was walking him to the door.

"Come again tomorrow, or some time later, when you like."

"But why should I not wait here until the coach comes?" asked Rubião. "The Empress mustn't get caught in the rain."

"The Empress has already left."

"She made a mistake. Eugenia made a big mistake. General— Why should you always remain a Major?— General, I saw the picture of your son-in-law; I wish to give you mine. Send to the Tuileries for it. Where's the coach?"

"It's waiting in the Campo."

"Send for it."

Dona Tonica, who was in the window, called:

"Here comes Rodrigues."

And she turned back to the street, bowing and smiling, while in the drawing room her father continued to lead Rubião to the door, gently, but firmly. The latter stopped to rebuke him:

"General, I am your Emperor."

"Of course, but come with me, Your Majesty."

They had reached the door; the Major opened the lattice, just as Rodrigues was setting foot upon the threshold. Dona Tonica came to receive her fiancé, but the door was blocked by Rubião and her father. Rodrigues removed his hat, revealing his graying, bristly hair; his peaked face was freckled, but his laugh was kind and unpretentious—more unpretentious even than kind, and, notwithstanding the insignificance of his manner and person, he was agreeable. His eyes did not show the startled expression of the picture; that effect had come from the fact that he made such an effort to have every part of himself just so, in order that the picture might turn out well.

"This gentleman is my future son-in-law," the Major said to Rubião. "Didn't you see a coach and cavalry squadron in the Campo?" he asked Rodrigues, with a wink.

"I think so, sir."

"Well?" continued Siqueira, turning to Rubião. "Go on, go on, turn up São Lorenço Street and go straight ahead to the Campo. Good-by, see you tomorrow."

Rubião went down three steps—there were five—and stopped in front of Rodrigues, looked at him intently for a few moments, declared that he was very pleased to know him and said that he should be a good husband and son-in-law. What was his name?

João José Rodrigues.

"Rodrigues. I'll send you an honorary decoration for your dress coat. That will be my wedding present. My regards, Siqueira."

Siqueira took his arm to make him go down the last two steps into the street.

"In the Campo, you say?"

"In the Campo."

"Good-by."

From the street Rubião still looked toward the windows, his fingers on his hat, in order to say good-by to Dona Tonica; but Dona Tonica was in the drawing room, into which Rodrigues had just come, fresh and charming as the first rose of summer.

CLXXXII

Rubião gave no further thought to the coach, nor the cavalry squadron. He suddenly found himself some blocks away and after walking for a while he turned up São José Street. He was coming from the Imperial Palace, gesticulating and talking with someone whom he supposed he had by the arm. It was the Empress. Eugenia or Sophia? Both fused into a single entity—or, rather, the second with the name of the first. Men who were passing by stopped; people came running to the doors of their shops. Some laughed; others remained indifferent; some turned their eyes aside to spare them the distressing sight of a madman. A gang of Negro boys accompanied Rubião, some so close that they heard what he was saying. Children of all sorts came to join the group. When they saw the general curiosity, they decided to give voice to the throng, and the jeering began:

"Crazy man! Crazy man!"

The clamor attracted people's attention, numerous second story windows began to open, curious faces of both sexes and all ages appeared, a photographer, an upholsterer, three or four faces together, heads peeking over one another, all leaning forward and peering, following the man who, with his grandiose and benevolent manner was addressing the wall.

"Crazy man! Crazy man!" shouted the urchins.

One of them, much smaller than the rest, grabbed the voluminous pants of another. That was in Ajuda Street. Rubião still heard nothing; or, if he did hear anything, he supposed that the cries were acclamations, and bowed in gratitude. The jeering increased. In the midst of the uproar, one could distinguish a woman's voice at the door of a mattress shop:

"Deolindo! Come home, Deolindo!"

Deolindo, the child who had grabbed the older boy's pants and had not let go, did not obey: it may be that he did not even hear, so great was the outcry and such was the glee of the little rascal who was clamoring in his faint voice:

"Crazy man! Crazy man!"

"Deolindo!"

Deolindo tried to hide among the others to avoid being seen by his mother who was calling him. However, she ran out to the group, and snatched him away. To be sure, he was too small to participate in street riots.

"Mama, let me see—"

"What do you want to see? Come!"

She put him inside the house, but she remained at the door, watching the street. Rubião had stopped; she could see him well now, with his chest thrust forward, gesticulating and talking and tipping his hat in all directions.

"Crazy people are funny sometimes," she said to a neighbor woman, smiling.

The boys continued to shout and laugh, and Rubião went on his way with the same chorus in his wake. Deolindo had come to the door of the shop, and when he saw that the gang was moving on, he tearfully begged his mother to let him go too or to go with him if she wouldn't let him go alone. When he completely lost hope, he gathered all his strength into one little shrill, whining cry:

"Crazy man, crazy man!"

The neighbor woman laughed. Deolindo's mother laughed too. She confessed that her son was a little pest, a little devil, who was never still a moment. If ever there was anything going on, he'd be right out in the street. He'd been that way since he was a little fellow; when he was only two years old he had nearly been run over by a carriage right there; he had escaped by a hair's breadth. Had it not been for a man who was passing by, a well-dressed man, who had quickly intervened, at the risk of his own life, he would have been killed, yes, indeed, killed. At this moment, her husband, who was coming up the other side of the street crossed over and interrupted the conversation. He wore a deep frown, barely greeted the neighbor, and went into the house; his wife followed and asked what was the matter. Her husband told her about the jeering.

"He went by here," she said.

"Didn't you recognize the man?"

"No."

Her husband folded his arms and stood looking at her intently without saying a word. His wife asked who it was.

"It's the man who rescued our Deolindo from death."

The woman trembled.

"Did you see him well?" she asked.

"Perfectly. I've seen him other times, but then he wasn't like this. Poor man! And the gang of Negro boys was yelling after him. We don't have any police in this country, apparently."

What most grieved the woman was not so much the man's derangement nor its mockery but the part that her son had had in it—the same child whom the man had saved from death. Of course, how could the child recognize him, after all, or even know that he owed him his life? What really grieved her was the coincidence. Finally she put all the blame upon herself; had she been more careful, the little fellow would not have gotten out and joined in the derision. The thought agitated her, and every little while she would begin to tremble. Her husband took the child's head between his hands and kissed it twice.

"Did you see the whole thing?" he asked his wife.

"Yes, I did."

"I would even have liked to offer the man my arm and bring him here, but I was ashamed. It was quite possible that the Negro boys would jeer at me. I turned my eyes aside because he might recognize me. Poor man! He didn't seem to hear any of it, though; and was going along contentedly enough; I believe he was even laughing— How sad it is to lose one's mind."

The woman was thinking of her son's naughtiness; she did not tell her husband and asked her neighbor not to mention it. Not until late that night did she fall asleep; for she had been suffering from the hallucination that many years had passed and that her son was becoming mad, and was tortured by derision; and that she, indignant and blasphemous, was spitting toward Heaven.

CLXXXIV

Two hours after the scene in Ajuda Street Rubião arrived at Dona Fernanda's house. The urchins were gradually disbanding; now the last three were combining their farewells in a single, formidable shout. Rubião continued on alone, scarcely noticed by the residents along the way, perhaps because his gesticulation was lessening or because he was becoming quieter. He was not addressing the wall, the supposed Empress; but he was still the Emperor. He would walk along, stop, mutter, gesturing only slightly, dreaming always, always, forever wrapped in that veil through which everything appeared to be something else than what it was, something else and something better; every lamp looked like a gentleman in waiting, every street corner was like a figure out of tapestry. Rubião went straight on to the throne room to receive some ambassador or other, but the palace was interminable, and it was necessary to cross through many halls and galleries, all carpeted, to be sure—and between tall, sturdy halberdiers.

Of the people who saw him and stopped on the street or

leaned from windows, many momentarily suspended their sad or troubled thoughts, their preoccupations of the day, their worries, their resentments, this one a debt, that one an illness, disappointed love, a friend's treachery. Every unhappiness was forgotten. Better forgetfulness than consolation; but the forgetfulness was over in a flash. As soon as the madman was by, reality took hold of them once more. The streets were again just streets, because the sumptuous palaces had gone along with Rubião. More than one pitied the poor devil; comparing their fortunes, more than one thanked Heaven for his own lot— bitter, but fully apprehended. Yes, they preferred their existing shack to the imaginary castle.

CLXXXV

Rubião was taken into a sanitarium. Palha had forgotten the obligation that his wife placed upon him, and Sophia, herself, no longer remembered the promise she had made Dona Fernanda. They were thinking about another house, a mansion in Botafogo, the remodeling of which was nearly finished, and which they wanted to open in the winter when the Chambers would be in session and everyone would have come down from Petropolis. Now, however, the promise was fulfilled. Rubião entered an institution recommended by Doctor Falcão and Palha. He occupied a special suite of rooms, drawing room and bedroom. He offered no resistance; he went with the men gladly, and entered his rooms as though he had long been familiar with them. When the men took their leave, saying that they would come again, Rubião invited them to a military review on Saturday.

"Why yes, Saturday," assented Falcão.

"Saturday's a good day," continued Rubião. "Don't fail to be there, Duke of Palha."

"I won't," said Palha, as he was leaving.

"Look, I'll send one of my coaches for you, a brand new one;

your wife must be the first to place her lovely body where, as yet, no one has dared to sit. Damask cushions and velvet, silver reins and gold wheels; the horses descend from the horse that my uncle rode at Marengo. Farewell, Duke of Palha."

CLXXXVI

"It's obvious to me," thought Doctor Falcão on his way out, "that that man was the lover of this fellow's wife."

CLXXXVII

"That man" stayed on at the sanitarium. Quincas Borba had tried to get into the carriage that took his friend away, and had started to run after it; it had required all the servant's strength to seize and hold him, and shut him in the house. The situation was just like that of Barbacena; but, after all, dear reader, life is composed of no more than four or five situations which only the accompanying circumstances appear to vary and multiply. Rubião immediately asked for his dog, and when the director consented to his having him, it was Dona Fernanda who took it upon herself to satisfy the patient's wish. She thought of writing to Sophia, but instead she went to Flamengo herself.

CLXXXVIII

"I'll send for him; it's not far from here," suggested Sophia.

"Let's go there ourselves. Why not? I've thought of something. Since the treatment may be long, will it be worth while to keep the house rented and ready for his return? It's better to let it go, sell it and its furnishings for ready money."

They walked from Flamengo to Príncipe Street, a matter of three or four minutes. Raymundo was out on the street, but when he saw people at the door, he went to open it. The inner rooms of the house had none of that precision or orderliness that seem to preserve some vestige of a life that has suddenly come to an end; they had, rather, a look of abandonment—the abandonment of neglect. The drawing room, on the other hand, with the wild disarray of its furniture, expressed clearly all the madness, all the distorted and confused ideas of its occupant.

"Was he very rich?" Dona Fernanda asked Sophia.

"He had something when he came from Minas," she answered; "but it seems that he went through everything. Look, pick up your dress; the floor looks as though it hasn't been swept for an age."

It was not only the floor that had been neglected. All the furniture, too, had its coating of dust. The servant, however, offered no explanation; he was merely watching and listening and softly whistling a popular polka. Nor did Sophia ask him anything about cleaning; she was dying to get away from "all that filth," she was saying to herself, and she wanted to inquire about the dog, which was the main reason for having come, and yet she really did not care to show any interest in him nor in anything else. It all seemed so trivial that it made absolutely no appeal to her mind or heart; nor did her memory of the deranged man help to make the time spent there more endurable. She was thinking to herself that her companion must be singularly romantic or affected. "What stupidity!" she thought, without disarranging the approving smile with which she responded to all of Dona Fernanda's observations.

"Open that window," said the latter to the servant. "Everything smells musty."

"Oh! It's unbearable!" agreed Sophia, sniffing disgustedly.

But, despite the exclamation, Dona Fernanda could not make up her mind to leave. Though no personal recollection was awakened by that wretched dwelling, she was stirred by a deep and peculiar emotion. It was not the sight of decay that occasioned it; for the old house did not bring her a realization of the fleetingness of time nor of the sadness of this world. Rather did it bespeak one man's suffering; the suffering of a man to whom she had spoken only a few times. And so she lingered, looking about quietly and sadly, absorbed in her feelings, devoid of thought. Sophia did not dare to utter a word for fear of displeasing so distinguished a lady. They were both holding up their dresses to keep them out of the dust, and Sophia, in addition to taking that precaution, was impatiently fanning herself as if she were suffocating. She did cough several times.

"And the dog?" Dona Fernanda inquired of the servant.

"He's shut in the bedroom in there."

"Go get him."

Quincas Borba appeared, emaciated and crestfallen. He stopped at the door of the drawing room and looked at the two women suspiciously, but he did not bark. He scarcely raised his dim eyes. As he was about to turn his body halfway toward the inner rooms, Dona Fernanda snapped her fingers; he paused, and wagged his tail.

"Let's see, what's his name?" asked Dona Fernanda.

"Quincas Borba," the servant drawled, laughing. "He has a man's name. Eh! Quincas Borba! Go over there. The lady's calling you."

"Quincas Borba! Come here! Quincas Borba!" repeated Dona Fernanda.

Quincas Borba went in answer to the call, but he did not go bounding with joy. Dona Fernanda bent down and asked him about his friend, if he were away, if he would like to go to see him; and, at the same time, while she was leaning over she asked the servant questions about the dog.

"Yes, madame, he eats now, but when my master went away, he wouldn't eat nor drink; I thought he was going to starve."

"Does he eat well?"

"He doesn't eat much."

"Does he look for his master?"

"He probably looks for him," replied Raymundo, covering a laugh with his hand. "But I shut him in the bedroom, so he'd not run away. He doesn't cry any more. At first he cried a lot;

it even woke me up. I had to beat on the door with a club to quiet him—"

Dona Fernanda scratched the animal's head. It was the first caress after long days of solitude and neglect. Even after Dona Fernanda stopped patting him and stood up, they still continued to look at each other, she and the dog; so intently and so deeply that each seemed to penetrate the other's innermost being. The dog was drawn and held by the all-embracing sympathy that was the essence of this woman, a sympathy so great that it did not hesitate to give of itself and enfold within itself this obscure little misery that was only an animal's. The woman, at sight of the poor creature, felt the same distress she had felt at the thought of the madman, as if both were of the same species; and feeling that her presence brought some comfort to the animal, she did not wish to deprive him of it.

"You're getting covered with fleas," remarked Sophia.

Dona Fernanda did not hear her. She continued to look into the dog's sad, gentle eyes until he lowered his head and began to sniff about the room. He had smelled his master's scent. The street door was open, and he would have run out through it had Raymundo not grabbed him. Dona Fernanda gave the servant some money to wash the dog and take him to the sanitarium. She gave instructions that he was to be given the best of care, and that he was to be taken either by the scruff of the neck or on leash. In this Sophia concurred, and ordered that he come and get her first at her house.

CLXXXIX

They left. Before setting foot in the street, Sophia looked up and down to see if anyone were coming; fortunately the street was deserted. Once away from the pigsty, Sophia reacquired the use of pretty speech and the delicate and harmonious art of captivating others. Affectionately she slipped her arm through Dona Fernanda's. She spoke of Rubião and what a sad thing madness is; she spoke also of the mansion in Botafogo. Why not go with her to see the work that was being done? They'd have a little lunch and start out immediately after.

C X C

There occurred an event that diverted Dona Fernanda's mind from Rubião; it was the birth of a daughter to Maria Benedicta. She hurried to Tijuca, covered mother and child with kisses, and held out her hand for Carlos Maria to kiss.

"You're as exuberant as ever," exclaimed the young father, as he complied.

"And you're as unfeeling," she retorted.

Despite her cousin's objection, Dona Fernanda stayed with Maria Benedicta during the latter's convalescence, and she was so good and kind and cheerful that it was a delight to have her in the house. She forgot Rubião's misfortune, such was the joy around her, but as soon as the new mother was well again, Dona Fernanda hurried back to the ailing man.

C X C I

"I expect to restore his reason at the end of six or eight months. He's doing very well."

Dona Fernanda sent this reply from the head of the sanitarium on to Sophia, and suggested that they both go to see the patient, if she thought it would be all right for her to go. "What harm could there be?" Sophia answered in a note. "But I'd not have the heart to see him; he was such a close friend of ours that I don't know whether I could bear to see and talk with the poor man. I showed the letter to Christiano, and he told me that he has converted Mr. Rubião's property: he realized three contos, two hundred."

264

"Six, eight months pass quickly," Dona Fernanda reflected.

And along they came, bringing their events—the fall of the ministry, the rise of another in March, her husband's return, the discussion of the law of the "free womb," * the death of Dona Tonica's fiancé three days before the wedding. Yes, Dona Tonica shed her last tears, tears of love and tears of despair; her eyes became so red that they appeared to have some affliction.

Theophilo, who had merited from the new Cabinet the same confidence that he had had from the old, had a large part in the debates of the parliamentary session. Camacho declared in his paper that the law of the "free womb" absolved sterility and certain crimes. In October, Sophia inaugurated her Botafogo salon with a ball that was the most famous of the day. It was dazzling. For the occasion she modestly displayed her arms and shoulder blades. Her jewelry was costly; she was still wearing the necklace that had been one of Rubião's first gifts, for truly, in that sort of adornment, fashion is most enduring. Everyone admired the charm of that young woman in her thirties, so fresh, so blooming; some men spoke (regretfully) of her wifely virtues and of her great love for her husband.

On the day after the ball, Dona Fernanda awoke late. She went to her husband's study, and found that he had already devoured five or six newspapers, written ten letters and set several books straight in the cases.

"I received this letter a little while ago," he said.

Dona Fernanda read it; it was an announcement from the director of the sanitarium that Rubião had been missing for

* *Translator's Note:* A law passed in 1871 enfranchising children born of slave mothers.

three days, and that in spite of all the director's efforts and those of the police, no trace of the man had been found. "This disappearance surprises me particularly," the letter concluded, "since there had been great improvement and I was counting on having him completely well in two months."

Dona Fernanda was very much perturbed; she persuaded her husband to write to the Chief of Police and to the Minister of Justice, requesting them to order the strictest search. Theophilo had not the slightest interest in whether Rubião were found or cured, but he wished to please his wife, whose kindness of heart he appreciated and, perhaps, too, he enjoyed corresponding with men high up in the administration.

CXCIV

But how could our Rubião or his dog be found since they had both left for Barbacena? A week before, Rubião had written to Palha to come and get him; the latter went to the sanitarium and saw that the patient was talking rationally, without the slightest trace of madness.

"I had a mental crisis," Rubião said. "I'm well now, perfectly well, and I'm asking you to get me out of here. I believe that the director will not be opposed. Meanwhile, as I wish to leave a few remembrances for the people who have taken care of me and my dog, see if you can advance me a hundred milreis."

Palha opened his billfold without hesitation and gave him the money.

"I'll try to get you released," he said; "but it probably will take a few days (it was the very day preceding the ball). Don't worry over that; you'll be out in a week."

Before leaving he consulted the director, who gave a good report of the patient. "A week is a short time," he said. "To have him well, really well, I still need about two months." Palha admitted that Rubião had seemed sane to him, but that the director knew what he was doing in any case, and if six or seven months more were needed, he should not hurry the release.

As soon as Rubião arrived in Barbacena and began to go up the street that is now called Tiradentes, he stopped and shouted:

"To the victor, the potatoes!"

He had completely forgotten both the formula and the allegory. Now, suddenly, as if the syllables had lingered in the air, untouched, waiting for someone who could understand them and put them together, he combined them into the old formula, and uttered it as emphatically as on the day he had accepted it as the true law of life. He did not recall the anecdote fully, but the phrase conveyed a nebulous sense of struggle and victory.

Accompanied by his dog, he continued up the street, and stopped in front of the church. He saw no sign of the sacristan. Quincas Borba, who had not eaten for many hours, pressed close against his legs and waited, with head hanging low. Rubião turned, and from the upper end of the street he looked down and far into the distance. Yes, it was Barbacena; the old city of his birth was being drawn out from the layers of his memory. It was Barbacena; here was the church, there, the jail, beyond, the apothecary's shop, from where had come the medicines for the other Quincas Borba. He knew when he arrived that it was the same old city; but as his eyes roamed about, memories kept coming until finally there was a whole flock of them. He saw no one; though there did seem to be someone peering out of a window to the left. But everything on the whole was as deserted as could be.

"Perhaps they don't know that I've arrived," thought Rubião.

Suddenly there was lightning, and the clouds piled up quickly. There was a more brilliant flash, and a clap of thunder. Then it started to rain, harder and harder, until the storm broke in full fury. Rubião, who had left the church when the first drops fell, was now going down the street, followed still by his faithful and starving dog. They were both dazed by the sudden, heavy shower, both without hope of food or shelter. The rain pounded them mercilessly. They could not run because Rubião was afraid of slipping and falling, and the dog did not want to lose him. Half way down the street Rubião thought of the apothecary's shop, and turned back, bucking the wind, which lashed his face; but after he had taken twenty steps, the thought was swept out of his head. Good-by, apothecary's shop! Good-by, shelter! He no longer remembered why he had changed his direction, and once again started down the street followed by the dog who did not understand what it was all about, but did not want to get too far away. They were both dripping wet and confused by the loud, continuous thunder.

They wandered aimlessly. Rubião's stomach was questioning, clamoring, crying out its need; fortunately the madness came along to deceive it with its banquets at the Tuileries. Having no such recourse, Quincas Borba started to prowl about, and when, from time to time, Rubião would sit down on the pavement, the dog, to forget his hunger, would climb onto his knees. Finding his master's trousers wet from the rain, however, he would get down only to climb back again; for it was night by now, the still hours of the night, and the air was cold. Rubião ran his hands over the animal, mumbling a few lean words of comfort.

If, in spite of everything, Quincas Borba succeeded in falling asleep, he would awaken immediately because Rubião would get up and start walking up and down the slopes once more. A mournful wind was blowing, sharp as a knife, and it made the vagabonds shake with the chill of it. Rubião was walking slowly, now; his weariness did not permit the great strides that he took at first when the rain was pouring down. He stopped more frequently. Famished and dead tired as he was, the dog could not understand that Odyssey; he did not know what it was for; he had forgotten where he was; he heard nothing except the muffled words of his master. He could not see the stars that had now emerged from the clouds and were shining brightly. Rubião discovered them; he had come to the door of the church, as when he entered the city. He had just sat down, and then he noticed them. They were so pretty, he recognized the chandeliers of the great salon; and he ordered them put out. He could not see the execution of his order, however, because he fell asleep at that very moment. The dog was beside him, and when they awakened in the morning they were so close that they appeared to have been made fast with glue.

CXCVIII

"To the victor the potatoes!" shouted Rubião, when he opened his eyes and saw that it was no longer dark and raining, and that the street was kissed by the sun.

CXCIX

It was Rubião's good friend Angelica who took him in with his dog when she saw them pass her door. Rubião recognized her, and accepted the lunch and shelter.

"But what's the meaning of this, Rubião? Your clothing is all wet. I'll give you a pair of my nephew's trousers."

Rubião was feverish. He ate little and without appetite. His friend Angelica asked for an account of the life he had led in the capital, to which he replied that it would take a very long time and that only posterity would finish it. "It will be your nephew's nephews," he concluded pompously, "who will see me in all my glory." However, he began a summary. At the end of ten minutes his friend understood absolutely nothing, so confused were the facts and ideas; in another five minutes she began to be afraid. When it became twenty minutes, she excused herself and went to a neighbor's to tell that Rubião seemed to have lost his mind. People began coming, then, in twos and fours, and before an hour was up, a crowd was peering in from the street.

"To the victor, the potatoes!" Rubião shouted to the curious idlers. "Here I am Emperor! To the victor, the potatoes!"

This obscure, incomplete phrase was repeated out in the street; and it was examined; but its meaning could not be apprehended. So that they might enjoy the fun all the more, several of Rubião's old enemies went right inside, quite unceremoniously; they told Angelica that she should not keep a madman in the house, it was dangerous; she should send him to the jail until the authorities put him somewhere else. To someone who was more compassionate, it occurred that it would be well to call the doctor.

"Why the doctor?" said one of the others. "This man is crazy."

"It may be the delirium of fever. Have you noticed how hot he is?"

Angelica, who was excited by so many people about, took his pulse and found that he was, indeed, feverish. She called the doctor—the same one who had treated the late Quincas Borba. Rubião recognized him and assured him that there was nothing the matter with him. He had captured the King of Prussia; he did not know yet whether he would have him shot or not; he would, however, exact an enormous pecuniary indemnification —five billion francs.

"To the victor, the potatoes!" he concluded, laughing.

A few days later he died—but he did not die in subjection or defeat. Before the onset of his agony, which was short, he placed the crown upon his head—a crown that, at least, was not an old hat nor a basin which might furnish the spectators with tangible evidence of his illusion. No sir, he picked up nothing and encircled his head with it; he alone saw the imperial insignia, heavy with gold, glittering with diamonds and other precious stones. The effort that he had made to raise himself partly did not last long; his body fell back again, but his face, perhaps, preserved its look of radiant exultation.

"Take care of my crown," he murmured.

Then his face became serious, because death is serious. Two minutes of agony, a horrible grimace, and the abdication was signed.

Here I should like to tell of the end of Quincas Borba. He, too, fell sick, whimpered endlessly, and ran about in frenzied search of his master. Early one morning, three days later, he was found dead in the street. But, seeing that the dog's death is recounted in a special chapter, you will probably ask me whether it is he or his late namesake who gives this book its title, and why one rather than another—a question pregnant with questions that would take us far— Well, if you have tears, weep for these two not long dead. But if you have only laughter, laugh. It is all the same. The Southern Cross, which the beautiful Sophia would not gaze upon as Rubião begged her to do, is too high in the heavens to distinguish between man's laughter and tears.